"Papa!" Kirsten screamed. "It's swimming underwater. It's coming toward us!"

Bjorn glanced at the water. "Keep away from the sides!" he called. His daughter's eyes caught his, and she smiled and softly shook her head. As he watched, horrified at what she intended, she stripped off her flotation jacket. Quickly she began to remove the rest of her clothes. "Stop her!"

But Kirsten, dressed only in panties, already stood on the air-filled side of the raft. Charles turned just in time to see her bend and then spring out and away from the raft. His jaw dropped at the sight.

Also by
Burt Wetanson and Thomas Hoobler

THE HUNTERS

THE TREASURE HUNTERS

BURT WETANSON AND
THOMAS HOOBLER

THE TREASURE HUNTERS

Published simultaneously in the United States and Canada by PBJ Books, Inc., formerly PEI Books, Inc., 200 Madison Avenue, New York, New York 10016. Printed in the United States of America. Library of Congress Catalog Card Number: 82-60692.

ISBN: 0-867-21235-7

First printing January 1983

Chapter One

Though he feigned sleep, Emperor Mkomo I had been aware of the plane's slow loss of altitude for some time now. When the Boeing 727's wheels touched down and the great plane slowly taxied toward the dim lights of the terminal, his hand slipped inside the pocket of his Burberry trench coat. There his fingers wrapped soothingly around the crosshatched handle of his Mauser automatic. They had been told that it was not necessary to bring weapons to the island, but Mkomo was not a man to leave things to chance.

The last time he had been careless, his most loyal servant, Prime Minister Lluanda—a man whose loyalty the Emperor thought he had ensured by personally reducing him to a eunuch—had betrayed him while the Emperor was abroad on affairs of state. It resulted in the Emperor's somewhat embarrassing current status as a stateless person.

Fortunately, the Emperor had thought to deposit a certain amount of the imperial treasury in a Swiss bank, and there had been more than enough to procure the Emperor's safe conduct to Paris. Paris has its attractions for a man like the Emperor, and he had found it a congenial place to organize an army of liberation to reclaim the throne.

Even so, Paris was not entirely safe, and the most recent attempt to assassinate the Emperor had underlined the need for greater funds. Mkomo disliked having to purchase loyalty, but the Paris authorities were uncooperative about allowing him the freedom to pursue his usual methods.

This promised hunt for treasure had been an unexpected opportunity. Mkomo had of course suspected that the offer of a hunting challenge was a crudely disguised attempt to draw him into a trap, but the agents for the supposed Treasure Island Resort had impressive bona fides. And the Emperor had never been one to avoid pitting his own skill against that of others.

The plane had completed its approach to the terminal, and the sound of the engines being shut off now brought Mkomo to action. He nudged the sleeping figure next to him—his heir, Charles—and stood up. Toward the front of the otherwise empty cabin the steward now made his appearance. He stopped at the sight of the Emperor's drawn weapon.

The steward recovered quickly, and his smiling face met the Emperor's cold eyes. "You will have no need for that, Your Highness," he said. "I'm sure you will find the accommodations quite comfortable."

Mkomo wordlessly gestured the man forward with the pistol and stood out of the possible line of fire as the steward unlocked the cabin door, now connected to the terminal walkway. It swung open to reveal an empty corridor.

The Emperor could hear Charles struggling to bring the heavy suitcase up the aisle of the plane. He hadn't liked to bring the callow sixteen-year-old along on this trip, but to leave him behind would have left him at the mercy of Lluanda's minions. Better to bring him along, where the Emperor could supervise his education.

Charles's earlier education had unfortunately been at the most exclusive British and Swiss schools. That training, the Emperor was reluctantly aware, had ill prepared Charles for the kind of swift decisions and actions he would need to govern the benighted people of the Biandran Empire.

Mkomo had originally thought that an education of this sort would give Charles the kind of Western polish that would make him a prospective suitor for a granddaughter of the current Queen of England, Elizabeth II. Unfortunately, Britain had been among those nations who broke off relations with Biandra in the wake of exaggerated newspaper reports about Mkomo's rule, and the Emperor had had to temporarily discard his ambitions for a connection between his family and the Windsors.

Mkomo roughly grabbed the steward's arm and thrust him forward along the corridor, using him as a shield. With Charles following, they reached the terminal without mishap. There, four other travelers were seated, their luggage at their feet and drinks in their hands.

One of them rose. "Damn it all if it isn't His Bloody Highness! Fancy meeting you here!"

Mkomo pushed the steward aside and trained his automatic on the standing figure. "I believe you have me at a disadvantage, sir," the Emperor growled.

The man ignored the Emperor's weapon and turned to his companions. He seemed to have had more than his share of drinks before the Emperor's arrival. "Allow me to present His Royal Highness Emperor Mkomo the, ah, First." He looked back with a wry smile. "The First, and perhaps the Only, eh, Your Majesty? I believe that overdressed fop standing next to him is the heir apparent, whose picture with his father's once graced the whole of the capital. I don't know whether you should all stand or kneel, but in the Emp's present, um, circumstances . . ." The man swayed slightly.

"Sit down, Ian," came a reply from a middle-aged woman seated nearby. "You've been tippling."

The man looked slightly abashed. "Oh, have I?" He looked around at the others and raised his glass. "My apologies, I'm sure." He checked in back of him to make certain his seat was still there, then retook it.

Mkomo trained his gaze on the woman. "Are you then one of my loyal subjects?" he said.

"Janet Gore," she said. "That's my husband, Ian. We couldn't in truth call ourselves loyal. Your henchmen butchered our workers on the farm that Ian and I owned for twenty years, but we managed to escape. 'Took the gap,' as the whites of Biandra called it. Since then, having been robbed of our livelihood and our country, we've been trying to raise the capital to buy a farm in Manitoba. I assume we're here for the same purpose you are."

Mkomo frowned. "It was not money that brought me here. An Emperor's greatest treasure is the love of his people."

"Quite so," said Janet Gore, "but your status as an Emperor does seem to be in doubt, doesn't it?"

Mkomo was tiring of this prattle. He let his gaze fall on the other two passengers. An old memory crossed through his brain, and with it his automatic settled on one of the two, an Oriental. "I remember you," Mkomo said.

The Oriental set down the cup of warm sake from which he

had been sipping. Mentally, he gauged the distance between the Emperor's gun and himself. His muscles tensed, but his face remained impassive. "I am honored," he said, and bowed slightly, keeping his eyes on the Emperor. "I am the photographer Kosho."

The Emperor's eyes narrowed into slits. "It was your false pictures of my subjects that were instrumental in prejudicing the Western nations against my rule."

"A similar complaint was made by American generals after my tour in Vietnam," Kosho replied.

The Emperor turned to the fourth traveler. "Since it seems that fortune has delivered my enemies to me, I would like also to know your name."

"Glassman," the man replied quietly. "I am afraid that I have never visited your country and know you only by reputation."

"I have never known a Jew who was a friend," said Mkomo. "Were you not responsible for the Israeli terrorist action against my country?"

"I regret that I did not personally command the group," said Glassman, "although I did have a role in training those who rescued Israeli tourists who had been held hostage by your barbarous regime."

Mkomo's lips curled in a sneer. "I am glad that my son is here to see the swift justice that the Lion of Biandra administers to his enemies." He looked toward Charles, who was at that moment relaxing in one of the cushioned chairs nearby, sipping a Dortmunder dark that the steward had brought.

"Pop," said the boy, "maybe it would be a good idea if . . ."

The Emperor suddenly whirled to face the steward, who had tapped his arm. In a swift movement, the steward stepped backward to avoid spilling his tray, holding a chilled bottle of Château d'Yquem. The Emperor now leveled his weapon on the white-coated steward, who bowed obsequiously, deftly balancing his tray as he did so.

"I am sorry to inform you," the steward said, "that the weapon you hold is not loaded. I believe this is your beverage of choice. Won't you have a seat and enjoy it until the others arrive?"

In response, the Emperor pulled the trigger of the Mauser three times. There were three empty clicks, and a subdued snickering from the direction of the four travelers.

The Emperor blinked. He had faced treachery before, and

would deal with it in his own time. The important thing was to maintain dignity. He placed the Mauser on the steward's tray and removed the bottle, along with a stemmed crystal glass. He leaned forward to whisper in the steward's ear, "I have one hundred gold Krugerrands in my luggage that are yours if you return it loaded."

The steward did not reply but withdrew hastily.

The Emperor smiled graciously at the small group around him, making a gesture of good cheer with his bottle. "A glass of divine spirits, and stimulating companions. What more could we ask for while awaiting adventure?"

Conversation revealed that each of the travelers had been flown to the island in an otherwise empty Boeing 727. Only a polite steward accompanied them. Kosho had flown from Tokyo, the Gores from Toronto, and Rabbi Glassman from Tel Aviv. For each, the journey had been a long one, and all had slept through a peaceful night. None of them knew the precise whereabouts of the island on which they now found themselves.

Each of the travelers had responded to a newspaper advertisement promising a handsome reward to anyone qualifying for a contest of skill and courage. On being invited to an interview, they had been informed that an international consortium of entrepreneurs was preparing to open a very private resort in a secluded location. The resort was described as a combination Club Med, Disneyland, wildlife park, and health spa. It was to contain five rough-terrain environments in which the jaded rich could compete in a test of hunting and survival skills.

For insurance purposes, the resort had to be tested before opening by a group selected for aggressiveness and survival ability. It was stressed that there would be an element of danger, for which each candidate had to sign a release form absolving the consortium of liability in case of accidents. All those completing the course, however, would receive a handsome fee of $20,000. And to sharpen the element of competition, the final leg of the journey would lead to a hidden treasure of a thousand ounces of .999 Fine gold—not a difficult burden to carry, slightly more than sixty-two pounds, but worth in the fluctuating gold market about a half million dollars. It would belong to the volunteer "contestant" who was first to complete the course.

It was not long before the sounds of a taxiing plane signaled the arrival of another group. Minutes later, the door to the admissions corridor opened. In stepped a tall blond couple in their late thirties, followed by a stunningly beautiful young girl who bore a clear resemblance to both her parents. Charles whistled loudly, and Mkomo glared at him. Mkomo stood and held out his hand to the man. "Emperor Mkomo of Biandra. I welcome you to our joint adventure."

The man took Mkomo's hand, and the two of them held the clasp for a moment longer than necessary, seemingly testing each other's strength. "Bjorn Halvorssen. My wife, Bibi, and my daughter, Kirsten."

"You'd take your daughter along on a trip like this?" exclaimed Glassman from his seat.

The Halvorssens exchanged glances and seemed to share a private joke. "Kirsten could hardly be denied the opportunity," her father explained. "She easily passed the tests that the owners of this resort devised. Actually, I think that her youth and agility may prove to be an advantage. We thought when she was very young that she would be a gymnast, but she grew too large for international competition, and took up water polo."

"Water polo!" said Charles. "That's pretty rough, although I guess girls' teams . . ."

Kirsten smiled at him. She brushed her hair back from her forehead. "My club in Stockholm makes no difference between boys or girls. We also play mixed teams. We *did* meet an all-boy team from England this year, and trounced them soundly."

Bjorn Halvorssen smiled at his daughter. "Watching the match, I had little sight of Kirsten. She has developed the ability to hold her breath for some minutes."

"Father means to say I was underwater poking them . . . where they didn't expect me to poke." She giggled; her parents beamed.

"Perhaps you can show me some tricks later on," said Charles.

"Oh, she knows plenty of tricks," chuckled her father, setting down his backpack. "Don't get in *her* way."

Charles ignored the advice and stepped over to help Kirsten with her pack. She shrugged him off and removed her quilted jacket along with the pack. Charles goggled at the curves that even a loose flannel shirt did not conceal.

Mkomo jerked his arm and muttered, "Time for that in Paris, ox-eyes. While you're gaping, the parents will be proceeding on to the goal." Charles gave his father a brief look of resentment.

The others were introducing themselves, and Mkomo hurried over to be part of the scene. "I had a curiosity what the others would be like,'' Halvorssen was saying, ''and I see now why the testers seemed to approve that we knew English.''

''Obviously we were meant to communicate with each other,'' said Glassman.

Mkomo glanced at the others. Already, he thought, the Israeli was attempting to gather the others around him to smooth his path to the treasure. Of course they would want to begin by forming into groups, and he who could gain the greatest number of followers could advance more quickly. It was not unlike politics, a sport in which he considered himself a world-class player. Still, thought Mkomo, there was an advantage to the one who might travel alone. He glanced at Charles, wondering if the boy would be more of a liability than he had thought.

The sound of another arriving plane drew their attention, and in a few minutes another couple appeared in the waiting room. Mkomo called out a hearty welcome. The newcomers appeared startled. The man doffed his cowboy hat and peered at Mkomo.

''Yeah, thought I recognized you from the newspapers,'' said the man in a flat drawl. ''I'm Bob Miller, from the U.S. of A. This here's my old gal Betty. She was Miss Mississippi not that long ago.'' He gestured toward his wife and then slapped her on the rump as if she were a prize heifer. '' 'Course she won't like me tellin' just how long ago.''

Betty Miller smiled at the group and turned around to let them admire her.

Her Neiman-Marcus tailored hunting outfit was as impeccable as if it had come out of Nancy Reagan's closet, but Mkomo searched her face for telltale lines of frustration. He had met women like this in Paris—the wives of men who were too concerned with making money to attend properly to the pleasure of their wives. Mkomo had found that such women could be suitably grateful to a man of potency.

''A lovely vision,'' Mkomo said, smiling at Mrs. Miller. He turned to her husband. ''Many men must envy you.''

''Yeah?'' said Bob Miller, wary at Mkomo's interest. ''Just make sure you keep *your* distance. We already read about your insatiable appetites in the *Dallas News Sunday Magazine*. And the way you butchered your own people.''

''If the Jews did not control all the newspapers and television networks in your country, my friend, I'm sure you would have read the true story. In fact, I was engaged in a struggle to eliminate Communist infiltrators from my people. In the battle against the Marxist beast, a man can give no quarter."

"Yeah? Sounds possible. I keep an open mind. We got quite a few of them traitors ourselves, but Ronnie Reagan will take care of them, you can bet."

"Indeed so. I have been a longtime admirer of your most courageous president. I am sure that if he had been in office instead of the vile peanut farmer, I would have been given help to overcome the Marxists that overturned my legally elected government."

Bob Miller shrugged, then paused. He suddenly realized his son was nowhere to be found. He looked behind him. "Wait just a second. Hey! Hey, Billy! What the hell . . . you get lost?"

Another figure shyly made its way around the corner to the passageway that led from the planes' embarkation connection. Carrying a small silver and blue flight bag with the marking DALLAS COWBOYS, he shuffled forward, head hung low, as if he would have liked to melt into the wall.

"My boy," said Bob Miller in a rueful voice. "Already got kicked out of Culver. Got him into Dallas Country Day, but he doesn't keep his mind on nothin'."

"Sons are a trial," murmured Mkomo sympathetically.

Miller nodded absently. "Took him to Vail, and he spent the whole goddamn week in the room readin' some smutty books. Cost me $4,000, that week, and it wasn't no more to him than a trip to the public library. Goddamn it, boy, get in here. Lookit this now! A real Emperor! We're goin' travelin' with a Emperor! Whattaya think of that?"

Billy looked for a fraction of a second at Mkomo, nodded just slightly, and mumbled something inaudible. Bob Miller shook his head in vexation and turned his back. "Where's the bar?" he hollered, and the steward rushed to bring his beverage of choice—a six-pack of Lone Star.

Billy took a seat apart from the others and played with the zipper on his flight bag. He was wondering if his father would notice if he took out his paperback copy of Jerzy Kosinski's *Steps* with the dirty parts in it marked by his friend Brian McConnell before he left. Billy decided against it. He had several books borrowed from Brian in his bag, but he didn't know how long this idiotic trip was going to last; he had noticed that the dirty parts slackened in their desired effect after six or seven readings, and there was no sense wasting one right out here where everybody was watching him.

Someone sat down next to him. Billy glanced over but quickly looked away when he realized it was a girl. He took a deep breath. She would soon notice him and move away.

She touched him on the arm. He jumped.

"Excuse me," she said.

He had to look at her now, and he forced his gaze upward to her face, then immediately looked down, realized he was now staring at her breasts, and looked away, wildly scanning the room. He moved his mouth, trying to think of something to say, but the only thought in his mind was that this was the most beautiful girl he'd ever seen. He knew enough not to say *that*.

"I was wondering how old you were," said the girl.

He struggled to answer. "I'm—" he heard the high, strangled pitch in his voice, and cleared his throat. He wondered if he should lie, but did not. "I'm sixteen," he breathed out in relief.

The girl clapped her hands and looked at him radiantly. "Isn't that nice!" she said. "I'm only fifteen, for another month anyway. That makes me the youngest on the trip."

Billy smiled and attempted to make his eyes meet hers. As he did, he saw that she had the palest blue eyes he had ever seen, paler than sky blue, and they seemed interested in him.

He searched his memory of the hours of advice that Brian McConnell had given him in case of situations like this. He recalled nothing except that Brian had said that if you rubbed them in the little hollow in the back where their buttocks began to separate, they would do anything. That didn't seem practical at this moment, except that thinking of it made it necessary for him to move his flight bag onto his lap.

"Where do you go to high school?" he stammered, to take her attention away from the flight bag.

"St. Berthilde's is my school," she answered. "Do you smoke marijuana?"

The directness of the question left him speechless.

"The reason I asked is that I heard all American kids smoke marijuana." She put her hand on his arm. He looked down at it, and desired it. He couldn't recall Brian saying anything about hands. He reached over and took it. Just like that, he thought, feeling the incredible softness of her hand in his, the warmth of another skin, a girl's hand.

"I hope you don't smoke too much," she said. "It's bad for the genes."

He looked at her dumbly, then nodded. She wasn't even noticing that he was holding her hand. Maybe he should let it go.

"Yes," he said. "I mean, no." He shook his head emphatically. "Just social. You know."

She nodded. "That is good. I admire people who like to experiment with life, but not fanatically."

Charles appeared in front of them. Billy looked up at the tawny, handsome young man. He wore an alpaca sweater from which emerged the long-tipped collars of the lime-green silk shirt underneath. Below he wore designer jeans that looked as if they had been sewn onto his body, and leather boots that shone. Billy sighed.

"I guess this is the young people's corner," said Charles, opening his lips to expose two rows of perfect white teeth.

"We were talking," Billy heard the girl say evenly.

Charles laughed softly. "I'll *bet*," he said sarcastically. "This fellow really looks like a together dude."

Billy felt the girl's eyes turn back to him. He met them with a tentative smile, as if to say, *It's all right. I don't mind if you go off with him.*

She turned back to Charles. Waving her head toward Billy, she said, "I think he looks a little like John Travolta."

Charles guffawed. Billy let go of her hand.

The girl's voice turned cold. "We're *really* having a private conversation."

Charles didn't seem to have an answer for this. His head jerked as if something heavy had landed on his neck. "I'll be around," he said, waving his beer bottle toward them in a vaguely threatening gesture, and walked off.

Billy could feel that his palms were wet. Kirsten's hand was still on his arm. He wiped his hands casually on his jeans and took up her hand again. It felt warmer, and he wondered if it was because his own hands were cold. "I really don't think I look much like John Travolta," he said.

She flashed her eyes at him. "It's your eyes," she said. "They're very deep."

He felt transfixed. They stared at each other, and he felt himself leaning toward her, slowly enough that she wouldn't have to notice. He tried not to think about what he was thinking about. Suddenly she moved her head forward and brushed her lips against his. He smelled her perfume before she popped away.

"Have you ever tried *aquavit*?" she asked. "They can bring us some, if we ask."

He didn't hear her.

Chapter Two

Seven slender figures clad in stocking-tight black garments sat in a space enclosed by a gray-green mist. To all appearances, they were in a cleared spot in the midst of a swamp, although the plants whose tendrils snaked toward the group bore no resemblance to plants that normally grew on earth. The surface on which they sat was composed of a spongy substance that provided comfortable seating.

To one side stood a pyramid of objects that any intelligent species would recognize as weapons—cleverly made slings; spears whose shafts were made of a golden wood that was hard and smooth and whose blades were hand-hammered to a point; huge, ugly clubs with fearsome-looking knobs and thorns.

To most of the People the camp was a meaningless display of ritual and myth, intended to flatter the egos of those members of a now highly sophisticated society who liked to recall their primitive origins. To these seven in the green mist, it was a satisfying sign that they were beyond the constraints—but also the assistance—of a society that had grown too soft for their tastes.

The Commander rose and indicated with a formal movement of his head and hands that he wished to address the group. The others indicated their assent.

In the oval space between them, the Commander summoned up the mental image of a globe on which were represented the surface areas of the planet. "As you can see," he said, "the land areas are concentrated in the central regions. One of the poles has no land at all, while the other has a landmass that is continually covered by ice. The distance of this planet from its rather feeble sun, and the specific concentration of the land areas, made it ideal for the formation of land-traveling life forms. There are, of course, water-based life forms, some as intelligent as the land-based dominant species, but they have not developed a social hierarchy, science, or tools.

"Curiously, the land-dwelling form of superior life was a single species, but as it spread throughout the globe, the individuals developed different types of aural communication. Since they have no telepathic communicative faculties, the lack of ability to communicate increased their tendency to band into mutually hostile groups."

The Aging Master raised his head in the traditional manner to indicate that he wished to speak, and the others assumed positions of attention toward him. "We were told, Commander, that the Hunt was to be conducted strictly according to the Old Rules."

The Commander indicated assent.

"Rule Three states that the game must have skills and weapons equal to those of the Hunters."

Again the Commander assented.

"My interpretation of this would be that they should have the power to communicate effectively with each other."

The Scientist started to object, but the Commander leveled a gesture of silence toward him. "I anticipated this objection," the Commander said, "and programmed the lures to select only those members of the species who can communicate in the most widely used language. It is now used for trade, and thus we were still able to obtain game from several nation groups."

The Aging Master indicated his approval.

"Where exactly on the planet are we?" asked the Golden Female, who was the youngest of the Hunters.

The Commander pointed toward the pole that contained a landmass. "We are on an isolated island which in the normal conditions of the planet is covered with ice. We have converted it for our purposes to a series of environments representing conditions of terrain and climate that are regarded as difficult by the dominant life form. As you will see shortly when we view the introduction to the Hunt by the guide we have supplied to the game, these environments consist of—"

"Do you mean," interrupted the Golden Female rudely, drawing an admonitory gesture from the Commander which she ignored, "that we will be operating in an illusion?"

The Commander indicated assent.

"Why doesn't that violate Rule Two? No one is supposed to use the Discovery on the Hunt."

The Commander was visibly annoyed, but the Aging Master again indicated his desire to speak. Though he was past the stage when a Female such as this one could have swayed his judgment by thoughts of mating availability, it was clear that he bore a special affection for the Golden Female, and was charmed by her evident interest in the subtle interpretations of the Old Rules. "Rule Two," he explained, "states simply that the Discovery must not be used *against* the game. Since we will be operating in the same environment as they, perceiving it exactly as they perceive it, then there is no advantage to us."

The Golden Female pressed her question. "Isn't knowing that it's an illusion—knowing that we could change the illusion at will—something of an advantage?"

The Aging Master indicated his approval of her perceptiveness, but said, "Of course it could be an advantage if any of us were to make use of that knowledge or violate our honor by acting on it. I trust that none among us will so dishonor himself—or herself."

Indicating his wish to speak, the Natural Hunter barely waited for the others to assent. When he spoke, however, it was in his usual slow and insinuating manner, as if he were questioning children. The Commander had disliked him from the first time they met, despite the Natural Hunter's reputation. "I take it that you will be maintaining these environments yourself, Commander."

"Correct," the Commander said, instead of merely indicating assent.

"If you should be careless enough so that . . . you would be disabled by the game, have you made any provisions for delegating the responsibility?"

The Commander glanced at the Mate, who nervously attempted to look capable.

"I see," said the Natural Hunter, following the Commander's gaze. "Of course, just in case the landscape should begin to appear to dissolve, it will be permissible for any of us temporarily to correct things."

"I hope you won't have to inconvenience yourselves," said the Commander.

"So do I," replied the Natural Hunter. "I would like to concentrate on the business at hand. At least," he added, "we won't have to discuss at tiresome length the possibility of Rule One applying."

The Commander uneasily allowed his gaze to flicker to the Scientist, to check his reaction. The Scientist asked permission to speak.

"The fascinating thing about these animals is how fast they have progressed from Class E to Class B. They first emerged as a recognizable species a scant 800 narlecs ago, little more than a million revolutions of their planet around their feeble sun."

"Perhaps they will make an equally fast progression . . . to the Discovery. That would be an unpleasant surprise."

"Not possible," said the Scientist.

The Mate realized suddenly that the Commander had concealed the fact that one of the animals on the earlier trip had been able to operate a Discovery-powered weapon. He felt a distinct sense of fear, for he knew as everyone else did the reason why the Guardians were careful to destroy all races who had reached the level of Class B—to keep them from endangering the supremacy of the People. Usually there *was* plenty of time for such a step, for it took eons for a race to proceed from Class B to Class A.

Here, there was need for haste, and yet the Commander had concealed the true ability of these animals—merely so he could command a Class B Hunting Party. If the Commander had miscalculated the speed of their development, then the wrath of the Guardians would make even a lifetime on this benighted planet infinitely preferable to returning home. That must have been why the Commander had brought the Scientist.

The Gray Female, who had been silently controlling her own emotions up till now, not wanting the others to sense her bloodlust, now indicated her desire to speak. At the Commander's indication, she said calmly and formally, "I feel we know enough about the creatures to begin the Hunt on equal terms."

The Commander assented. "We can now watch their reactions to the guide." He mentally summoned up the image of the interior of the terminal where the game were collected.

Chapter Three

Kirsten introduced Billy to the delights of aquavit. He found the effect immensely preferable to that of the pot parties in Brian McConnell's rathskeller. Pot had given Billy headaches and made him dizzy. He laughed uproariously with the others whenever something—anything—was said, but he woke up the next day feeling somehow that he had missed the joke.

With Kirsten, it was *she* who was laughing at *his* jokes. He had even surprised himself by casually draping his arm around her shoulder just as if he'd been doing it all his life. Billy looked around for the steward, thinking to order a third small glass of the aquavit, when Kirsten suddenly pointed. "Oh, look. Something's about to happen."

The stewards—there were several of them, Billy noticed, all looking even more remarkably alike than the waiters at the Dallas Country Club—were wheeling out large cases shrouded by blue velvet cloth.

Billy and Kirsten went to join the others who were coming forward to watch. Billy noticed his father and Mkomo jovially trading remarks about their prowess at hunting. He cringed, hoping that Kirsten wouldn't notice. When the group had assembled, the stewards removed the cloth, and the travelers fell silent.

The cases were filled with weapons of every conceivable sort, representing every culture on earth. There were modern small arms, machine guns, rifles, shotguns, and even a few portable rocket-launchers.

Numerous as the modern weapons were, they were dwarfed by the more familiar, older weapons. There were a hundred kinds of bladed weapons—épées, cutlasses, curved Arab scimitars. Kosho stared at a set of samurai swords whose blades were drawn half out of their scabbards to expose the shining steel of the razor edges. "Designs from the fifteenth century," Kosho muttered, "yet they show no sign of age."

Mkomo was equally fascinated by a selection of spears—Mongol, African, Native American, and even older ones that seemed to have come from cultures that had long ago passed into oblivion. Yet all appeared new.

Ian Gore dazedly inspected a display of medieval European armaments, complete with suits of armor, mace and chain, and a broad, two-handed sword that looked as if the young Arthur had just pulled it from the stone. Ian's hand reached out for it; he pulled it off the wooden rack on which it rested, and the weight of it pulled it out of his grasp to the floor.

The sound of the sword crashing against the terrazzo floor seemed to galvanize the others. Each reached for a weapon. Hesitating, Mkomo found himself unable to resist picking up one of the long African spears. He lifted it, testing its weight. "My father killed lions with one of these," he said. "I had one like it—that I too used—hanging behind the imperial throne. It was useful, but I never tried it on lions."

Kirsten nudged Billy and handed him a small Remington .25. She helped herself to a jewel-handled dagger that looked as if it had been made for a princess. "Don't you want a gun?" Billy asked. She smiled.

"I am an expert shot," she said, "but men do not shoot at girls. They rape them." She drew the flat side of the blade upwards through Billy's jeaned thighs. He jumped backwards.

Glassman, who was the only one still without a weapon, overheard their conversation. "You don't mean . . ." he said, then faced the others and shouted: "Wait! We have no need of weapons!"

The others stopped their excited conversations. Billy's father turned with a blue-steel Purdy shotgun in his hands. Kosho had withdrawn the exquisite samurai sword from its scabbard. Janet Gore stood as if on guard over her husband with a heavy Webley revolver. A red-faced Ian Gore brandished the heavy sword he had reclaimed. Betty Miller gracefully pulled the string on her tournament bow, thinking of her appearance as Diana the archer;

the bow's fifty-pound pull and its steel-tipped arrows made her look formidable.

Bjorn Halvorssen had shouldered a heavy-looking double-barreled hunting rifle; he knew that at close range its .470 caliber would bring down a charging elk. His wife, Bibi, like her daughter had been drawn to a blade, but hers was a Swedish-steel saber with an Italian grip. She was an experienced fencer, and the weight of the weapon hung easily in her hand.

Mkomo's son, Charles, was delightedly strapping to his waist a tooled leather belt and holster. When he finished, he practiced a western quick draw with a Colt Peacemaker, a movie six-shooter. His was a particularly handsome model, with filigreed engraving on the barrel, frame, and cylinder, and a pearl handle secured by diamond-tipped screws.

Glassman stared at the array of weaponry in dismay, as he saw the eyes of the others flicker around the group in suspicion. "No, no," he murmured, but his own gaze was drawn to the weapon rack, where he saw an Uzi submachine gun exactly like that he had used in the Israeli army.

"Oh, yes," replied a voice. They all whirled to face the speaker. It was a tiny gray-haired woman dressed in a flower print dress and Adidas running shoes. Her gray hair was pulled back in a bun, and she stared out at them from octagonal rimless glasses.

"Who the devil are *you*?" said Bob Miller.

She looked kindly at him, and said, "Why, I'm Granny."

The others relaxed the tension that her sudden appearance had caused. Even Mkomo chuckled, looking around at the others to see their reactions. He spun his finger meaningfully in a circle near his left ear.

Granny clucked in reproof when she saw the gesture. "Oh, don't be too quick to judge people by appearances. You trusted that cowering, quivering Lluanda, didn't you? Look where it got you?"

Mkomo frowned at the reference and raised his spear threateningly.

Granny clapped her hands. "And you, Rabbi, go ahead now—pick up the Uzi. We brought it especially for you—you did so well with the one you had in the Six-Day War."

Glassman's lips tightened. "Not 'rabbi,' if you please. A rabbi is a leader, a teacher; I am neither of those."

"As you like," Granny said with a wave of her hand. "Yet to your people, who talk of your exploits still, you are a rabbi."

"I taught, yes, and I led, but I am now beginning again to learn."

Granny surveyed the rest of the group approvingly. "I see the rest of you are a little in advance of me. I'm very pleased. There will not be much for you to learn."

Bob Miller laughed loudly. "You do remind me of my old sixth-grade teacher. But she never showed me how to bring down a boar with *this*." He raised his shotgun.

"No, and neither will I. You all brought your own skill with weapons and with trailcraft. Those skills come with practice, and you do not have time for practice. Tomorrow you will be testing your skills."

"Against each other?" inquired Kosho.

"No, that would be very unwise. I want you all to understand something right at the outset. You were *invited* here, and as you recall, were quite eager to come. There were . . . one or two little details that were omitted from your briefing. Until now. But I want you to know that when I speak to you I will not deceive you."

Kosho smiled. "However . . . a lie was told to us?"

"A little one. This is not really a resort, was never meant to be. There is no consortium. No one—in your world—knows that you are here, for no one knows where this place is."

"Well, by God, you're gonna quick get to tellin' us," said Bob Miller, raising his shotgun.

"Oh, there's no sense threatening *me*," said Granny, with a chuckle. "I am invulnerable." She turned toward Billy. "Don't get yourself in trouble with that pistol, now," she said with a tone that showed she expected obedience. "Come up here."

Embarrassed, Billy made his way forward, holding out the pistol, which he expected she would humiliatingly take from him. When he stopped in front of the old woman, he saw his father moving menacingly forward. Granny raised her hand.

"Shoot me now, Billy," Granny commanded.

His mouth fell open. He looked at his father, who seemed equally shocked.

Granny frowned. "I know you were chosen for your aggressive feelings. Are you afraid of me?"

"My boy ain't afraid of nothin'," said Bob Miller, "but he

wasn't brought up to shoot old ladies in a back alley for their pocketbooks."

"Your codes of civilization are still puzzling to us," replied Granny. "Though we know much about you. I see the Hunter's look on several of you, but among you there is one in whom it is very intense. Mr. Emperor," she said, pointing at Mkomo with a steady hand, "show us your skill with a spear."

Mkomo laughed from far back in his throat. He raised his spear, bringing shrieks from some of the others, who scurried out of his way. Bjorn Halvorssen tried to turn his rifle on the Emperor, but Kosho flicked it downward with a sudden thrust of the wooden sheath that had held the samurai sword. "Let her choose a destiny," the Japanese muttered.

Mkomo let fly. From a range of thirty feet, he could not have missed the target, but as the spear reached Granny, there occurred what appeared to be an optical illusion. The point of the spear touched the thin cloth of her dress and fell to the floor, its force spent.

"Protective clothing," nodded Bjorn Halvorssen.

"Not at all," said Granny. "If I had been wearing a defense garment, the force with which the spear was thrown would have knocked me to the ground. No, the truth is—and you remember I promised to tell you the truth—I am not flesh and blood."

The laughter this time was nervous, and echoed hollowly around the terminal walls.

Granny frowned. "I'm afraid you're being difficult students today. Let me have your pistol, Billy."

Meekly, he handed it to her. She pressed it to her breast and fired. The report was loud, and a small cloud of smoke rose into the air. She didn't even sway.

"I once saw a fakir in India do that," said Ian Gore, with the superior tone of one who has discovered the trick. "Blanks, of course."

Granny leveled the barrel of the pistol at him. "Would you take the chance?"

Gore smiled crookedly. "First one, blank; the rest, loaded charges."

"You tell me, then," said Granny. "How many should I fire into those seats?"

Gore licked his lips. "Three."

Three shots rang out, and three holes appeared in the row of plexiglass chairs. Granny held up the gun, and questioned Gore with a twinkle in her eye. "One more round in the chamber; two in the magazine. How many shall I fire at you, and how many at myself?"

Gore hesitated, looked around at the others, who watched in fascination. He felt a schoolboy's embarrassment. "All three at yourself, then," he said.

Three more shots. There was a slight rattling sound on the floor that drew all eyes. Ian Gore stooped and held up the three spent .25 slugs. Granny stood unscathed.

Kosho broke the spell that followed by stepping forward and bowing low. "You, then, are our guide?"

She smiled and nodded. "Among the group, you were thought to be the most adaptable. Except for the children, of course."

"And now," Kosho said, "you will tell us the real purpose of our trip?"

"Yes." Granny looked around. Bob Miller and Janet Gore were examining the bullet holes in the seats. Mkomo had reclaimed his spear, examined its point, and found it perfect. He squatted on the floor with the spear across his knees, in a pose that his son Charles recognized as one he assumed when he was in a particularly ugly mood. Charles grew nervous. On one occasion, the outcome of a similar mood was that Mkomo killed three of Charles's younger brothers whom he suspected of plotting against him.

Quietly, Charles checked the bullets in his Colt revolver. They were not blanks. He moved to a position out of his father's line of sight.

Granny clapped her hands to get their attention, and before long, most of them were seated in the chairs. Mkomo stayed in his squatting position on the floor.

"I am," the old woman began, "as one of you has guessed, your guide. You see before you a choice of weapons. You will be allowed to exchange your choices for other weapons at selected points along the way, and you will be provided with appropriate clothing for the environments through which you will travel."

"The environments?" said Billy, and immediately flushed, aware that people had looked at him.

"Those parts of the . . . park. Shall we call it the Park? I think that is a pleasant word in your language. There will be nothing that some or all of you have not already experienced. First, beginning tomorrow, you will find yourselves in the mountains. All of you have climbing experience, and the passes are not particularly difficult. There is only one difficult place, but I'm sure you are capable of traversing it. You will of course need to dress for the weather. After that—"

"How will we know which way to go?" interrupted Bjorn Halvorssen, who knew that a terrain of snow would present problems of visibility.

"Oh, they'll mark it with flags," said Betty Miller confidently. "Just like the course at Aspen."

Granny shook her head. "There will be maps that you can follow. Of course, you may find it necessary to go off the marked trails."

"Why would we—" Betty Miller began, but her husband shushed her. She shut her mouth and looked around, hoping that she hadn't been embarrassing Bob.

"I will be available to you in all the environments," said Granny, "and will give you good advice if you ask me."

"Isn't this supposed to be a *race*?" asked Kirsten. "Suppose we become separated?"

Granny nodded in approval. "I am glad the young people have so much competitiveness. Yes, you may become separated, but to call me you need only say, or think, *Granny, I need you*."

The group murmured among themselves; a feeling of doubt again became apparent. "The perfect *shabbas goy*," laughed Glassman.

"And after that?" said Janet Gore.

"After that . . ." Granny began. "Then those of you who survive will have another meeting with me, and we can discuss the next environment."

"Survive?" said Bibi Halvorssen. "I don't know about the others, but what you have described would not present a particular danger to my husband, my daughter, or me. We are experienced. As for the others . . ." She looked doubtfully at Billy Miller.

"Don't worry about the Millers, babe," called out Bob Miller. The others seemed to have equal confidence in themselves.

"Yes," said Granny. "The terrain itself will not be a truly dangerous challenge to any of you who are careful. You have, as you remember, been selected for a versatility of skills. But there is another danger."

Kosho nodded. *Granny, I need you,* he thought to himself.

Granny looked up, startled. "Mr. Kosho?" she said with a quizzical look.

"You do, then, know our thoughts," said Kosho, lowering his eyelids. "I do not have quite your ability, I can see, but I have developed my awareness, and I sensed a danger of which you have not told us."

"Yes."

A growl came from the squatting form of Mkomo. Charles's hand tightened on the grip of his Colt. "Mkomo fears no *danger,*" came the deep voice from the floor. "Mkomo fears *tricks,* fears *lies.*"

There was a brief silence. "I have not lied to you, Your Highness," said Granny.

"And the *treasure*?" said Mkomo with greater malevolence. "The others spoke of a thousand troy ounces of gold. Duped us. Lured us here for this pleasure trip. Mkomo does not perform like a trained lion for the pleasure of others. Is that a lie, too?"

"Oh, most assuredly not. I understand your concern. Would you just glance at that television monitor over there?" Without warning, a television screen at one of the ticket counters lit up. It was only a few feet away, and the picture was so clear that it must have been a closed-circuit telecast. The group gasped. On the screen were three shining bars of gold, shimmering against a blue background.

Mkomo grunted and rose. He walked to the screen and caressed the image lovingly with his hands. "So there *is* gold," he said. Then a renewed note of suspicion came into his voice, and he turned to face Granny. "It seems to be in water."

"That will be the final environment," said Granny. "The ocean. There will be diving gear for you . . . if you get that far."

Mkomo returned to the group and stood facing Granny. He nodded at Kosho. "And now," he said, "for I have felt it too . . . you will tell us of the enemy who waits."

"There's one of them now," said Granny. The group started collectively, but she was merely gesturing toward the television screen. On it now was the picture of a full-length humanoid figure, thin, wearing a black garment that seemed to cover its body from toes to neck. Gradually the camera drew nearer to the unmoving figure, until its gray face filled the screen.

The head was egg-shaped, with dark slits from either side converging toward the center, in the place where eyes should have been. There were two black holes in the place where there should have been a nose. Instead of a mouth, there was a thin slit that puckered at either end. The face was expressionless, yet carried the terror of an empty, fleshless skull.

"That!" cried Mkomo contemptuously. "That is an enemy? There must be many of them."

"There are only seven," said Granny, "against twelve of you, so you have the advantage in numbers. You have other advantages as well."

"Wait just a minute," said Betty Miller, sounding as if she were a little short of breath. She glanced at her husband. "Bob, I'm sorry, but . . . this has all been a little too quick for me. You mean these"—she shuddered, and could scarcely bring herself to look at the television screen—"these"—she caught herself. Her instinct had been to call them "niggers," but she remembered the presence of Mkomo and his son— "other folks are going to try to stop us from getting to the treasure?"

"That will be the effect," said Granny. "Actually, they are here to kill you."

Betty Miller put her hand over her mouth, but could not stop the wailing sound that emerged from it. The others watched her curiously, except for Billy, who looked away in furious embarrassment. His eyes met those of Kirsten, who patted his shoulder. "You'd better find a new clip for your gun," she murmured.

"Oh, my God, Bob, let's get out of here," Betty was now wailing, and in response her husband slapped her soundly across the face. She gasped in dismay, but she fell silent.

Billy nearly rose from his seat, his eyes blazing with anger, but Kirsten pushed him down. "Sometimes a woman needs a little shock to calm herself," she said. Billy stared at her, thinking of what it would be like to slap Kirsten. Reading his thoughts, she shook her head with a smile. "We Danes are quite disciplined already," she said.

Granny continued as if the disturbance had not occurred. "You see, it is *he* who has created the environments. He has brought the others here to your world for only one purpose—to hunt and kill you. They are Hunters, and you are a species of most promising game."

Glassman suddenly burst out laughing, and the others looked at him as if he were insane.

"You find this funny, jewboy?" shouted Bob Miller.

Glassman's laughter stopped at the epithet, then continued as his mocking brown eyes stared infuriatingly at Bob Miller.

"Yes," said Glassman, "I find it funny. You with your arrogance, the Emperor here with his hands of blood, and I myself . . ." His voice trailed off.

"Yeah, you're better than us, right?" said Bob Miller.

Glassman's smile was crooked now, and his voice lower. "I once thought so. I fought for a dream . . . a two-thousand-year-old dream, that there should be a place that would be free from persecution and pogroms." He put his hands to his face, as if he wanted to blot out something that he alone could see.

"And then," he continued tonelessly, as if it were a story he had told himself many times, "we found a new people, some others with whom we could not live as equals."

He shouted at them, the words pouring from him like a street corner evangelist. "Everywhere on earth, people quarrel, kill one another. Everywhere. Why? Aren't we really all one people? Jews, gentiles, Arabs, blacks, yellows. All one, yet we continually kill one another. I gave it up. Determined that whatever came, I would no longer go on with the killing. And now . . . here it is again. It follows me."

He fell back in his chair and hid his face. There was an uneasy silence. Granny regarded him with dismay.

"I know what he means," said Janet Gore. "In Biandra there was the same . . . killing. It was not just blacks against whites. That would be senseless enough, but when it became clear that the British would turn over control to a native government, then the blacks began to kill each other. It was hideous. We escaped, but wherever we went—even in Canada—I never escaped that feeling that nowhere were we ever going to be as safe again as when I was a child on my father's farm with his loyal native workers."

"Those people whom you exploited and wanted to rule as if they were children," said Charles.

Janet flinched. "Perhaps that is true," she said to him, "but we loved them as children. And when the killing started, your father was the result."

"Stop it!" shouted Granny. Her voice had enough authority in it to command their attention. "The history of your species has continually been that of groups warring against other groups. You fight each other, and sometimes regret what you have done, but you go on killing. And you also overlook that you have been only one species out of millions on the planet. And the *others* you have always exploited without compunction.''

''Life feeding on life,'' murmured Kosho.

Granny nodded. ''You have seen that. Yes, life lives on life, and you have been the dominant life form on this planet. You thought it your right to live from the life of the other species. Did you imagine you were alone in the universe? Surely you noticed the stars, and guessed them suns. . . .''

''Ah,'' said Bjorn Halvorssen, ''but we never guessed them threats. Like my lovely Denmark, we thought to survive because we did not invade others, did not provoke them.''

''And we certainly did nothing to provoke you,'' said Ian Gore.

''Do not think that way,'' cautioned Granny. ''It is not I who am your adversary. Do you understand?'' She looked around at the rest. ''Everyone! Listen to me for your own good! I am not to be thought of as the ally of those who hunt you. I am in truth their creation, but they have created me to serve you. You must believe that, for your lives may depend on it.

''The People, for that is what they call themselves, are not interested in merely slaughtering you. They could do that easily. But it would serve no purpose. They have many sources of life to provide for their physical needs, much closer to their home than your planet.''

''Where is that?'' asked Kosho.

''It does not matter. What matters is that you must understand the rules under which the Hunt is to be conducted.''

''Rules,'' spat out Mkomo. ''This is the only rule that I respect.'' With a howl, the famed howl of the hunting lion of Biandra, he flung his spear over the heads of the others toward the television screen, where it pierced and obliterated the image of the Hunter.

''Impressive,'' said Granny, as the others sat in shocked silence. ''And indicative of why you were selected. But there *are* rules, not rules for you, but for them.''

''Why?'' asked Bob Miller.

''Because they are the supreme species in the universe. None can touch their ability. But they found that when they deliberately limited themselves, there was a challenge to them.''

''There is the danger of boredom in absolute superiority,'' said Kosho.

''Exactly so,'' said Granny. ''The rules are designed to give you a real chance to survive. The Hunters will not wear protective garments. They will only use weapons that you yourselves have chosen. They will not use . . . other powers that they have to confuse or evade you. And they have given you a guide."

"Either that . . . or they have given us someone to confuse us," said Ian Gore.

She shook her head. "I will prove my usefulness, if you allow me. I repeat, you have only to say or think that you need me, and I will be available to you. I am as invulnerable to their weapons as to yours. I was created that way. And I was created not to lie." She took a step backward. "I *never* lie," she repeated, and as they watched, she began to fade like an old photograph. She vanished. Betty Miller gave a howl of dismay.

Chapter Four

Ian Gore was beyond drunkenness, and had entered a false nirvana. "I shay it's all a ruse," he said, the sword of Arthur resting between his knees.

The others ignored him. The stewards had shown them to private compartments with comfortable bedding and toilet facilities, and set out a sumptuous meal for them, including endless bottles of wine and spirits.

As the others ate, Mkomo displayed his prowess with a spear by destroying television screens at greater and greater distances.

Sweating, Mkomo gathered up some of the spears he had been using for practice. Unlike the others, who discussed their situation in puzzled, frantic tones, he had immediately accepted the truth of the situation and had responded by sharpening his skills.

From what Granny had said, he deduced that his own skill with a spear would be challenged by one of the . . . others. The Hunters. Mkomo was confident enough to believe that no one—in the universe, if that was the testing ground—could surpass his skill.

"The universe" was not a difficult jump for Mkomo to make. He had been born in a village in which no one guessed that there was a city of many thousands in their own country. They had not even known the name of the country. As a boy, he had regarded white missionaries' stories of Europe, Asia, and America with as little credulity as their tales of a white man who had died on a cross to save all mankind. For Mkomo, the only God had been himself. Yet he had found that, in fact, there were such places as

Europe and America. He had seen them himself. Why then might there not be people from another planet?

Kirsten, Billy in tow, had followed Mkomo as he gathered his weapons. "Could you really kill someone, if you had to?" asked Kirsten of Mkomo.

The Emperor laughed heartily. He saw an advantage in impressing these two children. "My enemies," he said, "charged that I personally butchered fifty-five schoolchildren and ate their inner organs while they still steamed with hot blood."

With a little cry of disgust, Kirsten reeled backwards into Billy's arms. She looked up into his face and wrinkled her nose.

Mkomo, aware of the jealous figure of his son standing nearby, regarded the youngsters with an amiable flash of teeth. "Now I ask you—could anyone really eat fifty-five hearts and livers and kidneys, all at one sitting?"

Charles intoned quietly, "He means his enemies may have exaggerated the number of schoolchildren."

Mkomo sent a glare toward his son, but, caught up in the memory, recounted grandly, "I think maybe my own Minister of Information may have exaggerated the number as well. The people like to believe their leader is a man of greater than normal appetites." He laughed uproariously.

Kirsten stood wide-eyed, no longer joking with Billy. "But—" she started. Billy pulled her away. Mkomo frowned.

"If you want to survive, better stick with me," he called after them. He thrust his spear playfully at his son, who jumped backwards.

"Dad, really . . ." Charles began.

"Shut up, bird-heart," his father said. "Look at the situation. The rest of them don't really believe that someone is out there waiting to kill us. They don't want to believe it. While they stumble along, they will make good targets for the Hunters. Meanwhile, we can get a good start toward the treasure. Keep that foremost in your thoughts. The others are to be used."

"I know what I'd like to use that little blonde for."

"Keep your eyes off the girl!" he said in a low voice. "Pretty bodies are for leisure. We leave early in the morning. Get to bed! I will wake you, and you'd better be ready to follow."

Charles sullenly walked off, enviously watching Billy and Kirsten, who had settled on two seats with some of the food. Mkomo returned to his practice.

The others continued to discuss the reality of their situation.

Bob Miller strutted through the concourse, announcing, "I think it's all a lot of bullshit," to no one in particular. His was a cry of wishful defiance, made slightly ridiculous by the two ammunition bands he had slung over his shoulder Pancho Villa–style, the powerful shotgun he still carried, and the twin pistols on each hip. Bullshit or no, he was prepared for something.

The women had drifted into a small quiet group, comparing their knowledge of the weapons they had chosen. Betty Miller was in fact an accomplished archer; bored by golf, she had found an unused stretch of land at the Dallas Country Club that could accommodate an archery range, and a willing teacher. Golf is a discipline honed by endless repetition, but in archery, unlike golf, the journey of the arrow from archer to target is swift. Success or failure is quickly seen. The swiftness held her interest, and she found the discipline to practice. She shyly demonstrated her skill to Bibi Halvorssen and Janet Gore. Their appreciation gave her a satisfaction that her husband's indifference to her skills never had.

In turn, Bibi showed off her talents with rapier, saber, and foil. Janet Gore demonstrated the use of a side arm, which she had been schooled in since a young girl. She carried one as the women of Dallas carry purses. The three women giggled together at the supposedly unfeminine display of lethal skills.

Kosho and Bjorn Halvorssen sat in the bar, attended by a wordless steward. Neither pressed the other to try the beverage each culture contributed. Kosho's sake was warmed to the correct temperature and served in delicate ceramic cups; Halvorssen sipped from iced crystal glasses filled with aquavit; the glasses had stems but not bases, and could only be set down when the drinker had drained the vessel. Each man watched the other for signs of drunkenness, but neither wavered.

"Both our nations have renounced war. Don't you find that interesting?" said Kosho.

Halvorssen smiled that inward smile of the Scandinavian that denotes irony and sorrow. "And here we are. They chose us. . . ." He trailed off.

"Yes," said Kosho. He let his hand clasp the hilt of the seemingly ancient, razor-sharp blade in the curved scabbard that rested against his thigh. He had seen wars on all the continents except Australia and Antarctica; violence held a fascination for him, but he had never yet tried to kill a man. "I wonder if . . ." he said.

* * *

Halvorssen nodded. "I, too," he said, touching the hunting rifle, similar to one that he had used to bring down bigger game than a man, seemingly more dangerous than the strange being they had seen on the television screen. He wondered if one of them now held a rifle like this one.

The rabbi, David Glassman thought to himself with a taunt. He had killed many men—more than he could count. As he sat alone in the terminal, he knew full well that he could kill again, with that. He looked at the Uzi submachine gun that still rested in its place in the case.

He tried to remember the men he had killed, some face-to-face, but he could no longer recall any particular face. They all blended together, forming one proud visage with the lips turned in a sneer, and eyes filled with hatred. He remembered the villages where the dead lay sprawled, cast aside by Israeli artillery like toys. Men, women, children, eyes closed now, but in his mind they stirred and began to rise, gazing at him with that same stare of hatred that burned among the Arab villagers of the West Bank.

This enemy, Glassman thought, at least had no eyes. The image on the television screen recurred to him. It was a threat, a deadly threat. He, who had done nothing to them, had fled the senseless killing, had come to this place—where was it? No matter; it was on earth—and found that he was expected to kill again.

For he believed the woman's story. It was fantastic, but what in life was not? His parents had lived quietly alongside their neighbors in Austria. One day the black-garbed SS supermen of the Third Reich marched in. His parents underwent the horrors of the camps, and miraculously survived and found each other again.

They had come to New York, a city that itself was as fantastic as anything they had seen. A child was born to them—again a miracle, for they were both well into their forties—whose brilliance and beauty were the light of their lives.

Happiness, security, and hard work brought them a good, new life, and a small store that extended credit to neighbors whose misfortune found them hungry and unable to pay. Yet many paid, even those who bought for a time on credit.

Their son yearned for Israel, but knew his departure would break his parents' hearts. Yet one evening, while he was taking a test at the free university of the city of New York—a crazy pair of young boys had, for no reason, shot his parents after they had already given the boys the contents of the cash register.

That was how David Glassman had, at last, found his destiny in Israel, where, more mystery than miracle, people now thought of him as a hero. And others cursed him as an oppressor.

Glassman continued to focus his gaze on the Uzi, believing as fully as Mkomo did that tomorrow there would be waiting other black-garbed beings who would try to kill him. Unless he killed them first.

He raised his arm, which he had sworn never again to raise in anger; it felt very heavy, very slow, very aged. His fingertips brushed the oiled metal of the ammunition clip. They grasped it familiarly.

The Rabbi of Death, the Arab villagers on the West Bank called him. At least the old woman—Granny—had not taunted him with that name. He pulled the Uzi from its resting place.

Ian Gore had found the strength to lift the sword. Whooping, he swung it about, feeling its weight pull him, as if it yearned for battle. He remembered the stories of Arthur and his knights that his father had read by the light of a flickering kerosene wick in their farmhouse in Biandra. Beyond that light, somewhere in the darkness—nearby, it had seemed to the boy Ian—was England. When he was old enough he went there, to find England, to read Classics at Oxford, and was tempted to stay. His mind still delighted in the ancient stories, and he wished to teach them, to dwell all his life in those buildings that had seemed as old as the stories of Arthur.

But duty called at home, and he was a man who responded to the call of duty. He left England, but carried with him always the memory of its heritage, though in Biandra he found a world that Arthur could never have imagined. No, not even Merlin himself could have conjured up the horrors of Biandra. The faithful ones who turned faithless, the ones who remained faithful and were slaughtered. The blacks rose as incredibly as if the rocks of the fields had risen to march into London, crushing and destroying as they went.

He swung the sword, seeking the enemies who had ruined his world. "Galahad! Gawain! The best of my men! At arms! The enemy is at the gates! On the morrow we will slay them all!" Though the last tiny rational part of him denied everything that

Granny had said, the part of him that had looked in vain for an enemy to stand against embraced the chance that here at last was an enemy who would stand and fight. The old woman might be lying, but if there *were* any gray beings out there waiting, Ian Gore would march forth, sword in hand, to vanquish them.

"To arms! To arms!" he called, holding the sword high above his head.

No one paid any attention.

Eventually, they all drifted off to their comfortable rooms to find sleep. All took their chosen weapons with them, even Glassman, who stared for hours at the Uzi propped against the foot of his bed.

Betty Miller had brought her bow and quiver of steel-tipped arrows to the bedroom, but forgot them when her husband staggered in an hour later, clutching a bottle of tequila and shouting Spanish phrases that he had picked up from their gardener.

Wearing nothing but his ammunition belts, Bob Miller had pounced on her with surprising vigor, and she admitted to herself later that his lovemaking had been more ardent than she had experienced in some years. She glanced over at her now sleeping husband, wondering how he could sleep with the brass cartridges pressing against his back, and thought that in spite of everything the trip might prove a boon to their marriage. *If only*, she thought, *Billy would do something that would make his father proud of him*.

In his own room, Billy, having parted with a quick kiss bestowed by Kirsten, had resorted to the onanistic literature supplied by Brian McConnell. To his chagrin, nothing, not even Hubert Selby, Jr.'s *Last Train to Brooklyn*, which Brian had said was a surefire turn-on, had worked.

His mind kept wandering back to Kirsten, and when his thoughts were on her, he remained in awe, and flaccid. He wondered miserably if this were love.

Chapter Five

The Commander awoke from a state of deep concentration. The others were stirring as well, and the Commander quickly checked their condition. It was rare that the strain of an intergalactic journey caused ill effects on the passengers, but this was not an ordinary crew of youthful tourists. The Aging Master, in particular, was an object of the Commander's concern. Though he probably had made more of these journeys than any of the others, he was also nearing that stage in his life span when prolonged effort could prove dangerous.

The Aging Master would have liked nothing better than to end his long life on a Hunt. The Commander reflected that his eagerness to go on this trip indicated that the sense of decay weighed heavily on him, though among the People he was respected—even revered—as the greatest living Hunter. Since the imposition of the New Rules, however, he had virtually ceased to Hunt.

That was not from loss of vigor. He still participated in the affairs of the People and was rumored to have led the most recent expeditions to eradicate rivals to the People. There were even whispers that he was himself one of the Guardians.

It had taken a certain amount of courage for the Commander even to propose the trip to the Aging Master, for if he had been a Guardian the Commander would certainly have found himself answering unpleasant questions. Not only the trip, but the Commander's career would have been jeopardized.

Yet the Aging Master had readily agreed, on one condition: that the Hunt be carried out under the Old Rules.

The Commander had hesitated at that. It was bad enough to be Hunting Class B game—when the regulations required that their existence be reported so they could be placed under steady surveillance—but that could be explained away. Not so this kind of violation. To risk the lives of any of the People by Hunting under the Old Rules was probably the greatest offense, short of misuse of the Discovery, that anyone could commit.

The Aging Master had been insistent, however. He offered not only to equip the entire Hunt at his own expense, but to recruit other Hunters. To the Commander, such an offer had been irresistible.

The Commander found himself slightly disappointed that his weak partner on the earlier trip bore no ill effects from the journey. It would have been convenient, and certainly no loss to the Hunt, if the Mate had somehow . . . But that was the perverse luck that seemed to follow the Mate. Inept as he might have been, he always emerged unscathed from the trouble he caused.

The death of the tourists on the earlier trip to this planet could easily have been blamed on the Mate. He knew it, and the Commander had earned his gratitude when his report exculpated the Mate from blame. That had not been out of benevolent feelings toward the Mate. The Commander had blamed the entire fiasco on the scouting reports that had classified this planet's principal species as Class D. Those responsible for the scouting reports reacted as the Commander had known they would—with an indignant defense of their methods and conclusions.

The whole matter had been quietly dismissed. The planet had been flagged with a notation that it might possibly be inhabited by Class C game, and no one was the wiser . . . leaving the Commander free to outfit a surreptitious Class B expedition.

For there were, he knew, powerful patrons who desired the challenge of opposing Class B game, a challenge that had been denied them for some time. Not from reasons of personal safety—for under the New Rules even Class B game ordinarily could be Hunted in safety. It was merely an extra precaution the Guardians thought best to impose. Though ordinarily it took eons for a race to progress to the Discovery from Class B status, there had been a close call with one obscure race on a little-scouted planet.

Wiser, the Guardians thought, simply to exterminate all Class B species as soon as they were discovered.

All very well for the younger Hunters, who thought themselves honorable by vanquishing Class C or D game—but there were still Hunters who had faced Class B species, or wished to, and were willing enough to reward a Commander who would take them on such a trip.

Indeed, the Aging Master had easily found three such ambitious Hunters. Two of them were young and the third a contemporary of the Aging Master's, or nearly so; yet his endorsement had been enough to convince the Commander that they were worthy of such a Hunt.

The Commander had brought along the Mate, for whatever else he was, the Mate was shrewd enough to realize the necessity of keeping silent about the whole matter, as long as he was promised a good share of the collectible. And as long as he was right there for the Commander to watch over. To leave him behind would have risked his letting the secret out while they were away.

In fact, when the Scientist had approached the Commander with his proposal to join the expedition, the Commander had suspected that the Mate had already spoken loosely. It was a surprise to learn that the Aging Master had been the one who shared the news of the prospective trip. Though the Aging Master would not endorse the Scientist's Hunting prowess, he had referred him to the Commander.

His proposal had made the Commander uneasy—he had had enough of dilettantes who wanted to see fierce game but had to be watched over and protected every step of the way. In fact, the Scientist was more familiar with Class B game than any of the younger Hunters. He had made a life study of species that showed signs of readiness to make the Discovery. For some reason, his work had brought him under the interdiction of the Guardians, and now the only way he could pursue his work was to hitch onto illegal expeditions like this one.

The Commander at first refused him—why heighten the risks? But the Scientist had persisted, pointing out that his knowledge of Class B species might well prove useful. And if by some unforeseen chance they were about to make the Discovery . . . but of course that was unthinkable. In the end, however, the Commander became convinced that at least he would not be a detriment, and the Commander wanted no one left at home to realize the purpose of their journey. He gave his assent to the Scientist, with the warning that in no way would his safety be guaranteed.

In fact, the Commander had to admit, the Scientist had been useful already. He had a strong, disciplined mind and helped to gather those less experienced in uniting their Discovery power to propel the ship to the incomprehensible speed necessary to break its mass down to near nothingness so that they could make the intergalactic trip.

He recovered quickly too, the Commander noted, and stood behind him now, eager to help as the Commander made the final preparations for contact with the surface.

"There is more water than I expected," said the Scientist. "The environment should be nearly like that of Home."

"It was not too unpleasant before," said the Commander.

"I read your report, of course," said the Scientist, "but I could not be sure if you were being absolutely truthful."

The Commander chose to ignore the implied insult.

"Are you going to follow the same methods for assembling the Game?" asked the Scientist.

"We needed a greater challenge," said the Commander. "I decided to cast a wider net."

"I would have thought the loss of several passengers on your earlier trip would have indicated you faced a sufficient challenge."

"Those were tourists," the Commander replied, irritated at the additional slight. "We were expecting—prepared for—Class D game. This time, there are experienced Hunters. Except for you. If you like, you can stay above the surface and observe in safety."

"Certainly not. For my purposes I need to observe them physically. I would like to capture one, if possible."

The Commander could not hide his astonishment. "We are not here to collect specimens. I think you will find them too fierce for that."

"There are ways," said the Scientist. "You captured one on the earlier trip."

"That was an immature specimen, and I held it only for a few moments to recover something we had lost."

"Still, it was possible. I perceive they have artificial satellites circling the planet. Is that a defense mechanism?"

"They are not aware of the need for defense of that kind. They are concerned with observing each other. They exist in a number of social groups that frequently make war on each other."

"Are you quite sure this is really a Class B species?"

"I will leave that evaluation to you. I know that they are innately aggressive."

"How did you disguise our approach?"

The Commander was profoundly irritated at having an amateur question him. "Our approach was concealed by the transmission of a double flash of atomic energy that simulated the explosion of one of their fission-type weapons."

"Won't that alarm them and alert them to our presence?"

"You'd better study their social system a bit more. In all likelihood, it will increase the suspicion that their social groups already have for each other. Each will suspect the others of detonating the blast."

"A familiar Hunting ploy," came the voice of the Aging Master. The other two turned to acknowledge his presence. The Master indicated his approval of the Commander's plan. "Instead of trying to sneak into the animal's territory undetected," he explained to the Scientist, "one assumes a familiar yet provocative disguise. During the distraction, the entry is made."

The Commander felt gratified by the Master's approval. He continued his explanation. "Other than aggressiveness, one of their chief traits is greed. In a society without the Discovery, the inhabitants find themselves in competition for possessions. Despite their numerous social groups, they have a universal form of exchange. We have offered what to them is a valuable commodity."

"In return for what?"

"In return for the chance to display their survival skills."

"That seems too obvious a display of our intentions."

"Their greed will overcome any doubts that they have."

"A good plan," said the Aging Master. "I can hardly wait."

Chapter Six

In the morning the travelers awoke and gradually reassembled in the terminal. First to arrive there was Rabbi Glassman, who carefully replaced his Uzi in the weapons case. He sat reading from a volume of the Talmud as the others emerged from their quarters.

Kosho came over and sat beside him. Around his waist, Kosho was wearing the superb samurai sword, and he adjusted it as he sat. For a time he sat in silence, not wanting to disturb the rabbi's reading. At last Glassman closed the book and looked at the Japanese. "You think we will have breakfast?" he asked Kosho. "Since these people can apparently serve up anything we desire, I thought of asking for New York lox and bagels. Tel Aviv's delicatessens were never so good as New York's."

Kosho smiled. "It may be an illusion."

Glassman pondered that, his mind attuned to ambiguities and nuances after his reading of the Talmud. "An illusion about the delicatessens . . . or about the lox and bagels?"

Kosho restrained his laughter. "The latter was what I was thinking of. If they create these . . . environments—which we have not yet seen—they must have great power. Not, in truth, the power we came here expecting. Not the Americans' kind of power. *They*, too, could create a real park, bring thousands of earth-moving machines and construction workers and transform a desert island into an adventure retreat. I do not think a truly advanced civilization—one that could produce someone, or some-thing, like that woman we saw last night—would have to go to all that bother."

"You think they are using some other kind of power?"

"The power of mind. Which can create far greater illusions than are found in amusement parks."

Glassman furrowed his brow. His scarred, weather-beaten face, with its sharp features, seemed perpetually morose, but the intellectual challenge the Japanese had thrown down caused a slight, very fleeting expression of amusement to appear there. It was clear that the rabbi enjoyed an intellectual problem.

"You have an interesting mind," he said to Kosho.

Kosho inclined his head. They sat in silence.

"Excuse me for asking. You do not have to answer if you don't wish to," Kosho said, breaking the silence.

A twitch about the mouth seemed to indicate the rabbi was smiling. Kosho was emboldened enough to continue.

"You have replaced your weapon in the case. I wondered what the significance was."

Glassman nodded, morose again. "I have decided not to participate in the journey."

Kosho gave an appreciative murmur. "You have considered that they may try to force you."

"I am prepared."

Kosho murmured again, sympathetically. "I believe that the stewards are coming now for our breakfast orders."

"Well, whatever else these people do, they sure do go first-class," announced Bob Miller, patting his stomach, into which he had just shoveled several fried eggs, three glasses of orange juice, two cups of coffee, three pieces of buttered toast, and six strips of lean bacon.

"Watch that cholesterol, Bob," cautioned his wife.

"Ah, what the hell—live today, die tomorrow. But enjoy it while you live. Ain't that right, there, what's-your-name?"

Ian Gore raised his head shakily from the coffee he had been downing. "I'm afraid I'm experiencing the sorrows of that kind of philosophy."

"Too much to drink last night, eh?" said Miller. He looked around. "Get one of them waiters over here; ask him for a couple of raw eggs in a glass of bourbon. Fix you up right away."

Ian Gore turned suddenly green and headed in the direction of the bathrooms.

Miller watched him go and then turned to Janet Gore, leaning over to whisper. "Tell you what, missus. I don't think your mister is in shape for this kind of thing. Maybe you and him ought to take the plane back, first thing. I don't think anybody'd mind."

Janet Gore sipped her tea with the disdainful look that is the special property of British women. "And then there would be two fewer competitors with you for the gold."

Miller shrugged and smiled roguishly. "Well, if you consider that a couple of senior citizens like yourselves would be serious competition."

Janet nodded. "That's true. You have far more serious competition to worry about. Mkomo and his son, for instance."

Miller looked around. "Shit, they're just like any niggers at home. They ain't even up yet."

Janet smiled softly. "I think you'll find that Mkomo has in fact stolen the march on you."

Miller looked at her in puzzlement. "Maybe I misperceive your meanin'."

"I heard them leaving quite early this morning. It didn't alarm me, because I know the journey will be a long one, and believe that we must conserve our energies, but—"

Abruptly, Miller stormed out of his chair and across to the personal quarters. He disappeared into the hallway for a minute, then returned shouting to the room at large: "Hey! Who's makin' the rules around here? I thought we were all set to get goin' together! Where the hell's that old woman?"

As if in answer to his call, Granny suddenly appeared. She clapped her hands. "Attention, everyone! Your equipment is over by the door. There are packs with sufficient supplies, and appropriate clothing for the first environment. I think you'll all do well to choose snowshoes, as the early contestants did."

With a howl, Bob Miller raced to the pile of equipment that stood waiting. "Betty! Get your ass over here. Where's that damn kid? Billy, get moving, and no bullshit. We're playin' catch-up ball!"

His shouts produced a hubbub of activity. Billy, in fact, had already outfitted himself with the assistance of Kirsten and her family, who had examined the equipment with approval at its fine quality. Granny passed the Halvorssens maps as they departed. Kirsten ran back to hug Billy. "Oh, I *do* hope you'll make it through the first leg of the journey. Promise me you'll take care of yourself so I can see you again. And Billy . . ."

He nodded dumbly, hoping she would say, "I love you."

Instead, she whispered. "I know you must love and respect your father. He's so . . . masterful, the way Americans are. But see if you can get him not to shout when we're in the mountains. He could easily bring an avalanche down on you." She patted his cheek and slipped on her parka. He watched her go with longing.

The Millers, with Granny's help, soon outfitted themselves. Kosho had finished his preparations at about the same time. Bob Miller whispered to his wife, "Better let the Jap come along with us, at least for now. He's likely to figure out some shortcut, and we can't let him get unfair advantage on us."

The group of four stumbled out into the snow, feeling the sudden drop in temperature. The air outside was frigid, but that made the snow hard and crunchy beneath the snowshoes, and before long they had made their way along the trail and out of sight.

In a few minutes, Ian and Janet Gore followed, she supporting him for a few steps. He had insisted on bringing along the sword, which kept throwing him off balance, until he secured it over his shoulder, held in place by the packstraps. Janet Gore felt in the pocket of her parka, reassured by the touch of the Webley .45.

Granny went back to Glassman. They were alone now. He was reading calmly to himself. "The others are getting ahead of you, David," she said.

"That is no concern of mine," he said.

"Does it say anything in your book about agreements?" she asked.

"It says a great deal about them. Agreements are a subject of much discussion for the law, and this is—among other things—a book of laws."

"I believe you made an agreement, signed a paper, which is the custom of your people, when you came on this trip."

"Very true," he said, remembering that they had been asked to sign an indemnity exempting the resort from liability if they should become injured. "But since many of the terms of the agreement were concealed, it was not a valid agreement."

"What terms were concealed?"

"That we were being asked to kill people."

She shook her head. "That is still not part of the agreement. It seemed *likely*, because of the aggressive tendencies for which you were tested, that you would *want* to kill someone who was attempting to kill you. And the Hunters are willing to give you that fair chance."

His curiosity pricked, he looked up from the book. "Truly? Is that true? That we have an equal chance of killing them?"

"There are strict rules about that, which the People, the Hunters, will faithfully observe, as you would observe the laws in your book."

"I have not always faithfully observed the laws in this book."

"You are unusually honest. That is your failing."

His mind played with the nuances of this. "Is it true that they will only use on us the weapons that we have available to use?"

"That is one of the strict rules. Of course"—she gestured toward the weapons case—"you have a wide choice of weapons. Your species seems unusually devoted to constructing weapons."

He smiled. "And you know"—his voice dropped to a whisper—"of my proficiency with the Uzi."

"We know it earned you the name—excuse me, because you asked not to be called 'rabbi'—the Rabbi of Death. You were apparently a well-known Hunter."

"Very well known. Not only the Jerusalem and Tel Aviv newspapers, but also the *New York Times* and the *Post* wrote articles about my . . . prowess."

"And you used this weapon against your own species. It is strange that you are reluctant now. The People are not even from your own planet."

"The ultimate Other," he murmured.

"Perhaps you would prefer to try your skill at another weapon?"

"No." He rose. "I do not suppose you would fly me back?"

"The only way to return is at the other end of the hunting course."

"So I will go there. But I will take no weapon."

She folded her hands. "I have no instructions about this eventuality. It is a strange choice. You may change your mind, and if you do, I remind you that you need only call on me—*think* of me—and I will bring you one or more of the weapons in this case."

"I will have no need of them."

"You will, at least, let me outfit you with proper clothing and equipment."

He nodded. "I have no desire to commit suicide. That is not the proper way."

She clapped her hands. "Good. And you'll see. You'll enjoy the Hunt. I can tell. You are a born Hunter."

"So it seems," he murmured. "But we can become something other than what we were born. We were born helpless infants."

"I'm afraid my programming does not equip me to argue Talmud, David," she said, picking out his snowshoes with a care that reminded Glassman of his own mother.

Mkomo and Charles had prepared a lookout for themselves near the top of the trail that led across the foothills. Mkomo had burrowed himself into the snow and hollowed out a cave from which they could watch the approach of the others.

"I wish you had left that cowboy outfit back at the terminal," he said crossly to his son. Charles had strapped the six-gun over his down-filled coverall, and now leveled the pistol out over the vast, apparently empty valley. "You couldn't hit anything with it, and it's probably so frozen by now that it wouldn't even fire at close range."

Charles recognized the truth of this, but the Colt gave him a feeling of confidence that he could kill anything he aimed at. He was more afraid of his father than of the black-clad figure he had so far seen only on a television screen. "It's no sillier than the spears *you* brought along."

Mkomo wanted to slap his son's face for insolence, but he needed at least one ally. "These spears are well weighted. They are . . . prize objects, obviously the work of great craftsmen. I could hit a target approaching us from any direction at a hundred yards."

Charles suspected that his father was, as usual, exaggerating his skill, but he admitted that the old man was brilliant at killing whoever stood in his way, and he had seen him practicing last night. "Who are we looking for? The other passengers, or the geeks in the black suits?"

"Both," said Mkomo. "From here we can watch their encounter, and determine the strength of our enemies . . . or our potential allies, if that is possible."

"Why don't we just get on as far ahead as we can, so we can get to the gold first?"

"Because, moth-brain, those who travel in front of the group make excellent targets for the Hunters who lie in wait for the game."

"The . . . game? Pop, you really think they're . . . serious? I mean . . . they think of us as animals?"

Mkomo gave a throaty laugh. "What man of stature thinks of his fellows in any other way? What better proof could we have that they are beings of superior intelligence?"

Charles swallowed. His father was continually surprising him. He wished he were back at school in Switzerland.

The Aging Master squatted so that he would not be seen. He seemed to the Mate to be dangerously close to the sheer bluff that overlooked the valley, but the Mate knew better than to warn him back. "They have separated into groups," the Master said.

"I must say they have chosen an odd assortment of weapons," said the Gray Female. She shot a look at the Commander. "Are you sure the information we are receiving from the Lure is accurate? I have had past experience with defective information gatherers."

"The Lure is most reliable," he said.

"We paid enough for it," said the Natural Hunter. He edged closer to the Master. "Perhaps they are close enough for us to try one of their primitive spears." He weighed the golden shaft of the spear in his hand. "I think I could reach them from here."

"A little closer," said the Master. "They wouldn't be able to reach us with any of their weapons from there. The spear artist has for some reason built a blind for himself and the young one who carries a primitive pellet projector."

"Why not attack them first?" inquired the Scientist.

"I think not," said the Master. "They appear to be the most cunning of the group. It would be a shame to take them at the very beginning of the Hunt." The Commander nodded in approval.

"Since I have the stringed projectile thrower," said the Golden Female, "I think I would like to oppose my counterpart." Coolly, she strung her bow, still a little unfamiliar with its operation, and stood up.

"Take care," said the Mate, in spite of himself.

The Natural Hunter made a contemptuous gesture toward him. "Nothing they have could possibly hit us from their position." The Mate felt embarrassment narrow his eyeslits.

"I think you may try it now," said the Master. "Even if you are not successful, we all know that sometimes the game needs a little persuasion before they realize that they are actually privileged to be part of a Hunt. Although," he added, with a glance at the Commander, "few of us have ever had the thrill of hunting Class B game. They may react in unexpected ways."

The Golden Female stepped closer to the edge. The Master pointed out for her the beast that was carrying a stringed weapon similar to hers. The Golden Female hesitated for an instant, deep in concentration, and then let fly.

Chapter Seven

Billy trudged along behind his parents. The trek had not so far been arduous, and the garments they wore protected all but his face against the cold. Kosho had showed him how to pull down the goggles that were part of the parka so that his eyes were protected. He kept looking ahead, hoping that they would catch up with Kirsten and her family, but his father kept warning them to take cover whenever the wind stirred up the snow ahead so that it seemed there was movement.

Billy felt that his father's caution was an act. Oh, he knew that something might be lying in wait for them—he had picked up that much of the speech that Granny had given them—but he still felt it was just one more of his father's make-believe adventures that he was supposed to get enthusiastic about but just couldn't.

As he walked, he was concentrating on thinking about the sensations he had felt the night before when Kirsten kissed him, imagining what he might have done in return to advance things a little, wondering what advice Brian McConnell would have given him, when he became aware of some kind of warning signal in his brain. He looked up. The others just at that time had their heads down to avoid a rush of on-blowing snow. Somewhere in the dense cloud of flakes that rushed toward them he sensed danger.

He began to run, and just before he reached his mother he realized that the danger was meant for her. It came from the air. Frantically, he began to wave his arms back and forth in front of his mother, as if to wipe away something poisonous in the flying snow.

His mother looked up in surprise in time to see one of Bill's arms glance against an arrow that flew from above. The arrow was deflected off to the side and lay point down in the snow. She shrieked, and her husband turned. "What's the matter?" he said. "Billy! What the hell are you doing?"

"No, Bob," Betty Miller said, putting her hand on her husband's arm. "Look." As she pointed to the arrow in the snow, Billy suddenly jumped forward and waved his arms, again deflecting an arrow in flight. Kosho, a few steps ahead, stood gaping at the scene.

"Take cover," Bob Miller shouted, pushing his wife off the trail toward a formation of snow-covered rocks. She began to run but tripped over her snowshoes and fell full-length in the snow. The others stepped more carefully to where she had fallen and helped her up.

Billy turned again. "Run, Dad," he shouted over his shoulder. "Get Mom behind the rocks." Betty had twisted her ankle, and Bob Miller and Kosho supported her between them, clumsily edging across the snow.

"What's that kid doin'?" Miller snarled, trying to look back without falling. Kosho, more agile, managed a glance over his shoulder. "I cannot be sure, but it seems to me as if he is brushing away arrows."

"You're crazy," shouted Miller as they struggled forward. "Nobody can do that. He'll get himself killed. Billy!" he shouted. "Get your ass over here on the double."

"It is crazy," Kosho murmured, realizing that Miller would not be able to hear him above the wind. "Either he has ability far beyond that of any trained adept, or . . ." He thought of the conversation he and Rabbi Glassman had had earlier. That had been an intellectual game, speculation on the reality of their situation that, Kosho knew, had the effect of lessening the harsh impact of reality itself. The mind is capable of denying anything, Kosho thought, but it was not capable of doing what he saw the boy doing. Or *thought* he saw, he reminded himself. They reached the safety of the rock at last, and huddled down.

"Billy!" hollered Bob Miller.

"Coming, Dad," came the response. Kosho and Miller looked over the edge of the rock formation. Billy was hurrying toward them. Behind him, in the snow, in a line that followed the footsteps that the Millers and Kosho had made, were four more spent arrows, point down in the ground. Kosho stared at them, as if to concentrate on them would enable him to deny what had happened.

Farther above them on the trail, the Halvorssen family had heard the shouts and turned to look. Because of the flying snow, they could see little of what happened to the Millers, but Kirsten's sharp eyes picked out the black-clad figures on the ledge above them on the other side of the narrow pass. She had seen the one close to the edge with the bow, loosing arrow after arrow toward the group just behind them.

Bibi spoke to her husband, lapsing comfortably into Danish. "The enemies are real, then."

He nodded and smiled at her. "You had the same thought I did—that perhaps this was some kind of ruse to persuade us all that the hunt for the treasure was more dangerous than it really was."

"Yet it seems strange, Bjorn," she said. "They only shot arrows, and from that range—"

"—and in this wind," he finished for her. "Yes, it would have been only a lucky shot to have actually hit anything."

"Yet a lucky shot was possible," she reminded him. "Certainly the archer had a good vantage point, and power enough to reach the . . . target."

Kirsten spoke anxiously. "Papa, Mama, they were shooting arrows. And it was Billy's mama who carried the bow and arrow."

"It was not her," her father said. "We saw the archer. It was one of the black-clad people like the one the old nana showed us."

"I don't mean that," said Kirsten. "Didn't the old nana say they would use our own weapons against us?"

Her parents were silent.

"Papa, couldn't you shoot them?"

He patted her head with his glove-covered hand. "No one has yet shot at *us*, beloved. It is not our way to provoke others."

"But they might have—"

"We will see," sighed Bjorn. "I think we had better move on quickly to the turning in the trail, where it rises into the foothills. We will be out of danger there." He and his wife set out with a quickened pace. After an anxious look behind, Kirsten followed.

* * *

The Gores struggled up the path. Janet kept a sharp eye out, but was concentrating on preserving her footing. Snow was strange to her, a girl who grew up in the heart of Africa, although once her family had gone to see Kilimanjaro. A helicopter had taken them to the observation post halfway up the mountain. She and her sisters had frolicked in the snow, and tried their hand at skiing, with laughable results.

What she was most worried about was fatigue. She had been stung by Miller's suggestion that they were too old for such a journey. Both she and Ian were hardened by years of farm work, and in relatively good shape, but she admitted to herself that there was a possibility that they would find themselves unable to go on. If that happened, she wondered if someone would come to rescue them. She glanced at her husband. To another's eyes, he would have looked quite foolish, carrying his sword across his back like some misplaced knight on a Crusade. She smiled. Whatever happened, they would bear it together.

They heard shouts. She strained to distinguish the voices from the howls of the wind. Off to their right they saw the Millers. Billy was standing up from behind a rock formation. "Get *down*!" he was shouting.

Ian turned to her. "Bit of a dust-up, Jan. They seem worried for us. See anything up there on the other side?"

She looked in the direction the boy was pointing, knowing that Ian's eyes were poor for distance, but he refused to wear his specs for anything but reading. She scrutinized the sheer bluff on the other side. There was a ledge up there; *that* seemed to be the object of the concern. But she could see nothing there, and told him so.

"Perhaps we could be of assistance," Ian suggested.

Janet looked back at the nearly frantic group behind the rocks. "They'll just slow us down, Ian."

He hesitated. "Suppose so. All part of the game, eh? Still, all for one and one for all. Safety in numbers, and so forth."

She frowned, and nodded. They left the trail and made their way to the rocks. Janet noticed the arrows in the snow and nudged Ian. He nodded.

"Get down!" the others were still shouting as they reached the rocks.

"Hush!" Ian shouted at them, in the same tone that he had used to calm frightened women and children during the rebellion in Biandra. They hushed. "That'll never do," he admonished them. "Danger's past. Better get on with it."

Slowly Bob Miller rose to his feet, looking warily upwards toward the cliff. "They were shooting at us."

Ian nodded. "Anyone injured?"

Miller looked around.

"From the ledge across the way?" inquired Ian.

"Yes, yes. We were like sitting ducks."

"Mother's hurt," Billy said, and Janet stepped over.

"Let's have a look at her, then. Must be bandages in these packs."

Betty was stretched out behind the rocks, holding her ankle. Janet rolled up the cuff of her down-filled pants.

"You're not wounded," Janet said. She pressed against the ankle and Betty cried out.

"I twisted it and fell. These damn snowshoes." Her southern accent had diminished under pressure, but there was enough of it left to amuse Janet, and to remind her that Betty came from a hot climate too. She set to work with an Ace bandage from one of the packs. She interlaced it with handfuls of snow packed tight and bound Betty's ankle.

"It's cold," Betty complained.

"You won't feel it for long," Janet said. "The cold will numb your ankle. We've got to move on."

"It was the . . . creatures. Like that old lady said. They tried to *kill* us."

"There, there, dear," said Janet. "They're gone now. I could see the ledge from the trail. Lucky we came along. You might have stayed behind these rocks for quite a long time."

They got Betty back on her feet and into thesnowshoes again, and she found that she could move without much pain.

After the group moved on up the trail together, Ian dropped back to speak to Janet. "Most amazin' story they told about the boy. Said he knocked the arrows right out of the air."

Janet humphed. "Americans," she said. For her, that said it all.

Mkomo and Charles had left their hiding place after witnessing the beginning of the attack, and they were now approaching the summit. "That's some of them gone, anyway," said Mkomo.

"Dad, we could only see the thin little people through the

snow," reminded Charles. "You had a perfect shot at them with your spears. I think you ought to have picked them off."

"Seven of them," said his father. "And only three spears. And they were eliminating those who wanted the gold."

"What happens when they come to eliminate *us*?"

"I think it is possible that we slipped by without being noticed. Let them have their hunt, if that is what they came for, as long as they are occupied with the others."

Charles choked off a response. He hoped they wouldn't get the cute little Dane.

His father gave a shout, and Charles hurried to catch up. Mkomo stood on the summit of the mountain; from that threshold he could see the afternoon sun shining against the other side of the mountain and the valley below.

"Halfway through," said Mkomo. "At the bottom, there is another trail, if this map can be trusted, that will lead us to shelter."

Charles looked around. "But Pop, it's a sheer drop. How are we going to get down? Fly?"

"Look inside your pack, ostrich-head. Ropes." Mkomo took the large coil of heavy nylon line from his pack and looked around, studying his map. He paced along the edge of the precipice, then turned back in the other direction. He dropped to his knees and brushed away a covering of snow. Underneath was a large wooden box. He grasped a brass handle and pulled. Inside were axes and sharp steel pitons and hammers. "Make yourself useful," he snarled at his son.

Charles proved to be too clumsy for Mkomo's liking, however, and the Emperor took the hammer and made the initial pitons secure in the rock at the edge of the cliff. He tied the rope through the head of the piton expertly.

"Pop, how do you know all this stuff?" asked Charles with a note of admiration.

"A man does not become Emperor of his people without developing his skills," said Mkomo, tying additional pitons to himself with knots that could be quickly slipped when necessary. "Our British rulers trained me in the native army. When I became Emperor—this was when I was a colonel, then later President—the Americans and the Russians implored me to let them train our democratic army, or our socialist army. I pretended to be undecided in those days. Naturally, I took part in the training. I attended War College classes in the United States and People's Liberation Army classes in the Soviet Union. By the way, you must tell me sometime what it was you learned at that school in Switzerland that cost me so much money."

"Well, we studied political theory and economics—"

"Not now, not now." He tied the rope around his son's waist and led him to the edge. "I will lower you to the first ledge and then follow."

"Down *there*?" Charles said, pulling back after a glance at the drop. "There isn't enough room for me to stand."

"It is enough," said Mkomo. "When you reach it, you must spread your arms wide and hug the side of the mountain, as if it were your dear father. Like this," he said, taking a step toward Charles with his arms flung out like a bear's paws . . . and shoved him backward.

Charles felt his feet slip on the ice, and then realized that there was nothing beneath them. He dropped, and screamed. Then, as the rope cut short his fall, his mouth jerked shut abruptly so that his teeth snapped together, catching his tongue. The pain of his bitten tongue occupied him so that he hardly noticed when his toes felt the presence of the ledge. Instinctively, he spread his arms and leaned against the cliff, feeling the frozen rock against his cheek. He started to look over his shoulder.

"Don't look down," shouted his father from above. "Look only at the rock in front of you. The rock is your lover, your father, your life. Kiss it."

Charles didn't know whether to take the instructions literally, but to be on the safe side he kissed the ice-covered bluff. He broke off a piece of ice with his teeth and rolled it around his mouth. It made his tongue feel better.

Presently he heard the hammering of steel. He hazarded a glance upward and beheld the amazing sight of his father's 300-pound bulk dangling from what seemed to be a dangerously slim length of white nylon rope. Using the toes of his boots to keep him clear of the icy face of the cliff, Mkomo expertly let out the length of rope until he was next to Charles. There was no room on the ledge for Mkomo's wide feet, but he wrapped the rope around himself to free his hands. Quickly he hammered another piton into the cliff.

"Don't move now, and *don't look down*," he ordered Charles. "I am going to free you from the rope. You will be in danger only for a second."

Charles closed his eyes. He knew that if his father had intended for him to die, he would long since have been a corpse. Like his brothers. It was only Charles's good fortune that had found him in Switzerland when they had tried to kill Mkomo. That had been a senseless act, for none of them was as wily or skilled at treachery as their father. Nonetheless, Charles knew that they would have persuaded him to go along with the plot if he had been in Biandra. He had always done as they wanted him to do, just as he had always followed his father's orders. He was the only one who hadn't wanted to lead. That was why he was the only one left.

"Now," said Mkomo. Charles opened his eyes. Mkomo showed him how to use the secured rope to lower himself down. Again Charles hesitated, only for a second, and then his father nudged his feet off into space again. Charles at first clung wildly to the rope, his body dangling in midair.

"*Move*, as I showed you," growled his father. "Or I cut the rope."

Charles found the courage, or the lesser fear, that enabled him to lower himself to the next ledge without breaking his legs. Above, Mkomo freed Charles's rope and attached his own to the piton. In a short time he too stood on the wider ledge below. There was room for both of them there, a little space in which to walk around, and a dozen sets of Head skis, boots, and poles. Following his father's lead, Charles began to strap on a pair of boots.

"Pop, look," Charles said suddenly.

Mkomo, struggling with the bindings, turned and looked upward to where Charles was pointing. From another point on the summit, several hundred yards away, seven black-clad figures appeared, one by one, and slipped off the gradual slope there. They were wearing skis.

"Hurry," said Mkomo, renewing his efforts with the ski boots.

"Pop, you're not going to ski *ahead* of them."

"If they get to the bottom before we do, we will be perfect targets for them as we glide down the snow. They can take aim at leisure and pick us off. There is no place to hide now, so the only escape is speed. Did they at least teach you to ski? After all, Switzerland does have mountains. Surely you noticed?"

"Of course they did, Pop. I'm a good skiier."

"Excellent, for I am a poor one. Go first, and I will follow."

Eager to show his prowess at something, Charles set off, only realizing after he had committed himself to the slope that by leading he would be first to face whatever weapons the black-clad figures had. He felt at his side and was reassured by the touch of the Colt Peacemaker there. He had learned from American movies that such a weapon was almost always deadly.

Chapter Eight

Mkomo did not like the sensation that skiing gave him. As they descended the slope, their speed gradually increased. He saw with approval that Charles was indeed a good skiier. Instead of prodding the snow with his poles to slow himself, as Mkomo tended to do, the boy swayed from side to side, and managed easily to slip by obstacles in their path. Once or twice Mkomo nearly fell and clumsily righted himself, using the poles as a cripple uses his crutches.

He glanced over his shoulder and saw the black figures approaching. They were drawing nearer. The frustration Mkomo felt came from the fact that his speed seemed out of control and prevented him from turning and making a stand with the puny spears. Better, he felt, to die fighting than to be cut down while slipping downward on these children's toys.

He remembered the old woman's speech the night before. He had accepted the situation more easily than the others, because he had experienced magic all his life. To a boy raised in a primitive village, the cities of the wider world had been filled with magic. He remembered traveling for the first time on an elevator. Airplanes he had understood from watching, and had prepared himself for—they were nothing more than huge birds inside of which you fastened yourself for a ride. But when the sudden feeling of flight had touched his stomach inside the small room that the elevator had seemed to be, he had thrown himself to the floor in surprise. His hosts, members of the British colonial office, had tried to conceal their mirth, but it was plain they regarded him as a savage.

He had experienced other kinds of magic, in the remote villages of his country where witch doctors, as the Westerners called them, or shamans or healers, as the people of Biandra knew them, practiced their art. Mkomo had known very many people who had been healed, or hurt, by their magic. He had assembled a number of them in his court to help him rule.

So what the woman said was not difficult for him to accept. Thinking of her now, he used the very simple incantation that she had advised: *Granny, I need you,* he thought, and nodded in acceptance when she appeared beside him.

"You can help me escape?" he asked.

She shook her head. "I cannot think for you. I am a machine, or at least that is what you would think me. I can only serve you. I can bring you what you ask."

He uttered oaths in the language of his village.

"I can bring you some of the materials you speak of, but they seem strange requests."

"No," he muttered between clenched teeth. "I am helpless on these sticks of wood. Is there nothing that will propel me where I want to go? Can you bring me an airplane?"

"You would not be able to take off in it."

He concentrated. "I saw something in a French magazine in Paris. Some device that the Americans use, one of their many ingenious playthings. It too has skis, but can be maneuvered like a car."

"You want . . . I think it is called a snowmobile."

"Yes, that sounds right to me. You can drive it? Like a car? Like my grand Rolls-Royce, outfitted for an emperor's use?"

"Not like *that*. It will be a standard snowmobile."

"It will have to do."

"Call to Charles. Would you like one for him?"

"Yes. Two of them. The fastest models."

"The path down the mountain narrows not far ahead. Turn off to the left there."

"We will be slowed down if we turn."

"But the snowmobiles will be waiting—although they will be dangerous if you try to use them to go farther down the mountain at this speed."

"I will take the chance."

Mkomo bellowed a call to his son as the woman slowed her

progress beside him and disappeared. Charles looked back and gradually reduced his speed to allow his father to catch up. "Pop, we can't stop. They'll be on us."

"No, I want you with me. I have found a way out. Up ahead, where the trail narrows between the ridges of ice. You see it?"

"Yes, but we can get through. They'll have to slow down too, and move single file."

"At the end of the gap, we will turn left. You can do that? Sharply left."

"But Pop, you can't ambush them. There are too many of them."

"No. Your father will show you the way. You show me how we turn, and I will follow."

The thought crossed Charles's mind that his father meant for him to turn off and stop, and then would himself continue on, leaving Charles as a target for the hunters. But Charles had always been the obedient one among his father's sons. That was why the other sons were dead, and he alone had been spared to take the role of heir apparent. Old habits are not easy to break, and Charles did as he was told.

The Millers, the Gores, and Kosho had finally made it to the top of the mountain. Janet was glad that Betty Miller had complained often and had called for frequent stops for her to rest her ankle. Her slowness had made it possible for the Gores to keep up without seeming to retard the progress of the group. And now Betty Miller was expressing what Janet, in her reticence, also felt but would not have liked to publicly confess.

"Oh, my *Gawd*, Bob! We don't have to go down those *ropes*! I can't do it, I simply can*not*! Can't you signal for help? Tell them we're giving *up*, or something?"

Bob Miller gritted his teeth. He was himself not eager to fling himself over the lip of the cliff. No telling who had planted the pitons there. Maybe it was some kind of trap, and once over, the pitons would pull out and they would fall. . . . He looked quickly away from the edge, as his stomach began to swim.

"*Looks* dangerous, no doubt about that," said Ian. "Yet not so difficult as it seems, no doubt. Had a bit of climbing myself, though that was some time ago. Tell you one thing, we're blessed that we don't have to climb *up*. Immensely more difficult than lowering oneself. Though from up here, the sheer drop, appearing all at once, *looks* harrowing, what?" He tugged on the rope that was still attached to the piton. "Feels secure enough," he said. He turned to Billy. "Like to give it a try?"

"Leave him *alone*," screamed Betty Miller. "He's only a *boy*. Why don't you try it yourself?"

"Actually, thinking of you, mum. Seems desirable to have a couple of us up here to lower you after some others establish a foothold."

"I'm not going *any*where," Betty said.

"Mm," said Ian, glancing at the sky. "Afternoon's pretty well along. Be a jolly bit colder out here at night than it is now. No wood to make a fire, and not enough time to get back to the terminal, supposing you'd want to make your way back the way we came. According to the map, once we reach the bottom of this drop-off, we can make good time skiing to the lodge. Warm fire there, no doubt. Good food, if last night is any indication. And a drop of brandy. I must say, *I'm* looking forward to it."

"Oh, shit," said Betty Miller.

Billy stood off by himself on the edge, trying to look down. Kirsten and her parents must have gone by here. She was probably down there, skiing by now. Maybe they were getting close to the lodge. "What if the black things are down there waiting?" he said, thinking aloud.

The others heard him and were silent. "They could as easily be behind us, pursuing," said Ian finally.

Billy smiled at the others, who seemed to be waiting for him. He was embarrassed to have the grown-ups watching him this way. He grasped the rope and, without saying anything, jumped over.

Betty screamed. "Good show," murmured Ian. Kosho lay full-length on the edge to watch.

"He's moving too quickly," said Kosho, describing Billy's descent to the others. "Slower!" he shouted. But if Billy heard, he gave no sign. With an agility surprising to Kosho, the boy switched ropes nimbly at the first ledge, barely letting his feet touch the rock. Kosho watched in admiration as the boy spun off the side of the rock, swiftly lowering himself to the wider ledge below.

Kosho rose to his feet. "He made it," he said, still staring at the edge of the cliff. He turned to Bob Miller and offered his hand. "You have an exceptional son," he said.

Awkwardly, Bob Miller removed his mitten, and Kosho, remembering that this was a Western custom, swiftly removed his own to grasp Miller's hand. "Like father, like son," said Bob Miller, swiftly replacing his glove, for the chill air had already begun to numb his fingers.

Kosho followed suit. "If you like, I will go next," he said.

"Let me give it a try," said Janet, thinking that if she went now, the others would not be conscious of her slowing them down later.

Kosho bowed, and the middle-aged woman slowly dropped herself over the edge. Her arms ached, and she hoped she would have stamina enough to last until the first ledge. She looked up to see Ian's face watching her with concern from the edge above. "It's all right," she whispered, knowing he could not hear her.

Billy's head swam as he sat by himself on the second ledge. He didn't know what had made him do that—nor what had enabled him to successfully lower himself down the cliff—except that he didn't want the adults looking at him the way they had. He wanted to get away from his parents, their expectations for him. They were always *on* him, wanting him to come on this stupid trip—or if not this one, another—and there were never any people there but other people like them and their children, who always shunned Billy. He wished he were back in Dallas, where he could tell Brian McConnell about this knockout chick he had met. Only, he knew that he would make up stories about what she had let him do to her, the way he suspected Brian did about the girls in their high school.

He'd feel bad if he did that. Even if he never saw Kirsten again, he'd remember the way she kissed him last night, and feel ashamed if he ever made up stories about her.

Billy looked back at the face of the cliff. He had already strapped on his skis, and the woman from Canada, and Biandra before that, was still struggling. He couldn't do anything to help her from here. The thought of Kirsten somewhere down below, maybe in danger from the black people, made him decide to go on.

He was still puzzled over what he had done with the arrows. Kosho had asked him about it, but he had just shrugged. Kosho wanted him to *explain* it, but he couldn't. He had just *felt* the arrows were coming. And he really had saved Mom. Even Dad had been impressed, but as usual he didn't say so. He had always wanted to do something that would impress his father, but no matter what he tried, things always seemed to turn out wrong. Kirsten was the first person he could remember meeting who had seemed to really admire him, for some reason. She thought he was really the person he wanted to be.

And she was somewhere up ahead. He didn't want to wait for the others. He took up the poles and pushed himself down the slope. He remembered something from the skiing classes at Vail that his father had insisted he attend. It *did* seem easy, as many things had since he met Kirsten. He lowered his goggles against the flying snow and began to watch for her.

Chapter Nine

Mkomo tried to turn and stop as gracefully as Charles had, but the abrupt change of direction caused him to lose his footing and slide farther down the slope. His son watched the fall with considerable alarm, for it seemed impossible that his father's mammoth bulk could sustain a skiing accident without serious injury.

Fortunately, Mkomo had had the presence of mind to break the skis away from their bindings, and the snow off the trail was deep and soft. He rose gingerly, testing his legs. Then he roared with delight. Charles turned to see what his father was looking at, and beheld the two shiny black snowmobiles parked just where Granny had promised.

Mkomo, his ski boots sinking deep in the snow, ran toward the machines. He joyfully leaped into one of them. In a minute, Charles had taken the controls of the second vehicle.

"Now, cowboy," Mkomo said to Charles, "have you tried to fire your six-gun yet?"

"No, Pop, but there's nothing to it. You just point and pull the trigger."

"May all things in your life be so simple. Shall we then show those slit-eyed vermin who they are dealing with?" He started and revved the engine, which made a deafening noise, and started back toward the narrow pass in the mountain. Charles, who knew that his father never chose to fight unless he was certain of victory, followed eagerly.

The Natural Hunter had selected the spears as his weapon, and claimed the right to the first Kill of the Hunt, now that the Golden Female had failed in her attempt. Though it was a violation of the Hunting Code to remark on the failure of another Hunter, he could barely conceal his contempt at the Golden Female's missing a virtually helpless target. True, the young beast's apparent ability to brush the arrows aside showed interestingly quick reflexes, but even so, the arrows must have been feebly shot.

In his eagerness, the Natural Hunter had moved far ahead of the others. He had had experience hunting on snow-covered planets, and he found the native means of transportation comfortably familiar. He was glad that his skill gave him an edge over the other Hunters, for the Gray Female was equally desirous of making the first Kill.

She had chosen the primitive projectile-thrower that the Commander had called a pistol. If she were closer to the game, she might have a chance of bringing down the young animal who traveled with the great black beast that was the intended prey of the Natural Hunter.

The Natural Hunter entered the narrow pass without slowing his speed. He expected that the two animals were still a good distance away, and was completely unprepared for the sight of Mkomo charging toward him, mounted in his suddenly acquired vehicle.

Catching sight of the Natural Hunter, Mkomo stood up, brandished his spear, and let out his hunting cry, the "voice of the lion" that had added to his legend among the people of Biandra. It could be heard even above the screaming of the snowmobile's engine, and had the same effect on the Natural Hunter as it had had on so many who had opposed Mkomo in battle. He swerved to avoid the onrushing machine-mounted beast, and as he left the trail caught his skis in the deeper snow and fell roughly.

It was fortunate for him that he did, for Mkomo's spear whistled overhead and lodged itself in the ice-covered rock. The Natural Hunter frantically tried to extricate himself from his skis, groping for the spears that he carried across his back.

Mkomo found that while standing to throw the spears, he could no longer maneuver or brake the snowmobile. The uncontrolled vehicle took him past the Natural Hunter, and he turned his head to bellow, "Finish him off!" to his son. He regained his seat and revved the machine forward. There were more enemies ahead, and if he exhausted his spears, he could run them down with this excellent machine.

Charles sped forward, drawing his gun, grateful to his father for leaving him a felled and apparently helpless target. He fired, from too great a distance, and found his faith in western movies shattered as the black-clad figure found his footing and rose with a spear in ready position.

Charles remembered his father giving him the advice "Charge a gunman; run from a knife," but his recollection of the advice came out backward, and he turned his snowmobile on a collision course with the alien. As the Hunter flung the spear, Charles threw himself downward on the seat of the vehicle, knocking the steering bars to the side. The vehicle jumped into the air as it struck the icy edge of the trail, and the Natural Hunter's perfectly thrown spear smashed through the windscreen of the vehicle, instead of through Charles's body.

Feeling and hearing the chain drive of the vehicle spinning against the deeper snow off the trail, Charles tried to rise, but felt himself pinned to the seat by the spear lodged in the windscreen. He wriggled out just in time to see the Natural Hunter raise a second spear. Charles realized that the six-gun was still in his hand, raised it, and fired blindly.

The Natural Hunter let out a cry that to Charles sounded like a high-pitched whistle, tapering endlessly like a punctured balloon. He saw the creature drop his spear and hold his arm to his side. The rocking of his snowmobile caused Charles to turn his attention to getting the vehicle back on the trail, and as he did so, it sped off again. He fired several shots wildly over his shoulder until the chamber was empty. He turned his attention to reloading. There would be more kills to make at the other end of the pass. He could hear his father's triumphal shouts already.

The Natural Hunter calmed himself. He was thankful that none of the others heard him shame himself by crying out, though it was not, he told himself, the pain that caused his childish wailing. It was the frustration, which was utterly new to him, of being wounded by one of the game. Since his first Hunt, it was he who had earned the name Natural Hunter by always carrying off the perfect shot that felled the fiercest, most dangerous animals. Now he had been wounded, and although he had been trained to steel himself against pain, he could not bear the humiliation.

Yet he *had* to bear it, for the others were already by now

making the first kills of the Hunt. In his heart, he wished that they would somehow miss the clumsy young one who had wounded him. On his own planet, and indeed in virtually every culture the People had visited throughout the known universe, there was a saying.

Every culture seemed to have a variant of it, even on the strange huge planet that moved alone, with a nearly imperceptible rotation, around a brilliant dwarf star. On that planet, one side was unbelievably hot; the other close to absolute zero. The sole intelligent life there had taken the form of rocks, which moved at a pace too slow for any but the most delicate instruments to register—moved to stay within the narrow band of moderate temperature and light that made life possible. Their colossally long life span was lived always in the same condition of twilight, yet they too had the saying that coursed over and over through his brain now: *There will be another day*.

Following behind the Natural Hunter was a group of three: the Commander and the Mate, who had both had training on snow-covered frozen planets, and the Gray Female, who carried the six-gun, wishing it were a blaster. Many mating seasons ago, before Class B game had been declared off-limits to Hunting parties, her intended mate had been killed by Class B animals. She had been in the party that wiped out the population of that planet, yet her thirst for vengeance had not been slaked.

Intellectually, she recognized the need for eradicating Class B species before they could make the Discovery, but the coldly scientific, painless method of extermination—a gradual increase in the radiation bombarding the planet—held no release for her anger. She only felt release when she personally killed with her own hands, and had eagerly accepted the Aging Master's delicate proposal of an illegal Hunt. He was trying to atone for his own part in the long-ago death of her mate.

She raised her six-gun instinctively at the bellowing call of Mkomo's lion's roar as he emerged from the pass. The sight of this unlikely monstrosity mounted on some kind of crude mechanism caused her to waver for a second.

In that second of hesitation, however, the Mate, whose remembrance of the animal's ability to use a Discovery weapon on the earlier trip had made him overcautious, swerved in fear. His ski caught the edge of hers, and they both fell. The Commander, just behind them, could not avoid crashing into them. The three struggled to extricate themselves from the pile of bodies and skis as Mkomo charged down on them like a bull elephant.

The Commander reached for his own spear and managed to turn in time to see Mkomo let fly. The Commander instinctively timed the flight of Mkomo's shaft and knocked it aside with the blade of his own spear.

Suddenly he remembered how the boy had struck aside the Golden Female's arrows in mid-flight. That was a feat that should have been beyond even Class B game. It troubled the Commander.

If members of this species were indeed ready to make the Discovery, then the Hunt would be a more serious breach of the Hunting laws than any of his passengers would be prepared to face. The Commander had confided the secret to the Scientist, and it had only increased his eagerness to study them. But the Mate could easily give the secret to the others.

Thinking of the Mate's knowledge, the Commander found it expedient at that moment to push him into the path of Mkomo's oncoming vehicle.

Regaining control of his snowmobile, Mkomo instantly saw the tempting target that lay sprawled in front of him. He forgot for the moment the remaining spear in his arsenal and ran down the Mate, hearing the thing's squealing cry as the chain tread dug into his body.

Mkomo felt the chain catch flesh. The snowmobile jumped into the air and then returned to the snow-covered ground with a satisfying thump. Mkomo struggled to turn his vehicle to finish off the other two, but it was not easily maneuverable, and his turn took him in a wide circle that carried him away from the others.

In the meantime, the Gray Female had kicked away the skis that hampered her movement, and she now angrily aimed her weapon toward the retreating beast. Just then, the noise of another machine emerging from the gap in the rocks caught her attention, and she turned to face it.

Charles, feeling confident, piloted his snowmobile into the open snow and saw the black-clad figure aiming its Colt Peacemaker at him. He raised his own reloaded weapon and fired. The figure fired back, and Charles ducked.

Neither of them were in effective range of the nineteenth-century weapon, but rage on the part of the Gray Female and fear on Charles's part made them fire again and again until both weapons were empty. Charles saw the Commander raise his spear, and swerved to get away.

In frustration the Gray Female flung her empty pistol at Charles. The well-aimed pistol was more effective than the bullets had been, for it struck Charles in the face, bloodying his mouth. He turned to follow his father, only to meet Mkomo flying back in the direction of the two aliens, standing once more in his snowmobile and brandishing his spear.

The Commander saw him coming and tensed for the encounter. As Mkomo approached, his lion-roar caused a spasm of fear in the Commander, but the Commander quelled it with the thought that he had faced worse and lived. He feinted a throw, with the desired result. Before he was within certain range, Mkomo let fly his spear. The Commander turned it aside, seemingly without effort, and again raised his spear, sure now of a perfect shot, for the beast was so large that he could not effectively hide within the small compartment of the vehicle.

Mkomo frantically tried to turn the snowmobile, but saw that its momentum would carry it too near the enemy. He pulled the steering gear as far to the right as it would go, but it still shuddered nearer to the raised weapon. He watched the being's arm for the telltale sign of tension that would betray the decision to strike. As he saw it, he moved, surprisingly quickly for a man of his massive size, and threw himself over the far side of his snowmobile, holding the steering gear with an iron grip. He hung there, inches from the snow and the flying, razor-sharp teeth of the chain belt that propelled the vehicle.

The Commander threw just as Mkomo made his move, and watched in frustration as the spear crossed over the now empty driver's compartment of the vehicle.

Hanging over the side, Mkomo saw the spear pass overhead and land harmlessly in the snow beyond. With a cry of triumph, he pulled himself back into the driver's seat. He concentrated and sent out the intense thought, *Granny, I need you.* Instantly, she appeared next to him.

"Can I help you?" she said sweetly.

"Yes!" he gasped, swallowing air from the exertion. "More spears! Quickly! Many more of them!"

"Oh, of course. There is a cache of them buried in the snow not far from the other end of the pass where I left the snowmobiles."

Mkomo uttered imprecations in his native tongue. "What

good will those do me, when my enemies are not there but here? I want them, now, here, in this . . . ski machine."

"That's quite impossible," said Granny primly. "It's against the rules of the Hunt to use Discovery powers, and I cannot transcend space and time, except to give you advice."

"Discovery? What is the Discovery?"

"Can't answer that," she said firmly.

"Then, advice. What is your advice? Should I go back and run them down? Do they have more weapons?"

"*Those* two don't, but if you want good advice, I'd say you shouldn't bother with them." She nodded up the slope. "There are more of them coming, as you can see. And they are armed, two of them with guns. Powerful rifles. My best advice . . . let's see how you would phrase it . . . is to get your ass out of here."

"Aarrgh," grunted Mkomo, dismissing her with a wave of his hand. He turned to look up the slope and saw that she was right. The other enemies were coming, and he could see the rifles slung over their shoulders. To charge them, even with the ski machine, would be suicide. Mkomo had never felt the urge for a suicidal gesture.

Charles had turned his vehicle and was drawing closer. Mkomo could see the six-gun in his hand, but he knew that was a puny weapon. They might well finish off the two aliens down here, but to do that would risk delaying their escape. He revved up the engine of his vehicle and propelled it into Charles's path. They could not hear each other, even if they shouted, above the noise of the gasoline engines, but Mkomo pointed toward the pass. Charles waved his gun and gestured toward the defenseless aliens to their left, several hundred yards away. Mkomo pointed up the slope, and his son turned to see the danger there. The two made their way speedily toward the mouth of the pass.

Charles thought that at least his father would see the body of the alien, but he was surprised to see that somehow the body had been removed. Or had it been dead after all? He began to rehearse the story of the battle that he would tell his father later.

They emerged from the other side of the pass and raced down the slope. Far below lay the end of the trail and, if the map was correct, the comfortable chalet where they would celebrate their victory.

Chapter Ten

The Aging Master was not given to rude exclamations; nonetheless, when he beheld the sight of the great dark beast and his son, mounted on unpleasantly noisy contraptions, wreaking havoc among three experienced Hunters, he uttered a phrase which in the language of the People translated roughly to "Goodness gracious sakes alive!" The Golden Female looked at him sharply, for even this mild epithet was a surprising break with the Master's customary dignity and tranquility. For a second, she even felt relief from her own shame at having missed the opportunity, a rare honor, of being allowed to take the first Kill.

She immediately banished the thought from her head, for it was unworthy of a true Hunter. If she betrayed her momentary delight, she would lose the Aging Master's respect. That respect meant a good deal to her; her family had a long tradition of Hunting prowess. In her youth, the Aging Master had been a guest in her parents' home, and she was fascinated by his tales of adventure and courage in strange places, on distant planets, encountering the fiercest and most challenging species in the galaxy.

It had been a crushing disappointment to her when the Old Rules had been abolished before she had been old enough to partake in a real hunt. By now she had participated in many supervised Hunts, and had dispatched Class C game with ease—so much ease that the final few Hunts had been boring. They had taken on the stupidity, for her, of casual slaughter. She found no opportunity for the courageous deeds of heroism that she had heard the Aging Master and her parents describe when speaking of their own Hunts.

When the Aging Master had confided to her parents the plan for the new expedition, she had been thrilled. Yet her parents refused the offer; since their decision to mate, they had not kept up their training. That was the way of the People: those who had mated seldom returned to the Hunt. It was rare for those who had been as skilled Hunters as her parents even to mate at all. The Golden Female felt the same aversion to the mating process that all true Hunters were supposed to feel, and she had already determined never to succumb.

The Golden Female had broken in on the conversation between her parents and the Aging Master—a breach of etiquette, but one that she knew her parents would forgive. She had always been their favorite child, because she had been the one with the qualities of a true Hunter.

She begged to be allowed to go along. It was not difficult to obtain her parents' consent, and the Aging Master was bound by the rules of etiquette: to extend an invitation to Hunt toward one member of a family and not to include all the others of his family in the request would have implied a judgment that one member of the family was unworthy.

So her request was granted. Yet before the Aging Master left, the Golden Female had heard her mother's last conversation with him.

"I am honored by your allowing my daughter to go on the great Hunt of your lifetime," her mother had said.

The Aging Master had ritually responded with a recitation of the great feats of the Golden Female's family. Her mother had shown the proper humility, and politely waited for him to finish. Both knew that she had something to confide in him, but the conventions were to be observed.

When he had finished, the Golden Female's mother said, "I know that under your leadership the Hunt will be a victorious one, and all the members of it will return in glory."

The Aging Master acknowledged the compliment with the proper gesture. "I must tell you," her mother had continued, "that you may not find her well prepared."

"She has partaken with honor in many Hunts," replied the Aging Master, "and she is the child of a great family of Hunters."

Her mother acknowledged the compliment. "Yet it has never been possible for her to train herself against Class B game."

"Unavoidable," replied the Aging Master. "But the lapse in her training can now, happily, be corrected."

"Even so," said her mother, "I fear you will find her without the proper caution that a Hunter should use against the highest class of game. I beg you to make allowances for what I fear may be her greatest fault—a lack of discipline."

The Aging Master acknowledged the implied request in the most dignified way possible. "I shall consider it an honor to be allowed to instill that discipline in her as the final step in her training."

Remembering that conversation made the Golden Female all the more eager to win the Aging Master's approval—and made her failure earlier in the day all the more shameful to her. The others had assured her that the unexpected ability of the young one to turn aside perfectly shot arrows was something that none of them could have foreseen. Yet she had seen the ill-concealed delight of the Natural Hunter, his arrogance offended by not being selected to make the first Kill.

Now, witnessing the equally unforeseen attack of the two dark animals on the Commander, the Mate, and the Gray Female, and hearing the surprised exclamation from the Aging Master, the Golden Female saw her chance at vindication. She spurred herself forward with several pulls at her poles, then slipped the poles under her belt and drew her bow from her back into ready position. She strung it with an arrow, and with a cry of disappointment saw that at her advance the two dark animals turned their vehicles and began to flee.

In her frustration, she loosed the arrow anyway, instantly realizing that it was a wasted shot, and one that would bring her the Aging Master's just reproof at the Hunting Council. Missing the beast earlier had been a justifiable fault; taking an impossible shot was not.

She saw the two animals guide their vehicles into the narrow pass ahead. Knowing that to follow them was foolhardy, because Class B animals were perfectly capable of waiting there for pursuers, against which they would have a clear shot, she drew herself up. She knew better than to offer her help to the wounded one; a true Hunter did not accept assistance.

The Aging Master and the Scientist soon reached the scene. Only the Mate had actually been wounded, and the scrapes on his back that the animals' machine had made could be easily mended. To the Aging Master's distress, however, the humiliation caused by this first close encounter with the Game caused some breaches of the Hunting etiquette.

"You . . . *pushed* me!" the outraged Mate, his back stinging with flaming cuts, accused the Commander.

"I guided you," replied the Commander coldly. "If you had any presence of mind, you would have instinctively moved to draw his fire so that I could have had a clear shot." He choked back further retorts, conscious of the Aging Master's disapproving glance.

"You had long-range pellet projectors," said the Gray Female suddenly, pointing to the rifles on the backs of the Scientist and the Aging Master. "Why didn't you use them?"

The Aging Master, conscious that she was accusing *him*, drew himself up with a show of the utmost dignity. He could not possibly reply to her in the heat of Hunting. "These are things we must discuss in the Hunting Council," he reminded her evenly. "In the meantime, we are forgetting our companion."

The others looked around. They were six. The Natural Hunter was missing.

"He drew far ahead of us," said the Commander. "He entered the pass, and then, a short while after, the two animals emerged in their vehicles."

"Look!" said the Golden Female suddenly. The others turned. Up the slope three other animals were approaching on their snow sticks. "We can take all three," the Golden Female said eagerly to the Aging Master.

"There will be time for honors," he reminded her gently. "The Hunt has only begun, and we are fortunate in discovering the extent of their resourcefulness. For now, we must look for our lost companion, and then repair to the Hunting Council."

The Golden Female, and the others, followed his lead, but she looked longingly at the apparently easy game that was speeding downward within range of their weapons.

The Halvorssen family slowed their progress at the sight of the black-clad figures on the slope below. When they had sideslipped to a full stop, they surveyed the scene.

"Something happened," said Bibi. Her husband nodded. "I heard the sounds of snowmobiles," he said. "But I don't see a thing."

As they watched, the creatures seemed to regroup, and several of them had to remount their skis. They returned the gaze of the Halvorssens for a short time.

"Use your rifle, Papa," said Kirsten.

He smiled indulgently on her. "I think you are getting a little bit like your American boyfriend, beloved. Why should I use my rifle when no one has attacked me?"

Kirsten blushed a little, so becomingly that her parents smiled. "Who said he was my boyfriend? Anyway, you saw that he was afraid to use the gun last night when the old nana told him to shoot her."

"Of course not," Bjorn said. "Americans don't like to shoot directly at lovable old ladies. They prefer to bomb them from so high above that they cannot see their faces."

"He isn't like that," Kirsten said.

"Maybe we'll find out," replied her mother. "It looks like he's coming now."

It was true. Up the slope they saw Billy, coming a bit too fast for conditions, and holding his feet somewhat too far apart, but not doing badly. He must have seen them after they had first sighted him (Bjorn wondered if he closed his eyes when he skiied, as some of the Americans he had taught to ski had done), for he sideslipped to a stop rather too quickly, and inexpertly showered them with flying snow from his too abrupt halt. He completed the effect by toppling over and sliding down in between them. As he rose, he looked rather like a comical snowman that some children had erected.

In spite of herself, Kirsten laughed. She put her hand over her mouth and rushed toward Billy. Brushing the snow off his face, she planted another kiss on him. It warmed him, and the embarrassment that he felt at falling quickly vanished. He gasped, and spit snow from his mouth. "I . . . I thought you might be in trouble."

"Did you hear?" Kirsten asked, turning to her parents. "He thought we were in trouble! And he came to help! Don't you like him for that, Mama? Papa? Isn't he brave?"

"Very brave," said Bjorn, nodding his head in approval. He winked at his wife. "And now that the creatures have vanished, I hope he will help us to find the chalet that the map shows lies at the bottom of the mountainside."

Discreetly allowing for Billy's clumsiness, they made their way to the opening of the pass, through which the Halvorssens had seen the aliens disappear. Bjorn held up his hand for them to stop. Billy managed his sideslip somewhat better this time, to Bjorn's silent approval, and succeeded in stopping without falling.

"There could be danger ahead," said Bjorn, when the others had gathered around him. He gestured toward the opening of the pass. "We saw some of the black-clad creatures go into there. They might well have set a trap, and could be waiting at the other end."

"We don't know that they really mean us harm," reminded his wife. "They retreated when they sighted us before."

"Oh, they do!" said Billy. "You weren't there, but earlier they shot arrows at us. At my mother! They tried to kill her!"

Bjorn nodded. "If we are prudent, we should operate on the advice that the old nana gave us—and that is that they regard us as some kind of animals in a hunt."

"I don't really understand that, Papa," said Kirsten. "It seems strange that they should want to kill us."

"You have already asked me to kill *them*," reminded her father. She blushed again.

"I can well understand it," he said. "I have been a hunter myself, an expert one, and I often found the game too easy for me. I wondered if there might be something else that would present more of a challenge. I longed for the money that would enable me to try an African safari. But say that I did, and that I found the game there no more challenging than the beasts I found in the northern countries? Where would I search for adventure then?"

"Oh, Papa, but you're not like that."

"I am, though," he said. "I expend my restlessness in physical exertion, in competition of a peaceful kind. But the thought has occurred to me . . . that there is no other pleasure quite like killing."

Kirsten was shocked.

"What shall we do, then?" said Bibi.

"One of us must test the trail," Bjorn said. "Since Kirsten is clearly the fastest skiier—the youngest and most agile—I think she should go through first, with us following. I will be able to guard her with this." He patted the hunting rifle across his back.

"You can't *mean* it!" said Billy, horrified.

"It is the most reasonable solution to our dilemma," Bjorn said. "One of us *must* lead the others through. Otherwise we stand here until night falls, and since we have no means to make a fire, we shall certainly freeze."

Kirsten nodded. She was not sure why he had suggested it, but she felt implicit faith in her father. She knew he would allow no harm to come to her. She prepared herself for the thrust forward that would carry her into the pass.

"No!" said Billy. "You can't! I'll . . ." He suddenly shouldered past her. "Let me. If one of us has to go first, I will."

Kirsten reached to stop him, but her father interceded, blocking her way. Billy used his poles to push himself forward down the trail. Soon he had picked up speed, and before long he had disappeared through the entrance to the pass.

"We'd better follow," said Bjorn. He pulled the rifle around so that he could aim it quickly, and then set off. His wife kept pace with him, Kirsten hurrying afterward.

"I really thought you meant for Kirsten to go," said his wife, poling close to him. "I had not expected the boy to have so much courage."

Bjorn smiled across at her. "I was like him once, when I met you," he said. "Americans are really not all that much different from us. He is an excellent boy. I would have been disappointed if he had not acted as he did."

"It is too bad that she loves him so," said Bibi.

"Because in his impetuosity he will certainly die on this trip?" murmured Bjorn. "Not so. A tragic love affair, when young, is not a bad preparation for life. She will remember him, in serenity, and the memory will give spice to the dull husband she will have later on."

Bibi blew him a kiss with her lips. "You are never dull," she said.

Inside the pass, the walls of snow quickly closed around him, and Billy felt a fearful aloneness. *Granny, I need you*, he thought, and was surprised to find her skiing next to him.

"I . . . didn't expect you," he said.

"Why not? You called me, didn't you? Didn't I say I'd come? What did you want?"

"Oh, I guess . . . I wondered what to do."

"What to do? Why, continue as you are. You've been doing better than anyone could have expected."

"Really? But what if they are waiting for me at the end of the pass?"

"Pshaw. Don't worry about the Hunters. They've gone on to their Hunting Council. They were really embarrassed. You'll hear all about it from that braggart Mkomo when you reach the chalet. Though I expect he'll manage to exaggerate what he did."

"Really? You mean there's no danger?"

"Not unless you fall and break your leg. I'd advise you to slow down." The old lady's skill on skis seemed uncanny until Billy reminded himself that she was not really human.

"Don't you think I ought to tell Kirsten and her parents? They'll be worried about me."

"No they won't. *Cer*tainly not the parents. And as for Kirsten, she thinks you can do just about anything."

"You mean it? Does . . . does she love me?"

Granny shook her head. "Such questions. Pay attention now, for I've got to go back and help your mother and the others. Just keep on as you have. I have a question for you. What did . . . what were you thinking of when you stopped those arrows?"

"This morning? I was thinking of helping my mother."

"Yes? And just before you thought of that, what were you thinking of?"

"Oh . . . Kirsten, I guess."

"Mm. Well, the best advice I can give you is just keep on thinking of her."

Chapter Eleven

The Millers, the Gores, and Kosho slowly made their way down the face of the cliff. Kosho, who had climbing experience, discreetly took command of the operation, gently checking Bob Miller's impulsiveness and overestimation of his own abilities. Kosho was really alarmed at the others' inexperience, and the fact that they seemed to think that the only real danger was from the Hunters.

Even after they had reached the point where they could continue down the slope on skis, Bob Miller, leading the way, kept holding up the party, clumsily and abruptly stopping and twice nearly causing the following skiiers to pile into him. At these times, Miller would hold his shotgun at the ready and scan the surrounding slopes for a movement that had caught his eye, fearing another attack by the aliens.

Kosho admired the beautifully crafted blue-steel Purdy shotgun that Miller carried, and well understood the temptation to brandish and handle it. A machined object, Kosho understood, could have an aesthetic delight to it—in the way it looked and felt when handled. Yet he also knew that the weapon Miller carried was ineffective beyond a very short distance and would be utterly useless in defense against an enemy firing a high-powered rifle from the slopes. The only real danger it presented was in the eventuality that Miller should fire it, for the percussion and noise it would create might well cause a slide of the snow—softer now in the afternoon sun—and bring an avalanche down upon them.

Kosho admitted to himself that his own choice of weapon was

equally impractical, if not more so—at least a shotgun could bring down a group of enemies at thirty feet. Of what use would the samurai sword be, except to continue to be an awkward burden for which he risked his life in the climb down the face of the mountain? He reflected that it was almost as if they were servants, and the weapons were cherished objects that they were carrying under the orders of some distant emperor.

Yet Kosho knew why he had chosen the sword: for the aesthetic pleasure it gave him and for the hope that he would find an opponent who chose the same weapon. Kosho had in his youth become enamored of the legends of the samurai, who occupied approximately the same place in the tradition of Japan as the Knights of the Round Table did in England. Kosho shot a sidelong glance at Ian Gore, feeling a kinship for the older man carrying his great bulky sword like a modern Don Quixote—ridiculous to others, but secure in the recesses of his own mind, which revered the ways that others had discarded.

As Kosho did. From his youth, one of his leisure activities had been to develop his skill with samurai weapons. Fortunately there were others in Japan who shared his love for the traditional mode of battle. They practiced against each other, using wooden swords that in themselves were beautiful and functional, crafted to have the heft, feel, and suppleness of a deadly blade. Kosho had received many uncomfortable bruises in the pursuit of this passion, but he was confident that there were now few, even in Japan, who could best him in a samurai sword duel.

The irony of this did not escape Kosho: there were no more samurai, no more sword duels; he was an expert at an art that was no longer practiced. The arrival of the American ships under Commodore Perry in Yedo Bay in 1853 had humiliatingly forced open a society that had been closed to foreign influence for two and a half centuries. Japan had embraced the West, and when it did so, the role of the samurai vanished. The samurai found themselves useless, and by the early twentieth century all of them had gone. There had been a resurgence of nostalgic feeling for the way of the samurai in the 1930s, but it had taken the form of a strident militarism, and resulted in Japan's catastrophic participation in the Second World War. Japan had used Western weapons against the West, and lost.

Kosho's hand went to the hilt of his sword. Knowing it a hopeless yearning, he nevertheless felt the wish that somewhere up ahead he would find someone who shared his wish to fight according to the Old Ways; and then he would discover if he could have been a samurai.

The Aging Master lifted the exquisitely curved and balanced sword in his hand. He thought it one of the finest examples of a native weapon he had ever handled. He raised it over his head and brought it down swiftly, narrowly missing the head of the Golden Female. She struggled to maintain control of herself, knowing that he was in full control of the weapon, knowing that he was testing her discipline.

"Our mistake," the Aging Master said to the group assembled once more in the misty swamp for the Hunting Council, "was in taking unfair advantage of the game."

The Mate's wounds, temporarily soothed by a healing preparation, flamed again at this accusation. He started to protest, then caught himself. It would do no good to protest; he would wait his time to reveal what he knew about this species' closeness to the Discovery—and to humiliate the Commander, if necessary. What did the Commander mean to him? He only hoped that some of the rest of them would see the necessity of getting out of here as quickly as they could and leaving this planet to the Guardians.

At any rate, the Natural Hunter spoke the retort that the Mate had choked back. "I seem to be a living example of the creatures' ability to defend themselves adequately." His sarcasm, all could see, was his way of disguising the deep shame that he felt.

"You did well," said the Aging Master, with a complimentary gesture.

To refuse to acknowledge it would be a breach of politeness, and the Natural Hunter did so after a significant pause that the Aging Master ignored.

"Are we then to discard all weapons and allow ourselves to stand helpless against these creatures?" asked the Gray Female.

"Not at all," replied the Master. "Still, we came here in a spirit of arrogance, delighting in the prospect of being allowed to hunt Class B game once more. Or," he said with a paternal gesture toward the Golden Female, "for the first time. However, many of us—and I accuse myself, forgot that the reason the Guardians gave for restricting this kind of Hunt was that there was danger. A real danger."

Though he had made no reference to it, the Gray Female felt

that the memory of the death of her chosen mate was being sullied. Had not the Aging Master implied that his death was due to a lapse in skill? She would not forget.

"We thought," the Aging Master continued, "that we could stand effortlessly above the game and dispatch them with the ease of a novice shooting arrows."

The Golden Female humbly acknowledged her failure.

"We failed to take into account that they, with the skills of Class B game, had developed their prowess with the weapons to a greater degree than we had."

The Mate sucked in a lungful of the thin atmosphere, made a little more like that of their home planet by the presence of swamp gas. He gathered what little courage he possessed. "That's not true," he said.

The Aging Master—indeed, all present including the Gray Female—recoiled from this breach of etiquette, but the Mate continued, desperately trying to justify himself. "It wasn't her lack of skill with the bow that was at fault. Her aim was true. It was the boy who struck the arrows down in mid-flight. And he could do it only because he is close to making the Discovery."

The Commander made a severe warning gesture toward the Mate. The Mate stared at him bitterly. "I *won't* be silent. They have got to know—because you didn't tell them, you couldn't have—that on that first expedition one of these animals was able to fire a weapon of the People."

There was a fluttering of confused and astonished gestures among the Hunters. Only the Aging Master stood aloof, still holding the insult that had been thrown down at him.

"Is this true?" asked the Natural Hunter of the Commander.

"Part of what he says is true," said the Commander. "Like the beasts with two heads on the planet of the red and green stars, one head speaks truth, the other falsehoods."

"I have only one mouth," replied the Mate, "and it speaks true."

"Part of what you said is not true," corrected the Commander, "for I did tell our companion the Scientist of the phenomenon we observed on our first visit here." He looked to the Scientist for confirmation.

The Scientist acknowledged this by uttering the superlative of the word "truth." He indicated his wish to be allowed to expand on his answer. The others granted permission, glad that one of them still was able to maintain the etiquette of the Hunt.

"We discussed the phenomenon mentioned, at Home," said the Scientist, "and, I confess, it was my chief impetus for making the trip. Some of you are aware, no doubt, but have been too polite to mention, that despite my preeminent skills I have been forbidden to participate in the extirpation of Class B species who are judged to be too near the Discovery."

The Golden Female started to acknowledge this, but on seeing that the others made no gesture, cut short her movement.

"As I thought," said the Scientist. "For that I thank you, for it has been a humiliation to me. And I must tell you that this action against me . . . to thwart my work and stifle the skills that I have developed over a lifetime . . . was taken because I attempted to capture and preserve a specimen—*several* specimens—of Class B game . . . to allow them to develop Discovery powers."

The Golden Female could not keep back her thought. "But why? That would be the death of our species!"

The Scientist acknowledged her remark approvingly. "So all of our young believe.That is why they assent to the brutal extermination policy of the Guardians. Because I disagreed, my voice was silenced, and my work was stopped."

"Not only our young believe it," warned the Gray Female.

The Scientist acknowledged this with an impatient gesture that the others recognized as a mannerism that was not intended to be insulting. "Virtually all of the People believe it now, even though"—he turned to the Aging Master—"in *your* youth, species close to the Discovery were regarded as worthy adversaries for fair combat."

The Aging Master acknowledged this. "I should like you to know that I argued with the Guardians that you should be allowed to continue your work." Again came the flutterings of astonishment, for the deliberations of the Guardians were supposed to be the most secret proceedings. None even knew the identity of the Guardians, and now the Aging Master had revealed his entry into their council.

Even, thought the Golden Female, *as he might himself be one of the Guardians.*

The Scientist opened his arms in the unmistakable sign of pleasure and gratification. "You know, then, that I believed that further study of species about to make the Discovery would give us new insight into the process by which we ourselves make the Discovery, and ultimately into the nature of the Discovery itself."

The Mate, warily sensing the turn the argument was taking, and feeling the growing acceptance of it by the others, replied impulsively, "*Every*one knows what the Discovery is."

The Scientist again made his impatient gesture. This time it was tinged with a hint of contempt. "You think you know, because you know its power, the power that knowing how to use it gives you. Gives *us*, alone in the universe. We think ourselves unique, and that thought has given us arrogance, even though we do not understand the powers within us that have enabled us to make the Discovery. I have for some time now believed that the Discovery rests on sexual activity."

The others flashed embarrassment, with the exception of the Aging Master. Sexual matters were never to be spoken of directly, not even between chosen mates.

"The Commander carefully noted on his earlier trip," continued the Scientist, not seeming to notice their embarrassment, "that only one of the game he encountered was able to use the Discovery-powered weapon. My theory is that he was at the height of sexual power. Among the People, of course, Discovery power is conferred in a ritual ceremony held at about the same time that the ability to choose a mate becomes manifest. We therefore acknowledge our sexual longing, without seeming to. We transfer that awakening to the Discovery-awakening."

The Golden Female was blushing furiously, turning her a tawny color that did indeed resemble gold.

The Scientist, noticing her distress without seeming to acknowledge it, said, "To spare you further embarrassment, I must tell you that I came here with the thought that I, or someone, could capture one of these beings alive so that I could study its development."

Again, the flutterings of confusion greeted his announcement. The Gray Female and the Natural Hunter gathered their wits and made ready to gesture contempt and disagreement, when the Aging Master flung down his left arm, palm open, toward the Scientist. It was the unmistakable sign of total commitment, and it stopped the Gray Female and the Natural Hunter. They withdrew their gestures before making them apparent.

"I am in complete agreement," said the Aging Master, "for I believe we must come into close contact with these worthy game to defeat them." He turned toward the Mate, who cowered before his glance.

The Aging Master made a gesture of conciliation, though not, the others noticed, the highest gesture. "I freely forgive you for insulting me," he told the Mate, "for there is a noble task awaiting you."

The Mate struggled to remember the correct gesture of acknowledgment. It had been a long time since anyone had assigned him a noble task.

"The advisor that we have given to the beasts," said the Aging Master, "informs me that one of them has declined to accept a weapon. It is apparently an inferior member of the species, for it does not seem to have the natural instinct of aggressiveness that Class B game nearly always has. It expects that we will not attack it, for our advisor has revealed to them that we will oppose them only with their own weapons. It ignores the fact that it has limbs that can grasp, rudimentary claws, and rudimentary food grinders that can be used in attack, or defense. It is sufficiently armed to face one of us in combat. You have been chosen for the task. Try not to kill it, for the Scientist's purposes seem to me to be worthy."

The Mate struggled again for the proper gesture. He made one signifying that he was not worthy. He thought of another excuse. "Others wish the first Kill, who are more skilled than I." He was conscious of a nearly imperceptible hostile gesture from the Natural Hunter.

"This will not be a Kill, if skillfully carried out," said the Aging Master. Then his voice dropped a decibel. "You do not care to add to your earlier insult by implying that I have improperly chosen you?"

The Mate carefully rose to his feet, conscious that he must not betray the pain the wounds on his back were giving him. He turned before he left the Hunting Council. "Does the rule against using Discovery powers still apply? Even now that we know that some of this species can use the Discovery?"

The Aging Master spoke sternly. "This particular beast—your prey—has shown no aptitude or indication that it can use, or even comprehend, the Discovery. I was told you were a noble Hunter."

The Mate bowed his head, made a tentative gesture of acknowledgment, and left.

The Commander was uneasy at the task the Aging Master had given the Mate, but there was no use trying to countermand it. With luck, the creature might even kill the Mate. As far as the Commander was concerned, that would be no loss.

There were other things for the Commander to worry about. As had the Golden Female, the Commander realized that the Aging Master's apparent access to the Guardians' council might mean that he himself were one of the Guardians.

If so, he might have assigned himself to this trip to monitor the progress of this species. If it were discovered that they were actually about to make the Discovery, then the Commander's disgrace was certain. The only way he could avert ultimate disgrace was to capture the boy for the Scientist, and hope that his investigations produced something of value to the People.

He turned his attention once more to the Council. The Aging Master was urging the others to choose once again from the group of weapons that the beasts carried. As the Commander watched, the Gray Female examined the different types of bladed weapons.

"You may choose the one I hold, if you desire a blade," offered the Aging Master politely. The Grey Female tested the curved sword that was a match for Kosho's, but she declined it. "This one, I think, will cut better," she said, taking up the heavy English broadsword that was like the one Ian Gore had brought down the mountainside.

Chapter Twelve

Kosho, the Millers, and the Gores approached the well-lit chalet to the sound of laughter and song within. They shed their skis and entered, to find an uproarious party in full swing.

Mkomo greeted them expansively. The Emperor was carrying a new spear, identical to the ones he had lost in the snow, and proceeded to reenact for the newcomers the same tale he had been telling for some hours to the Halvorssens and Billy Miller—the now epic tale of his victory over the aliens.

The sight of a grand table of warm food and drink proved more appealing to the new members of the group, and they drifted over there. Undaunted, Mkomo continued his story, grasping a chair to use as a prop snowmobile, and leaning perilously far over the side to show how he had dodged the aliens' weapons.

Bjorn Halvorssen drew Kosho aside from the hilarity and asked, "You are all safe? You saw none of the beings?"

Kosho shook his head. "This morning, there were some of them on a ledge who shot arrows at us."

Bjorn nodded. "We saw them too, but did not know they were shooting at you. Fortunately, their aim seems to have been poor."

"I think . . ." Kosho started. He shook his head. "It seemed to me that their aim was true, but the boy, the son of the Millers, seemed to deflect the arrows from their path."

Bjorn stared at Kosho, then across the room to where Billy sat in quiet conversation with Kirsten. He shook his head. "The boy showed bravery this afternoon, but I don't think . . . Have you ever had experience with snow blindness?"

Kosho smiled at him. "I appreciate your skepticism. I have not experienced snow blindness, but I have had experience with illusions. Usually, I was able to dispel a visual illusion by the evidence of my camera. An eye that records without passion. Unfortunately, I was told that I could not bring my camera on this trip."

Bjorn nodded. "That is a hopeful sign."

"How so?" asked Kosho.

"It may mean that they expect some of us may return . . . may be *allowed* to return. If so, they would not want us to be able to bring proof—such as your camera would provide—that there were black-clad figures, or the old nana."

"So that no one would believe us."

"Just so."

Kosho considered the matter for a moment, then turned to count the group. "There is still one missing," he said.

"The one from Israel," said Bjorn.

"He told me—this morning it was—that he planned to take no weapons along."

"None? I thought he was skilled in the weapons of war."

"He is, but he is tired of them."

"Then he has more courage than you or I. Perhaps, though, he has too much courage. It is night out there now."

Kosho glanced at the windows of the chalet. The sun had just been setting when his group arrived, but now it was pitch black. Night falls suddenly in high mountainous regions. He shivered.

Billy, having shared three glasses of aquavit with Kirsten, passing the little stemmed glasses back and forth the way she showed him, was feeling warm and content. Kirsten had giggled at Mkomo's antics and shared her jokes with Billy. "You're a *real* hero," she had whispered to him, "for going first through the pass—and you had no snowmobile."

Billy liked the way that sounded, although he truthfully didn't feel he had done anything much. He would have been terribly scared if Granny hadn't told him there was no danger. And as for going first through the pass—well, he wasn't going to stand there and let a girl take the risk. Especially not Kirsten. He looked at her now, closing one eye so that he could focus on her a little better. She thought he was winking, and gave him a wink in return. "Do you want to go upstairs?" she asked.

He gulped, and thought for a wild moment of calling for Granny. Somehow, though, he realized she wasn't going to be much help now. He wished he could call on Brian McConnell, but whatever Brian could tell him . . . His head swam, and it seemed somehow that Brian McConnell, back in Dallas, was even less real than Granny, than what was happening to him now. It was as if he had become another person. Someone that nobody he knew back in Dallas would recognize. *That* thought gave him courage, and he rose and took Kirsten by the hand. They started up the stairs. None of the adults, by now seriously engaged in their own conversation about the day, seemed to notice. Billy didn't realize that Kosho's eyes were on him.

Though it was dark now, Glassman could faintly see the lights of the chalet at the bottom of the hill. He was glad he hadn't picked up the Uzi, had finally left it behind; gladder still, now that he had come the whole route alone, without a sign of any of the supposed hunters the old woman had warned them about. Maybe it was all a lie. *Allevai!* He hoped so.

The disappearance of the sun beneath the crest of the mountain had brought not only darkness but cold, a cold that with a rising wind penetrated through Glassman's parka and ski pants. He urged his skis onward with a push of the poles, hoping that behind the lights of the chalet lay warmth and food.

He did not see the dark figure coming swiftly from an angle behind him until it was too late. The figure made no move to turn aside but ran into Glassman as if intending to turn him over and run him down. The collision, instead, brought both of them into a heap of skis and flailing arms. One of the dark arms of the figure rose swiftly through the distant lights of the chalet, and it was only the brief sight of it silhouetted against the light that caused Glassman instinctively to turn his head to the side. As he did, he heard and felt the thump of the pointed ski pole in the snow on the spot where his eye had been.

Glassman kicked upwards, his boot still attached to the ski. The ski cracked as it met some kind of flesh and bone, and Glassman heard a high-pitched squeal that unnerved him more than the sudden attack. He struggled to turn, and abruptly his head was covered by the body of the thing. He could feel its arm scratching at his parka, searching for a hold.

Glassman had a moment of panic as his air was cut off by the thin body of the alien. He gasped and struggled to free himself, inhaling a sickening odor that reminded him of some earthly smell, something repugnant to him. As he twisted away from the creature and thankfully gulped in the clear, cold night air, he realized what the smell was: shrimp.

Instantly he was straddled again by the wiry figure, feeling it tear at his head in a violent move that cut against his chin where the strap that held his hood momentarily strained before breaking. The being clenched Glassman's hair and jerked his head back and then slammed his skull against the icy snow—again and again. The Israeli struck with the knuckles of both hands at the place where the creature's neck must be.

Billy and Kirsten had found an empty bedroom upstairs and were half reclining on the bed. They were kissing, a longer kiss than Billy had ever had in his life. Finally they lay on the bed, their legs dangling over the side. Billy gathered up his courage and reached down to caress one of Kirsten's breasts. He was astonished that she did not push him away. His attention wandered when she slid her tongue between his lips.

Suddenly he tensed. A cry of pain ruptured his brain, and he found himself gasping for breath. His body abruptly felt cold, and he pressed her closer to him, hoping to capture the warmth that she emitted.

"What's wrong?" she said in alarm.

"I'm sorry," he mumbled, looking around the room as if someone had just come in.

"I love you, Billy," she said, thinking that he had somehow become afraid because she had been too forward with him. She remembered the experience she had had with the boy from the English water polo team, when she had taken him to her room the evening of the match, feeling a little guilty the way she had embarrassed him in the pool that afternoon. When he realized what she intended to allow him, he became panicky and ran out to rejoin his teammates. One of her girlfriends had told her that all English boys really preferred other boys for that sort of thing, but she had never heard that about American boys. Still, maybe he liked to be more in command. She wished she knew how American girls acted. She sighed at her inexperience.

"No, Kirsten, I . . ." He clamped his hands over his ears as the cry for help came again. "It's not *here!*" he cried. "Someone's in trouble!"

She touched his arm in concern. "Was it like this morning, like what you told me about your mother and the arrows? Maybe . . . but Billy, she is downstairs."

"No! It's not her! Can't you hear it?" He was standing now, looking at her on the bed, wanting nothing more than to lie back down there with her, but the cries inside his brain would not stop.

She stood up and quickly rearranged her blouse. "We must go downstairs and look." She took his hand and kissed him again. "We can come back."

Kosho saw them come down the stairs with surprise. He had not expected to see the two of them again tonight. He moved quickly but unobtrusively across the room, becoming more alarmed as he saw Billy's wide-eyed look of pain, the way he scanned the room as if something were wrong. Kosho followed his look, but all the travelers had settled themselves on comfortable couches in front of the two blazing fireplaces. Ian and Janet Gore had gone upstairs after finishing their meal. The others had settled into quiet speculation or noisy boasting.

"Is there something wrong?" Kosho asked politely, not wishing to disturb the two young lovers.

"Billy has heard something . . . someone in trouble," explained Kirsten.

Kosho's eyes quickly moved around the group, counting. All were accounted for, except for the Gores, who seemed to have gone to bed, and . . . Glassman.

"Perhaps we should have a look outside," said Kosho.

The cold air hit them with numbing effect as they stepped out the door. Kosho's eyes scanned the landscape above them. The moon had emerged, a quarter-moon that emitted only a little light, but his experienced photographer's eyes were comfortable with the black-and-white landscape. He pointed up the slope with a shout.

Billy and Kirsten followed his gesture. Two figures, both dark but one with the unmistakable slim-limbed alien form and the other filled out with a down ski garment, were struggling against each other.

Billy set off at a run, and Kosho cried out that he would freeze in minutes without protective clothing. The girl tried to follow, but Kosho held her back. "We can only help him by bringing him a ski suit," Kosho said. The sensible Kirsten agreed, and they went inside to snatch up their discarded garments and an outfit for Billy.

At first, Billy's feet dragged against the deep snow. He sank deeper and deeper and slowed nearly to a crawl. *Granny, I need you* came the thought, almost before he wished it.

"Go back," she said, beside him once more. "You'll injure yourself."

"No, Granny, he needs help."

"You cannot help," she said firmly. "Go back."

Utterly stuck now in the thigh-deep snow, he looked at her reproachfully. He remembered the question he had asked her that afternoon in the pass, and remembered that she hadn't answered it. "Granny, I found out!" he said suddenly. "She does love me!"

At almost the same moment, he found a resurgence of power in his body, a power like nothing he had ever felt before, and he felt himself charge forward across the snow, and knew that by willing it he could . . .

Before he realized just what it was he was doing, he had covered the three hundred yards between himself and the struggling figures and had landed square on the back of the wiry black-clad figure. He grabbed its thin neck and found that his hands completely encircled it. He squeezed with a death grip.

Suddenly he was holding the throat not of a black-clad humanoid but a huge scaly beast that turned its head with immense strength to snap at Billy's arms. The jaws of the beast were larger than any he had ever seen or imagined, the teeth long and jagged. On top of its head were three great horns, and, as Billy held on, the head jerked back and forth attempting to gash him.

Abruptly he felt himself far, far away. His head reeled with the thought that he was on some other world, around some other sun, but he knew instinctively that he must hang on to the creature, for the strange new thoughts in his brain—beyond his own thoughts—were flowing from the creature into him. With the realization, Billy felt the creature struggle more violently to keep him from seizing something . . . something that had a special name . . . a power. He read the source of the power, and knew that it would make him able to change himself.

* * *

Kosho and Kirsten, emerging from the chalet, were astonished to see the distance Billy had traveled in their brief absence. The figures struggling on the slope were now three, one of them unmistakably Billy. Kosho had brought his samurai sword, and Kirsten her jeweled dagger, and they rushed up the snowy slope; but without skis, they soon found themselves bogged down.

"His footprints," gasped Kirsten, trying to keep up with Kosho. Kosho looked. Stretching ahead of them, Billy's footprints spanned fifteen and twenty feet at a stride.

At the sound of the creature's howl, they looked up the slope. At that distance it was difficult to see, but the silhouetted figures had changed. One of them had somehow turned into a four-legged beast that was goring its horns at Billy. Kosho and Kirsten stood stock-still, terrified and unable to do more than try to see what was happening. Just then the moon went behind a cloud.

In the momentary darkness there was still a little light, but not enough for Kosho ever to be certain just *what* he had seen. He thought he saw the old grandmother in the snow, or rather above it, rushing toward Billy, and then he thought he saw *two* great beasts clashing. He heard the howls, the feral cries that were unlike those of any animal he had photographed on the continents of earth, and finally a terrible high-pitched scream that echoed off the peaks high above and died away. Kosho and Kirsten stood transfixed, their senses straining against the darkness and the sudden ghastly silence.

As the moon withdrew from the cloud, Billy stood before them, too suddenly near, pulling the unconscious form of David Glassman behind him. When he saw Kosho and Kirsten, Billy collapsed, falling to his knees in the deep snow, and they pushed forward to enclose him in the warm garment they had brought.

As he pulled one of Billy's arms through the sleeve of the coat, Kosho felt the slipperiness of a still warm fluid on the tips of Billy's fingers. He saw that it was green.

Kosho looked back up the slope as they half carried, half dragged the bodies of Billy and Glassman inside. Nothing remained on the hillside, illumined again by moonlight: only a wide path of snow which bore the marks of a struggle. There was no sign of a third figure.

Inside the chalet, the others gathered around. Kirsten started to explain that Billy had heard something, Kosho interrupted to explain that Billy had seen Glassman attacked by one of the aliens and had gone to help, and then the cries of accusation from Billy's mother and father began to rain down on them. Bob Miller demanded to know why Kosho had let Billy go out in the snow without telling the rest of them, and made some deprecating remarks about Glassman being the only one without the guts to carry a weapon and so he ought to have taken the consequences. Billy's mother's ire was reserved for Kirsten, for leading her son into some danger—an utterly irrational accusation that led to harsh words from Kirsten's mother.

The noise brought the Gores back downstairs, and Janet Gore, in her flannel nightshirt, sensibly ordered Billy and Glassman brought over to the fire. When their ski clothes were removed, they saw that Glassman had been battered, and his nose apparently broken, but was in no danger. They all gasped at the sight of the deep cuts and scratches that Billy bore on his arms and shoulders.

"What made those?" asked Ian Gore, looking at Kosho. "A knife?"

"I could not see clearly," said Kosho, "but there appeared to be some kind of animal on the slope. Billy was struggling with it." He bit his tongue to silence the tale of what else he thought he had seen.

"An animal?" said Bob Miller. "What kind of animal would be loose up here? I thought we were supposed to be able to choose our weapons. Where the hell's the old lady now?"

Granny strode up behind them, as if she had just come from the kitchen. She clapped her hands, and the others were silent. Bob Miller stepped forward, but she waved him off. The others parted ranks to allow her to advance toward Billy and Glassman. She touched each of them briefly, then turned.

"They will be all right," she said, the calmness in her voice convincing. She looked at Janet Gore. "There are bandages and medicine upstairs. Bind this on the young one's cuts." She held out a shining tube.

She turned to face the group. "The Hunters asked me to apologize to you. One of them broke the rules of the Hunt. The violation will not occur again. I will be here in the morning to help you begin the next leg of your journey." Looking at Bob and Betty Miller, she said, "Your son has achieved a singular honor."

"But is he going to be—" Betty began.

"He is not seriously injured," Granny assured her. She turned to look at Billy, who even then was enjoying the delightful experience of awakening with his head on Kirsten's lap. He smiled faintly. Granny stepped over to the two young people and patted Billy's head. "You have the honor of First Kill," she said.

Chapter Thirteen

After Billy and Glassman had been taken upstairs, Mkomo drew himself up to address Granny, who remained with them.

"There is some error," he said. "If there is an honor in making the first kill, and perhaps a cash reward, it belongs to me, or possibly to my own son."

"You deserve congratulations for being very brave and resourceful," said Granny. "My, yes. There are not many who would have turned back to face the enemy when outnumbered the way you were."

Mkomo momentarily forgot his protest. The way the old woman described his achievement, he wondered why it was he *had* turned back. "Nevertheless," he said, "I felled one of the creatures with my spear, and my son administered a merciful coup de grace with his pistol. Later I charged into the spears of the enemy and ran one of them down with my snowmobile. I felt his bone crack."

"Oh, you wounded them, all right. Let me assure you, there is one of the Hunters who won't forget that. He has great respect for you, and will be certain to seek you out tomorrow. As for the second Hunter, it was he who attacked Rabbi Glassman and whom Billy . . . overcame."

"I should receive credit then for weakening him so that effeminate stripling could so easily finish him off."

"Just a damn minute," said Bob Miller. "That's my boy you're talkin' about. If you ran off leavin' this wounded and half-crazed animal roamin' around so that he could come back to take one of us, then you're nothin' more than a black-assed coward."

Mkomo started to raise his spear, and Miller's hand went quickly for the shotgun that was beside his chair. "Gentlemen, please!" said Granny, stepping between them. "The Hunters would be very upset with me if I allowed you to injure each other. They went to a great deal of trouble to bring you here, and it was not so that you could kill each other. I might add that it would hardly be to *your* advantage either. The next leg of the Hunt will require a strong bond of cooperation among you."

As Miller and Mkomo continued to stare menacingly at each other, Bjorn Halvorssen said, "What *is* the next leg of the . . . Hunt?"

"White-water rafting," said Granny.

Betty Miller laughed, making a nervous, high-pitched sound that she cut off with a hand clapped to her mouth. She had drawn the attention of the others.

"Oh, my, I just thought it was funny, because . . . well, there couldn't be any kind of white water around *here*."

"Oh, dear, you're forgetting," said Granny. "This area isn't a natural formation. It's a Park, as I explained. The Hunters have the power to make it . . . take any form they choose."

The others stared at her, frankly skeptical, except for Kosho, who nodded. "Illusion," he said. "It is all an illusion."

"It was a pretty damn cold *illusion* today," said Bob Miller. "My wife's ankle, the arrows they shot at us, Billy's wounds . . . *they* weren't no illusion."

"Nor are life and death," said Granny. "I assure you of that. Now I can't stop you from enjoying the hospitality of your hosts. There's plenty more food and drink. But I would advise you to get as much rest as possible. The second leg of the Hunt will be longer. You will be on the water for two days, at least."

"On a white-water stream?" said Janet Gore. "That *is* impossible. We'd have to sleep sometime."

"There will be places for you to land and make a campsite," said Granny. "But please remember, the Hunt will be in force until you reach the next place of safety."

After a while, they took the old woman's advice, each with his or her own thoughts. Like the others, Kosho found that his room held a fireplace with a blazing, warming fire. It was a seldom experienced luxury. There were no open fires in the fragile, paper-walled houses of Japan. He dressed himself in a kimono and sat staring into the fire with his treasured sword lying across his legs. He tried to meditate, for him the most effective rest, for the mind became peaceful, ceased its questioning, but he was unable to banish the questions that plagued his mind. If all this were truly an illusion, then it was the work of the most powerful mind he had ever heard of—one capable of more than was claimed for the great Indian gurus or the Christian mystics who were supposed to have developed the power to transport their bodies beyond the boundaries of space and time.

Had the battle he had dimly seen on the mountainside been another illusion? The beast that appeared there was certainly not one found on earth: an illusion created by someone who had visited some planet where such beasts did exist? But the second beast, if it were indeed the man-child Miller—who had created that illusion? The Hunters would surely not have created that illusion to kill one of their own. Yet there seemed to be only one other possibility, and Kosho danced all around it without being able to accept it, as a moth dances around a flame.

There were others watching in the night. The Aging Master purposely allowed his step to make a noise so that the Commander could indicate his desire to remain alone, if he wished. The Commander turned and gestured his willingness to converse.

"I have seen that the remains of your Mate were properly disposed of."

The words "your Mate" shamed the Commander. He had brought the worthless fool along to keep him from making trouble. Instead . . . "He violated the Hunter Rules," said the Commander. "In death, he escaped the shame. I take it on myself."

The Aging Master acknowledged the correctness of this.

"He could not even dispatch an unarmed beast," said the Commander bitterly.

"It was not the unarmed beast that dispatched him," said the Aging Master.

"Even *two* of these creatures, unarmed, should scarcely have presented so great a danger," said the Commander.

"I have questioned the advisor that you gave the beasts," continued the Aging Master.

"Yes," said the Commander. "She reported that the Mate

attempted to use our powers to turn himself into something he thought invincible.''

''That was not all,'' said the Aging Master.

The Commander was uncomfortable under the probing stare of the Aging Master. ''The rest of her story is unbelievable,'' the Commander said. ''The Mate's use of Discovery powers must have deceived her as well.''

''It is possible,'' agreed the Aging Master. ''What is not possible is that one of us, even the Mate, using Discovery powers, could have been defeated—except by another being that had made the Discovery.''

''He could not have made the Discovery,'' said the Commander. ''He would have killed us all—at least attacked us—already.''

''The Scientist believes he may have been on the threshold. And witnessing the Mate use it, perhaps even coming into physical contact with him, as is done in our initiation ritual . . .''

The Commander sucked in the heavy air of his natural environment, recreated here in the Hunters' Lodge. ''That would be choicest irony: that the Mate actually made it possible for his adversary to make the Discovery.''

They contemplated this. The Commander gestured his willingness to obey the wish of another. ''Do you wish, then, that we leave and inform the Guardians?''

''And share with all the People the news of our disgrace?'' asked the Aging Master in a tone that carried unexpected anger within. ''We came here to Hunt. We shall complete the Hunt, using the Old Rules.''

Inadvertently, the Commander allowed his surprise to show. ''Including Rule One?''

''Rule One is the most important rule,'' said the Aging Master. ''Discovery powers must not be used against the Game.''

''It was not considered that . . . this situation would arise,'' said the Commander.

''He will be your responsibility,'' said the Aging Master.

The Commander nodded. It was an appropriate punishment. And a just one. As the Aging Master departed, the Commander drew upon his memories of many Hunts, and began to plan.

Each of the travelers' rooms had a window. As each awoke the following morning, the same astonishing sight greeted them: the snow had gone, and although the mountain loomed behind them, there lay in the other direction a swift-moving narrow river, fed by the melted snow. It led through the bottom of a high canyon of bare rock.

Granny was waiting downstairs, and she lectured them through a hearty breakfast. "The river journey should take you two days or longer. You might travel faster, but at a speed too great for safety. There are two large rubberized rafts waiting. Six of you will fit comfortably in each. Within, you will find a dozen paddles and two sets of oars. Even so, you may find that they will be used up rapidly."

"We won't need to paddle down that river," said Janet Gore.

"Indeed not. The paddles are to slow your course, and to ward the boat off rocks. The boats are steered with oars, although that takes an expert touch. The Halvorssens and the Millers both have experience at this kind of sporting travel. You are free to choose your own companions, but I should advise you to allow each family to be the leaders in one of the boats."

"I acknowledge no one over me as leader," said Mkomo.

Billy looked despairingly at Kirsten as he realized the import of what Granny was saying: they would have to be separated. He wanted to be next to her, not only because, as he had now discovered, he loved her, but because . . . he was afraid of what had happened last night. He had slept fitfully, with nightmares—not of the creature that had threatened him, but of what he himself . . . became. He had called Granny to him, but she had refused to answer his questions, telling him only that she was forbidden to. He was afraid, even when the others all morning had been congratulating him on "First Kill," that phrase that Granny had used. If they only knew . . . he was terribly afraid, and felt that if Kirsten were next to him he would at least know how to *act* brave.

"You must decide," said Granny firmly. "I can only advise. In addition, each boat will contain six high-powered rifles, with ammunition."

"Oh, I say," said Ian Gore. "I thought you promised we could choose our own weapons. I didn't carry Excalibur over that bloody mountain to discard it here."

"You may keep the weapons you chose," said Granny. "You may decide to use the rifles if you are fired upon from the cliffs."

"The cliffs?" shrieked Betty Miller. "That's not fair! They'll always be high above us."

"They may not be," said Granny. "The rifles are only a precaution. There is also camping equipment in each raft, and when you decide to stop for the night, you will have to find a part of the river where the banks are wide. The Hunt, as I told some of you last night, will continue then, and you may encounter the kind of hand-to-hand combat that several of you seem to favor."

The success of the first day had elated most of them; some were beginning to feel that there was in fact no real danger. Kosho, having seen what attacked Rabbi Glassman, was under no such delusion. He drew Glassman aside after they had finished eating. Granny was distributing flotation jackets and instructing them on what they should do if they were swept into the river.

"Have you changed your mind about the weapons?" Kosho asked Glassman.

Glassman shook his head. "I carried no weapon yesterday."

"Yet that did not preserve you from attack."

"The thing that attacked me had no weapon. I consider myself better off."

It was not your lack of a weapon that saved you, thought Kosho. But Glassman had been unconscious when Billy had arrived, and it was useless to question him about what had really happened.

The air was warm today, although those who dipped their hands in the river found that the water was icy cold.

"No one should embark on a river like this one without first scouting it," remarked Bjorn Halvorssen to Bob Miller.

"Hell, of course not," replied Miller, "but we ain't got the time for all that Boy Scout stuff. If it gets really bad, it looks to me like a man could scale those cliffs and come out on the other side."

"Some of us could," agreed Halvorssen. "And I suppose that the scouting of the river would be as dangerous for the scout as embarking on it in a raft would."

Kosho managed to secure a place in the Millers' raft, for he wanted to continue to observe Billy. The Gores were chosen to go with the Millers, since Bob Miller and Mkomo were still at odds.

Mkomo, Charles, and Glassman were left by default to go with the Halvorssens. "I'll take good care of the young lady," remarked Charles, bumping Billy aside. Billy stared at him in speechless anger. He thought for a moment that his hands were claws again, and he felt the urge to drive the talons into Charles's neck.

Billy looked down at his hands and thrust them into the pockets of his jacket so that no one else would see. Just for that second, he had remembered *exactly* what he had experienced when the stick-limbed creature had turned into . . . something else. Exactly. And he remembered how to do it. He stood on the bank as his father called to him. Mkomo and Bjorn Halvorssen pushed their boat into the water and started off with surprising speed.

"Billy," said his father. "Come *on*, goddamn it. Stop mooning around. We're still in a *race*, remember?" Billy looked at him strangely and finally moved.

Kosho helped Bob Miller send the boat afloat, then jumped in next to Billy. "Are you . . . all right?" he asked.

Billy gave him a surprised look. "Yeah, sure."

Kosho, who had seen Charles mutter something to Billy and guessed its content, said, "A master must learn to control his anger."

"I'm not a master," said Billy. His father was shouting for him to take up his paddle.

Just what a master would say, thought Kosho happily.

Chapter Fourteen

To the inexperienced, at first it seemed like great fun. Mkomo reacted with his lion's cry, the sound carrying upward to echo off the canyon walls far down the narrow chasm.

He might as well announce our approach, thought Glassman wryly. Glassman held fast to his belief that his determination not to carry a weapon would, if not save him from harm, at least free him from the burden of guilt. Only, he prayed God, if it was his fate to be killed on this fantastic journey, at least let him have the satisfaction of seeing that butcher Mkomo die first.

Bjorn Halvorssen was seated atop the rowing frame, which consisted of wooden supports for the oarlocks and a platform on which the rower could sit to get a vantage point on the rushing water. The others knelt or stood around the perimeter of the boat, supporting themselves by leaning against the inflated eighteen-inch tubes that kept the boat afloat. Each held a paddle in case it was needed to push the craft away from the sharp boulders that jutted above the surface of the water.

Mkomo had chosen the front position in the raft, at the urging of Halvorssen, who wanted his weight there to help balance the craft. If the front of the raft were too high when it encountered a rock beneath the surface of the water, the following current could push the rear below the surface of the water and the entire craft could flip over backwards.

The early part of the river was deceptively easy, and Mkomo continued shouting joyously at the thrill of the speed, the roller-coaster motion of the boat, and the craft's apparent ability to glide over or around any obstacle. He was shouting commands back to Halvorssen, warning of perfectly obvious obstacles. Halvorssen ignored him, for the experienced Dane knew that visible rocks and pools of flotsam were the least of their worries. The danger lay beneath the surface. Halvorssen knew how to identify the surges of water—seemingly small mounds on the surface—that indicated an underwater obstacle. He would steer the craft to avoid these if he could, but the steering oars were powerless in escaping a really strong current, indicated by a V-shaped pattern in the water, that would carry the craft inexorably over one of these underwater obstacles.

That did not necessarily mean disaster. They had already passed over a number of water mounds, experiencing no more than a sudden drop and a resounding slap on the bottom of the boat as the craft fell into one of the pools that formed in front of a surge. At this point the current would turn back on itself, sometimes forming a back wave that would spray harmlessly over those in front.

The abrupt change in current could, however, produce a teeth-shattering halt to the boat's progress. The momentum and weight of the boat had, so far, been sufficient to carry the craft through this backwash and into the main current again. But Halvorssen had seen boats as large as this one caught and held fast in huge suck holes created by a heavy backwash until the current coming over the surge from behind filled the boat and swamped it.

In that eventuality, they could remain in the useless craft, which might be only a foot or so below the surface, suspended there by the equilibrium between its buoyancy and the weight of water inside. Eventually, however, the frigid water would take its toll on their legs, causing their bodies to lose heat until they succumbed to unconsciousness and death. The alternative was to swim for shore, but in this current Bjorn doubted that even Kirsten would make it.

Bjorn knew that their safety depended on his keeping his eyes on the river constantly, watching for the signs the flowing water made, and making instant decisions as to the course they must follow. Whether the other craft was proceeding as well as they were, he neither knew nor cared; he hoped only that the arrogant American who piloted it knew enough not to follow them too closely. If one boat followed another immediately ahead over the top of a surge, there would be a collision—the following boat would land directly on top of them, swamping both rafts.

What added to Bjorn's uneasiness was the threat of the supposed Hunters on the cliffs. Just as he could not look back, he could not afford even a glance upwards. In the periphery of his vision, he could see that Bibi, Kirsten, and Charles kept rifles close to them. The utter fool Mkomo was continuing to bellow, now brandishing a spear in one hand and his paddle in the other. As if a spear could conquer either the current or enemies on the cliffs who could fire down on them as easily as if the rafts had been large, bright yellow waterfowl.

Bjorn turned his attention to Glassman. Although the Israeli manned his paddle with skill and strength, he refused to touch one of the rifles. What kind of man was he? wondered Bjorn. Even the Danish papers had carried stories about his exploits, but it was hard to credit them, given the man's unwillingness to take up a weapon.

The Japanese photographer had told Bjorn that the Israeli was tired of killing, had foresworn it. Bjorn could not believe that. A man kept the skills he had developed, perhaps with age became a little less swift, a little less sure, but the experience of age often made up for the slowness of eye and muscles. A man did not foreswear something he had trained his whole life to do, unless something happened to him that made him realize that with slowness would come death. That realization could produce a loss of nerve; Bjorn had seen it in others. Some called it cowardice. Bjorn was more tolerant. What it was—might well be in the case of the rabbi—was a reluctance to admit that the body's slowness meant impending death in any case, whether it came in a state-supported hospital bed or on a battlefield. Somewhere in the wise book the rabbi carried with him, a man must have put down the thought that you cannot run away from death—better to turn and face it, as a man should.

There was a curve in the river ahead, as the stream turned to the left. Bjorn concentrated on the water, keeping to the center as long as possible, knowing that the curling currents close to the left bank would carry their force outward and across the bend in the river. A boat caught in them would be hurled against the walls of the chasm at the end of the curve. He had to choose the right second to turn the raft and cut across into the main channel downstream. As he prepared to make the move, however, he saw Bibi raise her rifle. He quelled the instinct to look to his right, high up on the near cliff, where she seemed to be looking.

A shot rang out from above. Mkomo bellowed in surprise, and

Bjorn wondered if he had been hit. Bibi aimed and returned the fire, but as Bjorn saw the upward angle at which she was firing, he realized it was an almost impossible shot.

He hesitated. The chance for cutting through the swirling current shooting out from the left bank was almost gone, but if he made it through, the boat would be a perfect target, receding away from the marksman on the cliff to their right.

He used the oars to jerk the raft sharply to the right, taking it as close to the cliff as he dared. The water was deep there, for the cliff descended straight down into the water, and by following the edge of the rock, he could keep the current from dashing them against the cliff face.

The only drawback was that the twisting, swirling current on this side would cause the boat to turn. He had to pull in the right oar to avoid smashing it to bits against the cliff, but as he did so he lessened his control of the boat.

It began slowly. Mkomo, in the front, was first to notice it. He was staring upward, scanning the area where the shot had seemed to come from, when he noticed that the cliff had begun to revolve—then realized it was not the cliff but the boat. More and more quickly, the front of the boat turned toward the middle of the stream. Mkomo thought that Halvorssen was only turning the boat around the bend in the river, but the turning went on and on so that now the front of the boat was beginning to face back upriver.

Mkomo looked toward the rear of the boat to warn Halvorssen, and saw the Dane jumping down from the rowing platform. "Down!" shouted Halvorssen to the rest of them. "Pull in the paddles and get down on the floor of the raft! We're riding free!"

Confused and hesitant at first, the others began to follow his example. Glassman stayed at the perimeter, apparently with the wild idea that he could push the boat away from the cliff wall with his paddle. "That doesn't matter now!" Halvorssen shouted at him. "Get down or the centrifugal force will sweep you overboard."

For by now the boat was swirling faster, glancing off the cliff face, following it around the curve downstream in the whirling current. Halvorssen could only hope that the rapids directly below did not hold any dangerous surges. If not they would eventually be able to regain control of the raft. If they hit a surge while they were spinning . . . then he had lost the gamble. But it was their only chance.

As they moved away from the end of the curve, Mkomo tried to rise to see the marksman on the cliff, but the spinning was violent now and knocked him off his feet. All of them were beginning to feel the nausea caused by the endless, ever faster whirling of the raft. Halvorssen crouched on his hands and knees, knowing that to lie flat meant risking a broken rib or worse if the bottom of the boat struck an underwater rock. Several of the others began to vomit; he tried to hold his breakfast down, knowing he would need strength later. And still the spinning went on, and on, and on.

The Natural Hunter felt the urge to fire again, to empty his rifle at the crazily turning yellow craft below, but it would be a futile gesture, one that would only embarrass him further, for there was no way of taking sure aim at anything inside the raft. He knew that a bullet could not sink it. It had been his impulsiveness at seeing the black beast standing in the front of the boat, waving his primitive weapon and bellowing—making that sound whose pitch was unmistakably one of arrogance and triumph, triumph over *him,* the greatest Hunter in the galaxy—that had caused the Natural Hunter to fire too soon. If he had waited a moment longer, he could have had a perfect angle of fire, but that sound, and the memory of his humiliation, had caused him to abandon the proper patience.

He made his way back to the path that ran along the top of the cliff, parallel to the river. There would be another water craft following this one, but the Natural Hunter wanted only that beast in the first craft. He could not allow the others waiting downstream to get to him first.

The Millers' craft was still far upriver. Bob Miller was not the equal of Bjorn Halvorssen as a pilot, and from his seat in the rowing platform he tried to direct the raft around the surges, instead of risking going over the top. In the process, the raft frequently became tangled in pools of floating wood that marked the spots closer to shore, away from the main current, where the side currents spun endlessly, trapping small floating objects. They were struggling to push the boat out of one of these eddies with the paddles when they heard the gunfire echoing along the cliff sides from farther down the river. Everyone froze at the sound, listening for more. Several of them dropped their paddles and took up the rifles, scanning the rock face on either side of the river.

Kosho, watching to see what Billy would do, was not surprised to see the old grandmother suddenly appear beside him in the boat. Bob Miller, from his vantage point, glanced down after she appeared, but his reaction was less tranquil.

"Where'd *she* come from?" he shouted, pointing. The others looked, reacting in their own ways. "Hey!" called Bob Miller. "What's going on? Billy! Keep away from her!"

Billy paid him no attention. "I know what you want to do," Granny said quietly to him.

"Can I? Granny . . . I'm not sure I know how."

"Then don't try it," she said.

"But . . . last night . . . you know what happened last night?"

"I was there."

"But I mean, did it really happen? Did I . . . change?"

"Yes."

"And I . . . kind of . . . *moved,* without moving. I just went from one place to the other like there was nothing in between."

"You did. You conquered the earth and air."

"Show me how I can do it again. I have to go to Kirsten. She needs me."

"She does *not* need you. Be still. She's not in danger, not from the Hunters at any rate. Not just now. Think about her, and you will know."

He did think, concentrating on her, and received some feeling that made him draw back, embarrassed. "I . . . touched her. But she's afraid, Granny."

"Afraid of the river, yes. But she is safe."

"Granny, you've got to tell me how I can do that again."

"I cannot, Billy. It is absolutely forbidden. Even if it were not, it is not something that can be taught."

"What is? Is there more to it?"

"Much, much more. But . . ." She rubbed her forehead in annoyance. "Billy, I told you I am not human. I was created to be a help, a guide for you. A Hunting guide, and therefore I was made to look like someone any of you would trust. But I am programmed."

"Programmed? You're . . . you're really a computer?"

She chuckled. "Nothing so fancy, nor so simple. I am only

. . . something in your imagination. But there are rules I must follow, and . . . I cannot understand how I can follow them in your case. It seems to me that the Hunt is violating those rules."

"What do you mean?"

"I cannot explain it to you without violating those rules."

"Granny, *please!* I don't understand."

"You should not understand as much as you do. I can only tell you what I said before. Keep on as you are. Either it will happen, or it won't."

She disappeared. The boat, free of the eddy, suddenly found the current again and shot downstream. Bob Miller was occupied with the oars, struggling to keep the nose of the craft pointed in the right direction. The others flailed about with the paddles, trying to keep the raft off the jagged rocks that jutted up from the water.

"Amazin' thing, that," said Ian Gore, shouting over his shoulder to his wife. "Did you see the old woman come and go, just like that?"

Janet nodded, glancing nervously at Billy.

"Glad of that," said Ian. "If you hadn't seen it, I would have thought it was time to turn myself in."

"She said, Ian, on the first night . . . that we would only have to call to her and she would come," Janet Gore said in a puzzled tone.

"That's right, she did, didn't she? Oh, well, then, any of us could have summoned her up, eh? It wasn't the boy at all, really. Still, she doesn't seem to have done us much good."

Bob Miller had been unable to avoid a large surge that lay at the end of an inverted V of water, but in his attempt to do so, he had turned the craft askew, so that as it went over the top of the swelling mound of water, the left side of the craft sank abruptly downward, throwing those along the right side sprawling on the floor of the raft. Janet and Ian and Billy's mother were among these. The raft teetered in the backwash beyond the surge, its right side in the air, threatening to overturn. Billy and Kosho rushed across to weight down the right side, and the craft slapped its bottom on the water. Fortunately, the boat sprang free of the backwash at the same time. Bob Miller started to breathe a sigh of relief, but the renewed force of the current was now carrying them toward a large boulder in the middle of the stream.

"Get up!" Miller screamed. "Use the paddles!"

Chapter Fifteen

Downstream, Bjorn Halvorssen, a better pilot than Bob Miller, was trying to take advantage of a brief lull in the danger to rally his shaken crew. The spinning of the raft had finally subsided, and Bjorn had climbed back on the rowing platform, reset the oars, and guided the craft back on a straight course.

At this point in the river there was no bank on either side on which to attempt a landing. The cliffs rose straight up on either side. The sky was only a narrow sliver high above, and since it was past noon, the canyon was filled with shadows. Bjorn was conscious of the danger of a renewed attack from the dark sides of the cliffs, but he deliberately stalled the craft in one of the swirling eddies close to the edge of the river. The drawback of this method of slowing their progress was that it set the raft turning again, although more slowly than before.

''Moron!'' shouted Mkomo, struggling to get to his feet but slipping and falling back in the vomit and spray that covered the plastic floor of the raft. ''What kind of pilot are you? Get us out of this! I cannot stand any more of that turning!''

Bjorn looked contemptuously down at the filth-covered former Emperor. ''It was the only way out of the danger,'' he said, then chided himself for feeling the need to explain his decisions. Still, Mkomo was strong and brave—they would need him if they were to survive.

''We cannot rest here for long,'' said Bjorn patiently. ''I can't hold the boat out of the main current in this weak eddy. Help the others get on their feet, and use one of the bailing pails to wash the bottom with river water."

Mkomo glared at him, but did as he was told. Glassman, Bibi, and Kirsten were soon on their feet and helping. Charles lay shivering and twitching on the floor, still attempting to vomit, but bringing up nothing more than stringy spittle.

"How many were there firing at us from the cliff?" Mkomo asked Bibi.

"Only one that I could see," she said. "And I'm sure I didn't hit him."

Mkomo clenched his hands in fury. "If only they would give us a clear shot. They don't dare! Not after what I did to them yesterday."

"If so," Bibi Halvorssen said, "then there will be more of them waiting on the cliffs below."

Mkomo nodded. "That is so." He looked warily up at the cliffs, then at Bibi. "You are good shot?"

"Sufficiently," she said.

"So. And I think your husband is, as well. And you love your daughter"—he raised his hand, gesturing helplessly toward the recumbent Charles—"as I do my son. Though he is not, I fear, a warrior. I should never have sent him to Europe, but I wanted him to be prepared to deal with the Americans and the Russians, wanted him to become the ruler of a great Empire. An African Empire." He shrugged. "That is a lost dream now. Still, if our lives are spared, there may yet be a chance . . . somehow. The ways of nations are as strange as the ways of men. You understand?"

She shook her head.

"It does not matter. We both want to save our children. Can your husband, you think, move us closer to the cliff again? Without spinning? There must be no more spinning."

Bibi went to relay his request to Bjorn.

"It is possible," Bjorn said. "But what is he going to do?" As they watched, Mkomo stripped off his flotation jacket, his boots, and then the army fatigue outfit that he wore. Underneath, his heavily muscled black body was covered only by a dark elastic jockstrap. In spite of herself, Bibi shivered at the exposed raw power of the man. He began to strap his rifle and spears to his body, and they guessed his intention.

He turned and grinned to them, and pointed a forefinger

upward, to the top of the cliff. "A surprise for them," he said behind his sharp white teeth.

Bjorn shrugged, but behind his gesture his eyes flickered for a second in approval. He stood up, his feet braced against the pipe at the bottom of the platform, and used the oars to fight the current and keep the unwieldy craft still. Mkomo climbed to the top of the flotation tanks that encircled the boat, balanced unsteadily, and looked upwards, searching for a crack in the cliff face that could serve as a handhold.

He leaped, and stuck fast to the rock, hands gripping the crevice he had found. His feet scrambled underneath him and found a narrow support. As the raft was swept away, he began to climb. Even Bjorn took his eyes off the river for a second, watching his perilous ascent. "A man," said Bjorn thoughtfully.

Glassman watched him too, trying not to admire the attempt. He took a pail of the river water and let it flow on Charles. "Get up," he said gruffly. "Get up and watch your father."

"What are we doing up here?" the Golden Female asked.

It was an unexpected question, and the Aging Master, to whom it was directed, was annoyed at having his concentration on the swift-flowing stream disturbed.

"We are waiting for the game," he said.

"And when they arrive, what then?" the Golden Female persisted.

"We use these things—projectile throwers, guns, rifles—they have many names for them."

"There cannot be much danger in that," she replied. He could not ignore the impertinence in her tone.

"I am willing to accept your suggestions as to the proper conduct of the Hunt," he said.

She made a gesture of respect, seeing that his feelings were ruffled. "Honored One," she said. "Companion of my Parents . . ."

He acknowledged her politeness impatiently.

"You told us at the Hunting Council," she continued, "that we were taking unfair advantage of the game. Yet we had met them in open combat. Now we await them, await their floating crafts imperfectly controlled by manual power, and intend to fire on them from a position of comparative safety."

She paused, but since he did not silence her with a gesture, she gained the courage to go on. "Is there any difference between firing on them from here and slaughtering Class E game in an Initial Hunt from behind a protective blind?''

She had terribly offended him now, she saw, for he closed his sight- and speech-slits and sat unmoving. Yet his sound receptors remained open. ''May I go down and battle them in close combat?'' she asked. ''I know I am not worthy of the honor, after my mistakes, and I am willing to grant it to another.''

The Aging Master remained closed to her, and she looked up the rock to the Gray Female, who had ignored the conversation, training her senses on the swift-moving water below. *She is not truly a Hunter,* the Golden Female thought secretly, shocking even herself with the discourtesy of her opinion. *She wants only to kill.*

The Scientist, she saw, was watching the river from a protected spot, but he did not intend to kill. The Commander had gone off somewhere to fulfill some mission that the Aging Master had apparently given him. At least the Natural Hunter had risked going upstream alone, though everyone knew that was only because he craved so much the honor of the First Kill—even though it would not be the First Kill of the Hunt itself, only the first trophy taken. The Golden Female had wondered about that. There had been no discussion in Hunting Council of the skills that had made it possible for one of these creatures to overcome the Mate. There had only been the hint that the Mate had dishonored himself by violating Rule One. But if he had, how was it possible that he had been killed?

The Golden Female looked back at the Aging Master. He had not specifically reproved her for what she had said. He had only withdrawn into self-contemplation, which meant, formally, that he no longer desired her presence.

Well, then. She was free to act. She had not been invited on the Hunt as a novice, whatever her experience relative to the others' had been. She was a Hunter, and she must act, in the absence of direction, the way a Hunter should. She swung herself over the ledge and began to climb down. To her, it did not seem a difficult task. The danger was in falling, but if one's skill was sufficient to avoid falling, then there was no danger at all. There was another ledge farther down. She would rest there, and await the chance for honor. Honor, she well knew, was her only chance for reconciliation with the Aging Master.

* * *

Bjorn guided the boat along as slowly as the current would permit. Charles had gotten back on his feet, but his movements now were panicky and nervous. With the departure of his father, he had become what he really was—a rich schoolboy, who actually had no stomach for such a trip. Fortunately, Glassman was able to show him what he ought to be doing with the paddle, and Kirsten was there to give example. Even a boy like Charles had to feel embarrassed at letting a girl, a younger girl at that, accomplish tasks that he wouldn't. Bjorn calculated that if he could delay their progress sufficiently, Mkomo would be able to create enough of a diversion overhead for the raft to pass by the black-clad creatures that lay in wait.

Bjorn had quite forgotten the existence of the other boat. It was not until he heard the shouts behind him, and recognized the voices, that he realized they were not alone. "Wave them back," he called to Bibi. "Keep them from approaching too closely."

Bob Miller, on the other hand, having sighted the Halvorssen's raft, suddenly remembered that they were in a race. His competitive instincts aroused, he steered the boat deliberately into the strongest part of the current, willing now to take the risk in order to pass the others.

"Bob!" called his wife. "We're going too fast! You'll hit something!"

In response, Bob Miller gave a yodeling whoop. The raft rushed forward, hurdling over a high surge of water and slamming into the backwash beneath with a rolling, shattering motion that momentarily folded the raft in the middle as the front went over the surge and the back followed. Luckily, the front caught the downstream current in time and pulled the boat away from a fairly strong suck hole.

The raft shot forward, and Miller saw that if he kept to the main current he could easily pass the Halvorssens' raft, which was keeping closer to the side stream, before they reached the next surge a few hundred feet ahead. But Kosho, alarmed, ran back to the rowing platform and pulled at Bob Miller's leg. What he shouted was lost in the sound of the rushing rapids, but Miller's attention was drawn to the sight on the cliff face that Kosho was pointing to.

Near the very top of the cliff were three of the black-clad figures. One stood up, rifle in hand, and began to take aim. Frantically, Miller tried to use his oars to turn the raft, but the current held it in an unresisting grip, and all he was able to do was turn the boat sideways so that as it passed the Halvorssens' raft, and went over the heavy surge, the passengers were thrown to the floor. Bob Miller nearly lost his own balance, and dropped the oars to hold tight to the rowing platform.

"Fire! Shoot them!" Miller called to the others, but none of them held a rifle. Two shots rang out from the top of the cliff; one of them pierced the bottom of the boat, raising a small column of spray that continued in a stream like a particularly powerful water cooler; the other shot pierced one of the air tanks, the front one where Billy had been standing a moment before.

Halvorssen maneuvered his own raft closer to the cliff face from which the shots had come, trying to reduce the angle of fire from above. As he did, he became aware of something black in the air above. He glanced up and saw that one of the figures had leaped from the cliff.

Bjorn watched the dive with admiration, for it was a perfect one—he mentally scored it a ten—and the dark figure broke the water fifty feet in front of the boat without causing a ripple. Still, Bjorn realized, from that height the creature must have dashed itself to pieces on the rocky river bottom. More shots rang out from above, and he was glad that they did not seem to be aimed at his raft.

The Aging Master had seen the dive from his vantage point, and felt a thrill unlike any he had experienced in some time. He had known that the Golden Female would feel she would have to perform some noble feat to impress him, but her courage surpassed what he had expected. Her parents would be proud, had they been there to see.

He crawled to the edge of the rock and peered over, wondering how she expected to survive such a leap. He inwardly approved as he surveyed the river below and saw what she must have seen: at a certain place in the channel the water was a deep color, nearly black in contrast to the shallow places and white spray. The Golden Female had known that it indicated a deep hole in the bed of the river. He searched for sight of her, and realized that she was keeping hidden. Her plan flashed through his brain, and he rejoiced that one so young had the daring to try it. He drew his rifle into ready position.

Most of those in Bjorn's raft had now turned their rifles upward to the cliff face. Bjorn watched the spot where the alien had entered the water for a few seconds longer, but seeing no movement, returned his gaze to the swift-flowing current.

Only Kirsten, who also had appreciated the diving feat, kept her eyes on the dark part of the river. She was counting to herself, wondering if the alien creature could hold its breath for as long as she could. Suddenly she saw an ominous sign; in a place where the waters gathered in a pool, she saw a trail of bubbles.

"Papa!" she screamed. "It's swimming underwater. It's coming toward us!"

Bjorn glanced at the water. "Keep away from the sides!" he called. His daughter's eyes caught his, and she smiled and softly shook her head. As he watched, horrified at what she intended, she stripped off her flotation jacket, taking from it the jewel-handled dagger that she had brought from the arms cache. Quickly she began to remove the rest of her clothes. "Bibi!" called Bjorn to his wife. "Stop her!"

But Kirsten, now dressed only in panties, already stood on the air-filled side of the raft. Charles turned just in time to see her bend and then spring out and away from the raft, her body extended full-length above the water. His jaw dropped at the sight. He rushed to the side of the boat, and a bullet from above smashed into his shoulder.

Mkomo had struggled along the rocky top of the cliff and reached the scene just in time to see the shot that felled his son. With a roar of rage, Mkomo flung one of his spears, but the range was too great and the spear shattered against the side of the cliff only inches from where the Aging Master lay.

The Master swung his rifle around and fired without aiming. Mkomo heard the slug pass within inches of his ear. He took cover and unstrapped the rifle from his back.

The Aging Master looked to find the Gray Female scurrying to join the Scientist behind his rock shelter. Mkomo began to fire wildly in his direction. He rolled swiftly across the surface of the cliff toward the shelter that concealed his companions. Over his head, the Gray Female was returning Mkomo's fire.

In the Millers' raft, they were struggling to keep afloat. As the bottom slowly filled with water, the leak receded against the countervailing pressure of water from above. But the air tank was gradually collapsing, threatening to bring more water in.

"Beach the boat!" Kosho called to Bob Miller. "We have to repair it or we will sink." Miller nodded and looked desperately for a strip of sand wide enough to pull the raft onto. They had passed around the cliff without suffering further damage, although the sound of rifle fire had convinced them that the others were now under attack.

Billy was standing on the upstream side of the boat, straining to see what was happening. He could not see any sign of Kirsten in the other raft, and was horrified at the thought that she might have been hit.

He closed his eyes and let his mind search back in the way it had done before. He was afraid to do it, for what he had earlier felt was a perception that he was inside Kirsten, part of her, more than that, *really* her, and the intimate sensation had made him feel strange. He didn't understand how he could do the things he had been doing, and only one person could tell him how to control them. *Granny, I need you,* he thought.

Chapter Sixteen

The old woman was beside him again.

"Granny, Kirsten is really in danger," Billy said.

"Yes, she is," Granny acknowledged.

"I have to go to help her," he said. "Tell me . . . tell me how."

"You cannot help. Your command is not complete. You have command of earth and air. Water comes last. There is . . . another test for you before you can help her."

"Tell me what it is."

"I cannot. You can only experience it. Only one can tell you."

"Who?"

She put her hand to her forehead. "He is Hunting you. If he can, he will kill you."

"But Granny! I need to know *now!* Kirsten needs me."

"She can do better without you, for now. She is in the water, and she has better command of it than you. You can't swim as well as she."

He laughed, nearly hysterically. "I can't fly at *all*. But I did it last night."

She shook her head. "You must ignore such concepts. You still cannot fly. What you did . . . was conquer the air."

"Then I can conquer the water. Can't I?"

"That is the way it progresses. Billy, your . . . friend . . ."

"I love her."

"Yes. This is a concept that I have not been programmed to

understand. But I know that you feel a mating affinity for her. Strengthen that affinity. It seems to add to your power." She disappeared, leaving him in frustration.

He howled backward at the raging waters of the stream. "How can I strengthen my affinity if she's going to *die?*" The others in the raft turned to look at him, and he lowered his head. *Think of her,* he told himself. *Think. Be her again.*

The underwater world was familiar to Kirsten. She knew that near the bottom the current flowed weakest, and she stroked down there, her eyes comfortably open in the clear, clean water. She clenched the knife in her teeth. The stream was shallow enough here so that she could see a fair distance in front of her. The water was cold, however, and she realized that within a few minutes her strength would ebb, even if she rose to the top to replenish the air in her lungs.

Suddenly she felt a warming sensation. She thought of Billy, and realized the sweetness she sensed in him was somehow touching her. She felt almost as if he were there with her. She swam ahead more rapidly, and then she saw the dark figure.

It was not expecting her, and Kirsten was upon it before it could defend itself. She gave a final kick forward, and took the knife from her mouth. As she moved beneath the figure, she gave a slash upward, willing her hand to move through the heavy water.

She felt her blade tear the creature's flesh, and saw the water fill with a dark streak. But Kirsten also felt the power of the body that recoiled away from her, nearly carrying her blade with it. With a sudden clenching and unclenching of its body, it moved surprisingly swiftly to the bottom.

Kirsten followed it with her eyes and saw it show its own small blade like the one she carried. It sprang up at her, seemingly as effortlessly as if they had been moving in air. Kirsten dodged its lunge just in time, but the creature turned quickly, still trailing the dark liquid of its wound, and slashed at her. Kirsten felt a searing pain along the lower part of her leg.

Instead of retreating, Kirsten struck back with her own knife, bringing the blade through the water again and again, until she realized she was striking at empty water. She swore at herself for panicking, and regained control of herself. She rotated her body swiftly, trying to see where the next attack would be coming from.

She looked up. The creature, which had been in the water far longer than Kirsten, had finally risen to the top for air. Kirsten estimated she herself could last another minute without needing to fill her lungs, but if she took advantage of her position and attacked, the other being might hold her down below the limits she could endure. It would be stronger now that it had filled its lungs.

It was a chance she decided to take, and she swam upwards with all the power she could muster. She could feel Billy's thoughts as she cut through the water, felt strangely that somehow he must know what was happening. The thought encouraged her, and added to the strength of her last kick upward with both her hands holding the dagger directly in front of her.

The creature lowered itself from the surface, and Kirsten struck it, feeling her blade plunge deeply into its body. It writhed in pain and jerked away again. This time, Kirsten could feel that she had weakened it, and she sensed it would not return. She looked back as it sank slowly to the bottom, trailing bubbles.

Kirsten gave another kick, and her head broke the surface of the water. Not far away was the gladdening sight of the yellow raft. Her mother saw her first and stood up, waving her paddle. Kirsten struggled against the current, trying to reach her mother's waiting embrace.

The Natural Hunter cursed his luck for being too slow to arrive when the action was taking place. He had heard the shots as he made his difficult journey down the opposite bank of the cliffs. He imagined the others taking many trophies while he, who had gone upstream for the opportunity to be first to sight the game, had missed his shot and been the only one without a Kill. He knew the Gray Female would, if she could, leave none of them alive.

His elation, when he finally came in sight of the yellow raft bobbing helplessly in the stream below, made him forget to ask himself what had happened to the other Hunters.

When the single beast exposed itself on the lip of the raft, for some reason stretching a paddle over the side, he raised his projectile thrower hastily, took aim, and fired. He saw the shower of red liquid that was its lifeblood cascade over the others.

"Mama!" screamed Kirsten, as she saw her mother's face dissolve in front of her, just as she was reaching for the paddle.

Her father rose, stricken with shock, from his place at the oars. The raft suddenly pulled away from Kirsten.

Charles was a quivering imbecile, staring over the side at Kirsten. Only Glassman was left to act. He turned in the direction from which the shot had come, and saw the black thing silhouetted against the narrow strip of sky above the cliffs. The thing held a rifle, and quite clearly was aiming it a second time, whether at him or at the girl in the water Glassman could not tell.

His movement was instinctive. He picked up the rifle that Bjorn Halvorssen had left in the bottom of the boat. Another rifle shot rang out. Charles quivered in fear on the bottom of the boat, but Glassman did not waste a glance at him to see if he had been hit.

Glassman felt the power of the huge .470 hunting rifle as he shouldered it, and with that feeling of power realized its ability to kill. He adjusted the sight to allow roughly for wind and distance, and sought to bring the creature on the cliff within his sights. Then he realized what he was doing. Remembering that he had pledged not to kill again, he hesitated, and as he did so, heard yet another shot. But this one came from behind him, on the opposite cliff.

He turned and saw Mkomo firing. Across the chasm, the black creature who had killed Kirsten's mother sought the safety of an overhanging ledge, and as Glassman saw it flee, he threw down the rifle and picked up the bloody paddle that Bibi Halvorssen had dropped. He held it out for Kirsten to grasp, relieved that he was spared the decision of whether to take another life.

Glassman helped the girl into the boat, and she stood dumbly looking at her mother. He covered Bibi's body with a flotation jacket. It seemed more important than covering Kirsten's young, alive body, although Charles's stares soon roused Kirsten to cover herself.

Bjorn distractedly carried on, guiding the raft down the slowest part of the current until they came to the sand spit where the Millers' raft had been grounded.

They buried Bibi there, using the paddle to dig a hole in the soft, damp sand. Bjorn lowered her into the grave himself, lifting her body for the last time, and sliding it carefully down the side of the pit. Through his mind flashed an image of the times he had lifted her, laughing, and carried her to their large feather bed back in Denmark.

Though he had been aware of the danger, he had somehow never thought that Bibi could die. Her family was very long-lived; her parents were still living in the coastal village where she had grown up. He wondered how he was going to tell them what had happened, feeling the looks they would give him. Bibi was strong, healthy, and self-reliant; she had wanted to come on this ghastly trip, but a husband was supposed to take care of his family. He glanced at Kirsten, glad at least that she had been spared. He hugged her close, and the two of them stood watching Kosho and Bob Miller fill in the hole. When they had finished, the group stood instinctively around the grave. No one wanted to be the first to move away.

Charles's groans were the only sounds that punctuated the rushing of the nearby water. The boy still lay in the bottom of the boat, where Janet Gore had dressed his wounds. No one looked toward him.

"Would you say a few words?" Bjorn said, looking at Glassman.

"I?" Glassman was as astonished as the others. "But you . . . she . . ."

"We were Lutherans," said Bjorn. "But not very observant. I cannot remember comforting words from our service. But we share a tradition with you, and you have your wise book with you. Perhaps there are words there."

Glassman reached in his pocket, taking out his book. "The words are in Hebrew," he said, leafing through the pages. "I will try to translate, for it is we who need the comfort."

His fingers found a passage that he recognized. "The Psalms of King David," he intoned. "The Third Psalm." He read slowly, translating roughly as he went:

"See, Lord, how my enemies surround me, rising up in arms against me, their voices jeering, saying that His God cannot save him now. Yet, O Lord, you are my champion, the source of the pride that keeps my head high. I have only to cry out, and my voice reaches Him in his high place, and there he hears me. Safe in his hands, I lay down and slept, and woke again. Now though a multitude of my enemies set upon me from all sides, I am not afraid. Come now and save me, Lord: smite my enemies, and break their fangs. For from God all deliverance comes. Let your blessing, Lord, rest upon your people."

They were silent again. "Thank you," said Bjorn. Gradually the group broke up, leaving father and daughter standing alone at the grave.

The others conferred. There seemed no way of continuing. The Millers' raft had to be repaired. Night would soon be upon them, and there was no certainty of finding another spot to land farther on.

There was much to recommend this spot as a camp. The dry ground extended back under the cliff, giving them safety from that side. The opposing cliffs could be scanned easily, and it was doubtful that the things could attack by coming up or down the river. Some of them began to set up the tents that were stored in the boats.

Bob Miller and Kosho began to work at patching the boat. Everyone worked silently, for the reality of death had brought home to them the possibility of their own deaths. "You believe in God, in Japan?" Bob Miller asked.

Kosho shot him a look. "Most Japanese do, in one form or another," he said. "I myself find the existence of God an insoluble problem."

Miller digested this. "I don't believe, myself. The Dane was right, though. The words can make you feel better. When I was a kid I was in B.Y.P.U."

Kosho turned his head quizzically.

"Baptist Young People's Union," explained Miller. "Maybe the kid would be better than he is if he had grown up in a little town the way I did. I went there, to B.Y.P.U. to meet girls, but maybe the other stuff rubbed off too. That was from the Bible, that stuff that the J—that Glassman read."

Kosho nodded. "Your son . . ." he struggled to find the words to explain to this man.

"I know he ain't much to look at," continued Miller. "He surprised me last night. You saw what he did. What gets me is, I can't figure out how the hell he had the nerve to kill *anything*. What the hell happened out there?"

Kosho shook his head. "I think your son is very brave."

Miller considered this. "He seems to have the hots for the girl. Nice little piece of ass, too. Maybe it'll be good for him. Maybe he was showing off for her. You think?"

Kosho smiled.

"He better watch himself if he tries too much of that. These customers mean business. If only I hadn't been busy with the oars, I think I could've put a hole in one or two of them. If only they'd get closer. I'm just itching to use that damn Purdy shotgun. Anything within thirty yards of me, it'd blow 'em clean away."

Kosho thought of his sword, kept dry with oilcloth in the luggage in the boat. He glanced over his shoulder to the spot where it stood. "Why would they let us choose such weapons if we were not intended to use them?"

"You think?" asked Bob Miller. The thought seemed to cheer him, and he chuckled as they continued with their task. "I just wish," Bob Miller said, "that he wouldn't keep on talkin' to that old woman."

"She promised to help us, and the advice she has given has been good. She said she would not lie to us."

"Yeah. I know a few in business back in Dallas like that. They don't exactly lie. They just don't tell you everything."

Night fell, and they built a fire, more for warmth than for cooking. The provisions the old lady had put in their packs could be eaten cold. But with the setting of the sun, the chill wind blew down the stream from the mountains, whistling and howling along the narrow passes.

Suddenly a figure leaped down from above, landing with a thump on the sand beyond the fire, near the river. Bjorn and Bob Miller instantly raised their weapons.

"Hold!" came a familiar, deep-throated voice. It was Mkomo. He strode toward them, nearly naked, still carrying his rifle and one spear. "Idiots!" he shouted. "Your fire makes you a target from anywhere on the cliffs on either side."

Bjorn and Bob Miller admitted the truth of this by their silence. "We're cold," whined Betty Miller.

Mkomo spat out his contempt. "Cover the fire from sight by placing a tent over it. Let the open side be toward the cliff face. It will direct the heat toward you."

They rearranged things to his satisfaction. "While you have been sitting here at leisure, I have been hunting our enemies," said Mkomo.

"My mother was killed," said Kirsten. "And your son . . ."

Mkomo cut her off, raising his spear threateningly. "I left my son in your care," he growled at Bjorn. "If you have let him die, then . . ."

"Pop," came Charles's voice from one of the tents.

"He was shot," said Janet Gore. "But not badly. The wound was clean. The bullet went through. I bandaged him up."

Mkomo looked at her. "I thank you," he said.

Glassman stood up. "And I must offer my own thanks to you," he said. "You were on the cliff face, and fired at one of them when he was about to kill me."

Mkomo laughed. "Was he trying to kill you? My mistake. I could only see that he was aiming at the boat that carried my son. But why did you not fire yourself? Are not all you Israelis great warriors? Or is it our luck to be traveling with the only Jew afraid to carry a gun?"

Glassman gritted his teeth. "The girl was in the water."

"Why was that?"

"Because one of them had leaped into the stream. She dove in before we could stop her. She thinks she killed it."

"Indeed?" Mkomo looked at the girl with sudden respect, then back at Glassman. "It was fortunate you had a girl along to defend you. Now I understand why the Zionists use girls in their army."

Glassman turned away, his hands trembling.

"Were you able to kill any of them yourself?" Kosho asked.

"I fired many times." Mkomo shrugged. "There were many of them, and only one of me. Fortunately, the rest of you were able to paddle by in safety while I held them off."

"And did you kill any of them?" Kosho persisted.

Mkomo's eyes blazed. "They must have carried off their dead. When I emerged from my shelter, all had gone. They are cowards. Remember that."

"Granny said they might come hunting us at night," Billy said.

"Ah, you of the First Kill," said Mkomo, recognizing the boy. "Yes, and we will have to guard against that. I am weary, and wish to be with my son. Suppose you take the first watch. Perhaps you can duplicate your kill."

Billy's father started to intercede, but Billy said, "Let me, Dad. I can do it." Bob Miller looked at his son, and put his hand wordlessly on his shoulder. Billy felt terribly embarrassed.

Chapter Seventeen

The Aging Master sat in the mists of the swamp they had created for their resting place, gaining comfort and strength from the moist air. He had closed his sense receptors, indicating his wish not to be disturbed.

The others respected his wish. The Scientist was off somewhere, twittering over the observations he had made that day. The Natural Hunter was exulting over his own Kill, the first, indeed the only Kill that the Hunters had made.

The Aging Master had thought it a poor Kill. Had the Golden Female succeeded in her plan, her exploit would have put the Natural Hunter to shame.

Instead, she was dead. The Aging Master was saddened, not because he had allowed her to come on the Hunt—her parents would be delighted to learn that she had died while upholding the tradition of the Hunt in the highest degree—but because with her, his hope for the People seemed to vanish. There were too few like her.

He shifted his position. His limbs ached. There was a time when he could sit motionless as a stone, in wait for a quarry to approach, thinking him a lifeless object. He knew what the other Guardians would say: he was too old, and had encouraged others to Hunt who were too unsuitable by temperament to engage in a Hunt conducted by the Old Rules.

The Golden Female had had the correct temperament, but she had been deprived of the correct training. She had never been on a Hunt conducted under the Old Rules before.

The Guardians abolished the Old Rules because Hunting under them had become dangerous.There had been other Hunts on which some of the People had been killed. Their race was not a prolific one. The aggressiveness that was part of their nature overcame sexual affinity. For a sexual contact to be successful, there had to come that moment when both partners surrendered themselves to the other. The Aging Master, like so many of the People, had never been able to bring himself to make that surrender. He had no issue.

The Golden Female's parents, both superb Hunters, had found the courage to mate not only once, but three times. Their other two children, sons, had become like the New Children—only interested in the Hunt as a diversion, an exercise in slaughter, a feeble imitation of the ancient rites of the elders of their race. Their real interests lay in pleasure, a pursuit that they could comfortably occupy themselves with, because the People were supreme in the galaxy, taking what they wished from other worlds to provide comfort for themselves.

It was to ensure the continuance of that comfort that the Guardians had banned Hunting under the Old Rules. They ruled the galaxy now through their sole possession of the Discovery, swiftly moving to wipe out any species that seemed capable of the same Discovery.

The Aging Master was, as he had rashly allowed the others to guess, one of the Guardians. He had been the sole member of the Guardian Council of Seven to protest the abolition of the Old Rules. His reasoning had been that it would eventually lead to the dissipation of the values that made their species worthy of the Discovery. The six who voted against him had been more concerned with the continued existence of the People, even if they were New Children.

He had accepted the Commander's invitation, knowing the Hunt would be illegal, because he wanted to prove the others wrong. He had chosen the two young ones, and the Gray Female, thinking that they would uphold the tradition.

Now, his dreams lay shattered. The Natural Hunter had shown that he had earned his reputation by killing only those beasts who were helpless to defend themselves. He had not responded to the challenge.

The Gray Female . . . was as he might have expected. He had owed her this chance, but felt that her skills would be a model for the young ones. Instead, she had only showed her desire to kill, the desire for revenge that had nothing to do with the ideals of the Old Hunt. He thought of her the way she had been . . . when the two of them had considered that they might mate.

The Aging Master shifted position again, angry at his body's loss of discipline, at his sight receptors' inability to function as they should in the absence of light caused by the setting of the planet's sun. He admitted to himself what he could not admit to the others: he could no longer Hunt in darkness unless he used his Discovery powers.

The Gray Female still had excellent night vision. Angry at the Natural Hunter's success, she had gone seeking prey, taking a heavy-bladed weapon. If she should manage a kill, at least she would do it in close combat.

And there was the Commander. In him, perhaps, there was hope. Though he would earn a rich fee from the trip, there was something in the Commander's character that made the Aging Master believe that he Hunted according to the Old Rules because he had a sense of what they meant to their People. The Aging Master had resolved that he himself would not return. He had seen enough of this species to convince him that he could die worthily by engaging one of them in open combat. Return for him would mean shame, but the Commander had taken willingly the most difficult task—and the only one that could reconcile the other Guardians to the purpose of their trip. The Commander would engage the one member of the species that seemed to be acquiring Discovery powers. He was still out there, stalking, Hunting.

Billy sat close to the rushing of the water, his rifle across his knees. The sound of the water was lulling, made him forget the yearning he felt for Kirsten, sleeping peacefully now in one of the tents. It would be too gross, he knew, to approach her tonight, after her mother had died. Still, he thought of the touch of her breast, and the thought stirred him enough to produce an erection.

A voice behind him startled him. He scrambled around on his knees, not wanting to get to his feet for fear that his tumescence would show.

"I hope I did not startle you," said Kosho.

"Are you going to take the next watch?" asked Billy. "I didn't think it was time yet."

"It isn't," said the Japanese, sitting down next to Billy on the sand. "I came early because I wanted to ask you something."

Billy was uneasy. Kosho saw his discomfort. "I hope I have not disturbed your meditation."

Billy laughed. "I'm glad you didn't know what I was really thinking about."

"Then you must have been thinking about . . . Kirsten."

Billy flushed. "Does it show?"

Kosho spoke gently. "Lovers are always obvious, except to each other."

They sat silently. Kosho was content to sit with Billy and watch the water flow by.

"Kosho?"

"Yes."

"Do you believe in God?"

The Japanese laughed.

"I guess that was a stupid question. I'm sorry. Except that you have so much experience, and I'm . . . just a kid. That was stupid, wasn't it?"

"No, no, no. Please believe me, I would think nothing you asked stupid. It was just that . . . your father asked me the same question."

"He did? Dad? I can't see him asking anybody that."

"I cannot quite think of the American saying. Your father used it earlier, when he was proud of you. Fathers are like their sons? That does not carry the colloquial meaning."

"Like father, like son? But, Kosho, my father and I . . . we're not alike at all. He's not proud of anything I do."

Kosho inclined his head. "All sons bear the mark of their fathers. Many . . . most of the people of the earth know this, and accept it. For some reason, you Americans resist it. I think that is why so many of the rest of us find you strange. You think that each new child has the . . . ability . . . what am I trying to say?"

"Potential?"

"Ah, yes." Kosho rubbed his hands. "That is a particularly American concept. You have the potential to be anything that pleases you, as if the genes of your ancestors meant nothing at all. Do you believe that?"

"I guess so. Or no, I mean, there's lots of things I'd like to be, only I can't make myself be that way."

"Because that takes practice, discipline, will. You Americans

. . ." Kosho sighed. "You want to wish something, and then the wish comes true. You have always been lucky. But, Billy, you . . . perhaps that was why you could do what you did last night."

Billy shook his head. "Kosho, I don't know *how* I did that. It makes me afraid."

Kosho hesitated. "I don't want to . . . interrupt your learning . . . but did you ask the old woman how you did it?"

"Oh, sure, but she wouldn't tell me."

"No? Did she tell you that all this"—he gestured toward the river, the cliffs—"is an illusion?"

"An illusion? You mean it isn't *real?*"

"I am not sure what you mean by real. It has power, it is tangible. We can put our hands into the stream, and feel water, cold, motion. The great question is whether reality is what the mind perceives. What do you think?"

"Me? You're asking me? I don't even know *what* I think. Sometimes I can't tell if *I'm* real."

Kosho nodded. It was amazing, for one so young to have already advanced so far along the lines of thought that the great masters had developed over centuries.

They sat in silence for some time. Kosho was waiting for Billy to elucidate further the labyrinthine channels of his thought.

Billy was worried. The things that Kosho talked about . . . whether or not any of this was real . . . as though the mountain, the river, the water were only figments of somebody's imagination. It was dangerous to start thinking that way. You could drive yourself crazy. If it was really imagination . . . *whose* imagination would it be? His? Kosho's? Or was it the imagination of one of the alien things, like that horrible thing he had killed—*he! killed!*—last night. He shivered as he remembered it, recalling a little more of what happened. He had held the creature, the gray-skinned thing, like a man, and then it had changed. And Billy had learned how to make the change too. It was as if he had stolen the other creature's imagination. Did that mean he was now one of them? Or partly one of them? He remembered the story of Dr. Jekyll and Mr. Hyde, where in the end Dr. Jekyll couldn't help changing back—he couldn't control it.

Billy stood up abruptly. "Is it time for you to relieve me now? I'm tired."

"Ah, yes, you must be," said Kosho. "Try to sleep. Don't

tax yourself. You must be fresh for the dangers we will face tomorrow. And Billy, don't worry. I think it is going well for you."

Billy wandered back to his tent, wishing he could imagine himself out of all this. Suppose he imagined himself back in the public library in Dallas, and then woke up to find himself really there? He almost felt like trying it, but then remembered Mom and Dad. What would they think if he just disappeared? And maybe . . . maybe there really would be something he could do to help them. And Kirsten.

The thought of her made him calm. He was surprised, for up to now thinking about Kirsten had made him nervous. He kept worrying that he would do something stupid or crude that would make her laugh at him the way the girls back in Dallas always did. But now he felt calm, because . . . because he knew he would somehow be able to help her. Just now, he wasn't sure. The others had said she had jumped into the water and killed the alien that was going to attack their boat. *He* wouldn't have been able to do that. Granny had told him so. What was it she said? He hadn't mastered the water yet.

Kirsten certainly had. In fact, it seemed crazy to think that he would be able to do *any*thing that she couldn't do better. But he would. He started to concentrate on remembering. Remembering how to change. He thought of asking Granny to help, but she had always refused. "Keep on as you are," she said. He would try.

Kosho's watch was uneventful. He waited in vain for something to come near, some warrior that he could challenge with his sword. He was disappointed when Ian Gore came finally to relieve him.

"Any action?" asked Gore.

"Very much silence," said Kosho.

"That's when the danger's greatest, we always used to say," said Ian Gore.

Kosho noticed that Ian Gore had brought his heavy broadsword as a weapon. He thought of cautioning him, telling him that a rifle would be better, then checked himself. How improper it would be for him, after wishing for an opponent with a sword, to now caution this man, with his own dream of a noble combat. If the strange Hunters were to come, they would at least be opposed by Ian Gore, who was without doubt a man of courage. Useless as his broadsword might be, he would be able to make enough noise to awaken the others, who would bring more efficient weapons.

During Ian Gore's watch, the moon passed over its zenith, crossing the narrow strip of sky far overhead between the cliffs. The light illuminated the river valley, making Ian think of the cliffs of Dover. He realized that for a brief time he would be able to see intruders afar off, and the security allowed him the leisure to think again of the legendary exploits of the Knights of the Round Table.

Oh, the scholars had proved it all a myth. They said that Arthur, Lancelot, Merlin, and the rest never did exist. They had proved it all a forgery made up by Geoffrey of Monmouth, embellished by various monks and minstrels. Ian paid them no heed, for the story of Arthur was a story of the beginning of a great people. If Arthur hadn't existed, then whence came the courage of millions like him—those who died at Agincourt, Crécy, the Somme . . . ?

The blood of Arthur flowed today, in him, in Ian Gore, and in the many like him who awaited only another leader, a noble cause, to call them to arms, to rise and fight again.

That was the whole trouble. There were no more noble causes. This business in Biandra—there was nothing but ugliness and senseless bloodshed in that. Many of the blacks had been good fellows. This Mkomo was himself not a bad fighter, he was simply bursting with courage. Completely unsuited to lead, of course. He had no judgment, none at all. Were the blacks any better off under him after they had driven out the Gores and the other whites who had been part of Biandra from its beginnings as a nation? Look what they got. They said the whites exploited the blacks economically. No doubt some had. But they never slaughtered them by the thousands, tortured them. . . .

Yet the blacks had fought for Mkomo. Bravely and well. Their trouble was that their cause . . . it wasn't noble. Wasn't their fault, of course. There was nothing, anywhere, worth fighting for any longer.

All in all, it was not a world he enjoyed living in. Good old Jan kept the fire burning . . . make some money, start again, she said. Well and good. But were they going to find a place where people didn't want to butcher each other? Not Canada. Soon enough the trouble would spread there, too.

This now, this wild adventure . . . suppose they were fighting against something that came from another planet? Now that would be a cause, something that would make people all over the world stand up and take notice. They would turn to the British, of course, because throughout history they had been the people who could organize things. It wasn't a bad thought to Ian that he might well be fighting in the vanguard action against alien invaders. The last noble cause.

The moon's passage through the sky above was over. As it dipped beyond the other side of the cliff top, the valley was again thrown into darkness, waking Ian from his reverie. It was then he noticed that what he had thought was the reflection of the moon on the water was still there. It wavered, shimmered, and then moved.

Quite clearly. Ian glanced overhead, thinking that the angle of the moon might still allow its reflection. But above were only the stars, and darkness. He looked back, saw that the shimmering light had crossed the river and stopped at a point far down at the tip of the narrow sand spit on which they were camping. It wavered there, looking as if something were carrying it. Ian drew his sword and stood up.

The light moved, but not toward the camp. It wavered from side to side, lowered to the ground, then up again. Clearly it was motivated by something that had a brain. It held still at about the height of a man's head, then waved back and forth again. For some reason, the movement appeared to be a gesture, as if it were signaling someone.

Ian began to move toward it. His own feet moved soundlessly in the damp sand, and he was sure the darkness offered him some safety. Perhaps this was a scout, sent to see if the coast were clear. He'd bloody well be the first to show that it wasn't.

He padded farther down the sand. The light stood still now, although its beam was too weak to illuminate the area. He was still well beyond the point where he might be seen.

Yet he stopped. Perhaps it would be good to go back and awaken some of the others. After a moment's thought, he realized that that would also give the intruder time to assemble his companions. Better to go alone, since there appeared to be only one opponent. If he could catch it unawares . . . He moved on.

He was within thirty feet of it now, and saw from the dim glow the form of one of the creatures, humanlike but unmistakably not human, with arms too thin to be a human's except in the advanced stages of starvation. And the head: oval, between two shoulders, as a human's, but with long narrow slits where the eyes ought to be.

Ian surveyed his position. To go closer would surely invite being seen. He wondered if he could press himself against the side of the cliff, and slowly move down, keeping out of the circle of light.

Suddenly the creature threw down the light. Ian tensed, expecting it to go out. Instead, it flared with intense brightness, and he could see that it was a glowing globe of some milky, glasslike substance. Its intensified glow clearly marked the scene, and Ian realized that he was expected.

Old fool, he thought. *It could probably see you all the time you were coming.* For the creature faced him squarely, and held a weapon identical to Ian's. There seemed to be more than coincidence in that, and Ian's spirit rose at the offered challenge. It was his chance, at last. He lifted his sword, using two hands to do so, and noted that the creature lifted its own with one arm.

In strength, then, he was at a disadvantage. Skill would have to tell the tale. Ian moved forward, raising the sword as high as he could. The other waited. Ian struck first, only to have his downward blow parried and driven back. Ian felt the immense strength of his opponent, but was reinforced by the strength of his own determination.

Steel rang out against steel, echoing up the cliffs, but those in the tents were too far away to hear. No one watched the battle on the sand but a second black-clad figure high above.

The Commander had no desire to intervene in the battle. He watched calmly for a few minutes, noting that the creature was giving the Gray Female a good fight. She had not expected one, the Commander knew by now—she wanted only kills—but the Commander had no doubt about the eventual outcome. The Gray Female had picked one of the weakest of the group on which to make her first Kill.

The Commander watched only to see if the young one's Discovery powers would be strong enough to bring him awake. If he intervened, then the Commander would act.

Chapter Eighteen

When Bob Miller went to relieve Ian Gore on the watch, he was annoyed to find that the other man was not on duty. Miller assumed that Ian had been "nipping," as Janet Gore called it, and had tottered back to the tent. He had a good mind to go find him and read him out for leaving them at the mercy of the aliens.

Since nothing seemed to have happened, Miller decided to let the matter wait until morning. It was a good indication that the creatures wouldn't be back tonight, at any rate, and Miller felt quite safe taking a catnap of his own while he waited.

Bjorn Halvorssen woke him as dawn was breaking. "A quiet night," the Dane said wryly.

Miller told him of finding the post unattended when he came on duty. Halvorssen frowned. "You did not search for him?"

Miller shrugged. "Where was there to search?" He waved his hand. "There isn't much room for anyone to go far—" He stopped, as both he and Halvorssen saw the body at the far end of the spit. They looked at each other and began to run.

There was a dark stream of blood flowing from Ian Gore's body to the river. He lay facedown, and his sword was stuck in the sand, upright, at his head. They left him that way as they went to awaken the others.

Janet Gore, controlling herself, waved the others away. The circle of onlookers parted, allowing her to go to her husband. Kosho turned his eyes away, wishing he had the courage to lead the others back to the camp. There were some private things that strangers did not watch.

When she turned his body over, brushing the sand from his face, those who watched saw unmistakably that he had died with a smile. Janet lifted his shoulders and hugged him. It was the smile that made her cry. "Well, you found it, didn't you? Found it when you thought it was lost," she whispered.

After a time, she wiped her tears with her handkerchief and stood up. She looked around at the others, silently watching. "We'd better get the paddles, hadn't we?" she said in a voice surprisingly strong.

As they dug, she drew Billy aside. "I want to ask you something," she said.

He hung his head, embarrassed that she had singled him out, but knowing that it was something he had to go through.

"Do you know the old stories, about Arthur and his knights? Do they teach such things in American schools?"

"They don't teach them," he said. "But I know the stories."

"Do you remember what they did when Arthur died?"

He couldn't remember, and cast his eyes everywhere else, trying to avoid Janet's anxious gaze. He saw the sword, still standing in the sand. Janet had not let anyone touch it.

"It's the sword you mean, isn't it?" he said.

"Good boy," she said, patting him on the head.

"They threw—" She shushed him with a touch across the mouth.

"*You* must throw it," she said, her eyes glinting fiercely.

He nodded.

When they had finished digging the grave, they turned to Janet. She asked Kosho and Bob Miller to lower him into the grave. When they did so, she scraped the first bit of sand on top of the body. The rest helped, and soon he was covered.

The group instinctively looked at Glassman. Embarrassed, he stepped toward Janet. "Would you like . . ." he began.

She shook her head. "No more words," she said. "There were too many words. I know many of them by heart myself, and if I could wish words, if words would bring him back, I would recite the whole of Malory on this spot. No. He died for that," she said, nodding at the sword. She looked at Billy.

"Now," she said.

He stepped forward, conscious of the others' surprised eyes on him. He pulled the sword from the sand, struggling with its unexpected weight. He swung it with both hands, around his head several times till the momentum seemed to overcome its weight. The others stepped back out of his way, uncertain of his intention.

He let it fly. It sailed out over the swift-flowing stream, reached the length that the force of the throw would take it, and then gravity pulled it down. It cut through the surface of the water with hardly a ripple.

He turned to Janet. "I'm sorry," he said. The others watched, puzzled.

"There was no hand," she said, as if greatly relieved.

He glanced back to the water, but there was nothing there.

"I'm glad," she said.

Billy looked at her. She did not meet his eye. He did not believe her.

"Still," she said. "The bravery was real. And you are a proper boy." She patted his shoulder. "He would have been proud to have a son like you."

As she touched him, he recalled the story more fully. He realized that she wanted it to end *that* way. He remembered the dream he had had the night before. He had *known* someone was in trouble, and if he had gotten up instead of wishing the dream away . . . maybe he would have been able to help. He looked back out to the surface of the water, still feeling the touch of Janet Gore's hand on his shoulder. If he could only imagine it in the right way. . . .

"Look!" called Kirsten, following Billy's eyes to the water. The sword was emerging from the water, first just the tip of the blade, then gradually the whole blade, and finally the hilt.

There were cries and gasps from the group as they saw that the hilt was grasped firmly by a hand, a woman's hand. Slowly the hand moved, as the group of humans stood transfixed. It waved the tall heavy sword in a circle, once, twice, a third time, and then sank beneath the surface of the water.

Janet Gore cried out and sank to her knees on the sand, her hands over her face. Billy sucked in a lungful of air, then expelled it with a sigh of relief. It had taken an effort. He glanced at Kirsten, and saw that she was staring at him.

She knew. No, he couldn't tell her . . . he would deny it. It was too weird, it would make her afraid of him. And then he saw that Kosho was watching him too. He turned and walked away from them. He didn't *want* this. He didn't want Kosho's questions. He couldn't answer them. He just wanted everyone to stop *looking* at him.

The Commander still watched from the cliff, unseen by the group below. Why on earth had the boy done *that?* It must be connected to some kind of ritual that his limited study of this species had not prepared him for. It would make an interesting story for the Scientist, but the event caused the Commander great uneasiness. It meant that the boy was progressing, moving much faster than he had any right to.

To have full use of such powers, one had to go through the Initiation Ceremony. It was the most solemn moment of a young Person's life, the admission of the Person to full membership in the community, the bestowal of Power. How could this primitive beast be accomplishing it? Could he, in his battle with the Mate, somehow have uncovered the Mate's own memory of the Ceremony, and that way . . . but to probe the Mate's mind that deeply, he would already have to have made the Discovery. According to the assigned guide, the boy was touching the Mate when the Mate transformed himself. It was certainly possible that the boy mimicked that change, in the way that children were taught by their parents. That much, even a child could do. But now he was creating original illusions of his own. How long would it be before he grasped the power behind the illusion of the environment itself?

The Commander considered this as he watched the group of beasts begin to make their preparations for resuming the journey downriver. If only the Commander could probe the boy's mind, or more safely, simply wipe him out using his more highly developed control of the Discovery.

But the Aging Master had forbidden him to use the Discovery. Perhaps the Aging Master was simply using this tactic to punish the Commander. Perhaps the Aging Master was acting, after all, for the Guardians, and they would use his punishment as an object lesson to anyone else who might consider concealing the existence of Class B game.

The Commander reflected with irony on the feelings of disgust he had had on his last several Hunts—leading a pack of tourists armed with Discovery weapons against helpless Class D or C game. He had been disgusted with what seemed like a mockery of a real Hunt. There was no contest between animals who had nothing but physical skills and Hunters who had the Discovery. That was why he yearned to take part in a Hunt by the Old Rules.

Well, he had that now. And the tables seemed to be turned. It was he who was helpless against a being who seemed to be reaching Discovery powers with alarming speed.

The only advantage he had was that none of the other beasts seemed at all ready to make that evolutionary step. He remembered the tactic he had used on his earlier Hunt to this planet, when he had to recover the Discovery weapon. The creatures had strong affinity bonds toward family members. On the earlier trip, he had held a child hostage. Why not, now, capture one of the boy's loved ones?

Bjorn Halvorssen readily agreed to allow the Millers' raft to proceed first. He would rather have the less experienced pilot in front of him.

Janet Gore had taken Kirsten under her wing, out of her own need, and also because she felt someone should look after her in place of her mother. Bjorn quite approved of that. Janet had wanted Billy to go along on the Halvorssens' raft, but Bob Miller wouldn't permit it. That left Glassman to go with the Millers and Kosho, while Mkomo and Charles stayed with the Halvorssens. Bjorn was not unhappy at that either. Though Charles had recovered sufficiently from his injury to sidle up to Kirsten, no doubt with romantic intent, Bjorn was confident in Charles's ineptitude and Kirsten's ability to handle herself not to worry about that. And Mkomo had proved himself to be an asset in case of attack.

Even Janet Gore had once more strapped her .45 Webley to her hip. Bjorn felt what she did—the urge to avenge the loss of a loved one. Today, he would steer toward any of the invaders he spotted. Just close enough to allow him to use his own hunting rifle. It would not hurt to have the other boat go ahead as a decoy. Bjorn instantly felt bitter sadness. He was changing. The struggle to survive was changing all of them.

Bob Miller was running scared. He had figured out that both of the deaths had occurred when they were standing still. Bibi Halvorssen had been an easy target, and the old colonial had been taken by surprise in the middle of the night. To Miller, the obvious course was to move as rapidly as possible. Today his handling of the raft was as reckless as it had been cautious the day before. He ran the boat into the swiftest part of the current, ignoring even the highest surges.

They made swift progress, even though the passengers were somewhat unsettled by the roller-coaster ride, and it was not long before the sheer cliffs began to recede. Farther down, the river ran into a wide valley. Soon they began to see vegetation growing in the areas beyond the narrow strips of sand that the river lapped. At first it was only a few stands of grass, reminding them that the whole previous day they had seen nothing green. Then appeared small bushes, and finally trees.

The river still ran rough, but the appearance of what seemed like friendlier country made them relax a little. Betty Miller stood up in the raft suddenly. "Look!" she cried. "It's a deer!" The others' eyes followed hers. A gorgeous doe, feeding on some of the vegetation close to the river, looked back, startled, and then bounded into the woods.

"Did you see it, Bob?" called Betty Miller. Her husband nodded, but steered the boat past the spot as quickly as possible.

Kosho nudged Billy. "There is something strange there."

"What's that?" Billy said warily. He had been dreading Kosho's questions.

"This is our third day in wild country. The first day, among the mountains, we were not surprised at not seeing any other life. But yesterday, I watched for fish in the river. There were none. Something else. In country like this, there should have been many insects. Mosquitoes. There were none. This morning was the first time I saw something else that was alive. A hand. And you created the illusion of that."

Billy did not reply. He knew that the clever Kosho was trying to get him to admit that he had made the hand appear above the water. He would not respond. Let Kosho think whatever he liked.

But as Billy sat there, he began to think that the Japanese man was right. They hadn't seen anything else alive. Except for the black-clad people. They didn't count.

"Why?" he said, in spite of himself.

"Excuse me?" said Kosho.

"Why didn't we see anything else that was alive?"

Kosho nodded. The boy knew, of course, but he wanted to see if Kosho could discover it for himself. Kosho chose the words of his response carefully.

"Because it is more difficult to create the illusion of something that has life. I thought you looked as if your effort this morning cost you some . . . strength."

Billy nodded. "I didn't have anything to do with the deer," he said.

"Then," Kosho said, "they did."

They turned to look toward the rear of the boat. Betty Miller was arguing with her husband. "Damn, Bob, I'm hungry. We hardly had enough food in those packs for a decent breakfast. There's nothing left."

"We'll be fed when we get to the end of the river. There's supposed to be another lodge there," he shouted at her, trying to keep his eyes on the river.

"Who knows how long *that's* going to be? I could have brought down that deer. So could you. Maybe we're supposed to be living off the *land*. You always said we took that survival course so we could live off the land in case of atomic *attack*. We could have some nice deer steaks for lunch."

"And get killed ourselves?" He looked down at her, taking his eyes off the current, missing the impossibly large surge that lay at the end of a V-shaped current ahead. "They want us to stop. Don't you understand? You want to wind up like—" He blinked, and the expression on his face changed. He grabbed frantically for the oars. The others saw his movement and looked forward.

The heavy surge lay at the head of a drop that was so large that it could properly be called a fall. "Hold on," Kosho shouted, but it was the wrong advice, and too late. The raft stood nearly vertical, tumbling all of them but Bob Miller, who held on to the rowing platform, toward the front of the boat. It overturned.

There was an air bubble underneath the raft that enabled all of them to rise to the surface, finding that they were in a darkened hollow filled with the sound of shouts and screams that were nearly inaudible with the spattering sound of water pouring down on the overturned bottom from above. Eventually, they figured out that they could make their way to the still inflated tanks at the edge of the boat and swing around to the open air above.

They circled the boat, holding onto the sides like swimmers around a float. The flow of water from above was powerful, and continued blasting down on them inexorably, making the surface worse than the sheltered darkness underneath. Fortunately, the water was filled with rocks, and they were able to use them as handholds to pull themselves to the side of the fall.

They huddled there, perched on a rock like a group of drenched and ugly water birds. They looked upriver, but they had left the Halvorssen boat far behind. If they waited long enough, the other boat would come by to rescue them, but a wind blew up, chilling them all to the bone.

"Bob," shouted Betty Miller. "We've got to get ashore."

Everyone recognized the truth of this, but the swift-flowing river looked too daunting to allow them to swim.

Billy felt Kosho's eyes on his. *Jesus*, he thought. *He thinks I'm going to find us a way out of this*. Thinking that, however, gave him the confidence he needed. What was it that Granny had said? He had conquered the earth and the air, but not the water. Well, it seemed like the right time to try. He looked back at Kosho, closed his eyes, and jumped.

Underwater, he found that he could open his eyes. He had never done so in the chlorinated swimming pools in the yards of his parents' friends in Dallas. It was as if he had . . . lived here. Instead of rising to the surface, he sank deeper, instinctively knowing that near the bottom the current flowed less strongly. His body changed. He felt it changing, wanted it to change, saw things differently, knew for a second before the change was complete that it was because his eyes were on opposite sides of his head.

He swam. It was not swimming. It was movement. He did not feel arms or legs. He felt no arms, no legs. He had none. All of his thoughts were concerned with swimming, except for a tiny, tiny voice in the back of his brain that told him he must not follow the current joyfully as he wanted to do, but to make his way for the shore. He could hardly remember what the shore was. He had almost no memory of land.

But as his mouth touched the bank that marked the limits of his world, he changed again. Hands! Clumsy things, they reached out, touched . . . touched with the tips of fingers. . . . He had to concentrate to remember what fingers were.

The others, watching anxiously, thought that he must have drowned. Except Kosho. Watching the shore, he gave a cry of triumph. Because he had been looking a second before the others, he saw just a glimpse of the silver scales falling away as Billy broke the surface of the water.

Now what? thought Billy, still alive with the keen senses of an animal. He saw the coils of rope that lay not far from the bank. *Granny?*

She did not appear, even to him, but her voice sounded in his ear. *Don't be so stupid,* she said.

Chapter Nineteen

Billy dragged himself to his feet, took up the rope, and uncoiled it, his hands feeling strange and clumsy. He had to throw one end of it out to the others . . . no, first tie the other end to something here. A tree. He wrapped the end of it around the small trunk of the nearest tree. He felt something touch him and looked up in surprise. He realized that the touch was not a physical one; it was inside his brain.

Farther in from the shore, half hidden among the larger trees there, was a deer. It was watching him strangely—not the way a deer, wary of people, would give a quick look before darting into the forest. It seemed to be surveying him calmly—the eyes intelligent, calculating. Billy stared at it for a long moment.

The shouts of the others distracted him. He wanted to move inside the deer, feel what it was thinking . . . but he was tired; he couldn't concentrate. He turned away from the deer and began to look on the ground for a rock he could tie the other end of the rope to.

The rocks were all wet from the spray of the river, and he couldn't manage to keep the rope from slipping off them. He thought of the pistol inside his jacket pocket, the Remington .25 that Kirsten had picked out for him. He groped and found it. It was wet, but it would be good for something. He thought of the deer and turned with the pistol in his hand—just in time to see the white tail of the deer disappearing into the woods.

It hadn't been afraid of him until he thought of the gun. As if it knew what a gun was for. No, it had been quicker than that. As if it knew what he was going to take out of his pocket.

He tied the rope around the small pistol and weighed it carefully. It was a long throw, and the rope would make it even more difficult. It was harder than throwing a baseball. He knew what he would have to do. He drew back his arm, aimed at Kosho, who was nearest to the shore, and *thought* of the pistol in Kosho's hands.

Kosho was so surprised that he wasn't able to raise his hands to catch the object. Billy hadn't even *thrown* it; Kosho was waiting for his arm to come down, which would have given him a second or two to gauge the throw and raise his hand. Instead, suddenly the rope was unfurled across the distance between Kosho and Billy, and the pistol was in his hand, which closed in reaction. Kosho wasn't even sure if he himself had willed his hand closed. Kosho stared across the water at Billy, but the boy shook his head, his eyes pleading with Kosho not to speak.

Kosho tossed the end of the rope lightly to Bob Miller. Miller held it steady while, one by one, the others used it to hold themselves against the current and make their way through the stream to shore. Then Kosho and Glassman pulled Bob Miller ashore.

Billy had collapsed, and his mother was huddled beside him. "Bob, he's shivering. He's half frozen, and I am too. We've got to build a fire."

"With what?" said Miller. "We lost everything in the boat."

"I have these," said Glassman. He pulled a watertight container of matches from his pocket.

"Let's gather some wood then," said Betty Miller.

Bob looked around nervously. He had just realized that they had stopped, and it made him uneasy. "Listen, fires make smoke. We might draw a pack of those killers down on us."

"Damn it all, Bob, I'm freezing," said Betty. "And what about Billy? He saved us. Do you realize that? We'd be stuck out there on those rocks if it hadn't been for him. My God, Bob, the way you treat that boy it's no wonder he's always mopin' around. Let me tell you—"

"Okay, okay," Bob Miller said, raising his hands to stop her. "I was worried about your safety."

"At least I've still got my bow," she said. When the raft had dumped them, she had been wearing both bow and quiver over her shoulder. "And he's armed too," she said, pointing at Kosho, who had saved the oilskin-wrapped sword from the raft.

"Oh, great," said Bob Miller. "You can be Maid Marian, and he's got that pigsticker, but what happens if they start blasting at us with rifles?"

"You'll have to worry about that," she said. "If you hadn't turned thc boat over, we wouldn't be in this mess." She looked at Kosho. "Will you come with me?"

"Perhaps your husband is right," said Kosho. "I think you should stay here with your family so there will be some protection. Glassman and I will look for wood."

"Why should you have all the fun?" she said. "I saw a deer back in those woods. You couldn't get it with that sword, but I have a chance of bringing it down." She angrily stared at the rest of them, then stamped her foot. "If there's a man here, let him come with me," she said, and started toward the woods.

Kosho spoke softly to Glassman. "Go with her. But do not let her shoot at the deer."

Glassman looked at him quizzically. "The deer would be good to eat."

"If it were really a deer," said Kosho.

Glassman shrugged, and followed Betty up the bank.

Bob Miller sat down, watching the opposite shore. "I don't know what's happenin'," he said. "Betty never acted like this at home. She never went in for that women's lib nonsense." He looked around at Kosho.

Kosho felt sorry for him. "Perhaps we should call the old woman."

Miller stared at him as if he had made an obscene suggestion. "You got this business figured out, then?" said Miller. "How did she do that? Was she really in the boat yesterday?"

Kosho smiled. "So it seemed to me. What did you see?"

Bob Miller sighed. "I don't know what to think." To Kosho, the other man's face seemed suddenly old. "I thought they must have put somethin' in our food. Drugs, maybe. To confuse us. I thought it was all some kind of joke, until they killed those two people."

Kosho sat with him, leaving the other man to his thoughts.

"I'm scared," said Bob Miller after a while.

"That is nothing to be ashamed of," said Kosho. He looked at Billy. The boy seemed to be sleeping quietly.

"I mean I'm afraid to call the old woman."

"She has never harmed any of us."

"No, I mean I'm afraid she would come. I wonder, I mean you don't have to . . . could you call her?"

Kosho paused. He would never really understand Americans. Their culture was too different. *Granny, we need you.*

They heard her voice, and turned around. She looked impatient. "You're not making any progress just sitting here, you know," she said.

Bob Miller watched her, his jaw slack. He struggled to find words.

Kosho spoke for him. "What should we do now?"

"Why, you have to make your way downriver to the lodge as best you can. The bank is open from here on. You'll have to walk, unless your friends in the other raft stop for you. But ten of you won't fit."

"I want my gun," said Bob Miller. "Can you bring me a gun?"

"There's another shotgun, just like the one you lost, waiting in the lodge for you."

"No, I mean I need it now."

"I'm afraid that's impossible. You lost the one I gave you. It's all part of the fun of the Hunt. If you lose your supplies, you have to be ingenious enough to survive without them."

"This is *stupid*," shouted Bob Miller. "It isn't fair."

"It's quite fair. The rules apply to all."

Miller reached to grab her. She stepped aside, and he slipped on the sand. When he looked up, she was gone. "Where'd she go?" he said.

Kosho shrugged. "She is gone. Unless she was never there."

Glassman didn't like the forest. It reminded him of New York's Central Park. He had assembled an armful of sticks and small branches, but Betty Miller was moving farther into the woods.

"Mrs. Miller!" he called.

She turned. "Y'all call me Betty," she said. "Since we're the only brave ones."

"We've got enough wood for a fire. We'd better go back."

She shook her head. "I want a shot at that deer. Don't make so much noise. You've got to come up on them moving across the wind, so they can't scent you. They're skittish creatures."

"But your son. He needs some warmth."

She paused. "That's so. You take it on back. I'll be there directly."

He laughed, thinking of what Bob Miller would say. "Please, Mrs. Miller."

She looked at him. "You're just like Bob. Think I can't take care of myself. It's always been that way. I was supposed to be some harmless toy. My father treated me like that. All I was supposed to do was look pretty and know how to keep the boys talkin'. Oh, I was good at that. You know what happened?"

He shook his head. "I looked in the mirror one day, and I saw that I wasn't so pretty anymore. I was a middle-aged lady."

"You're still quite beautiful," he said.

She shot him a glance to read his intentions. Satisfied that he wasn't up to no good, she continued. "And you know, I realized that I didn't really care to hear what the boys had to say anymore. They were just a bunch of drunks lolling around the country club. A bunch of good ol' boys. You ever been in a country club?"

"Um . . . no."

"It's the most *boring* goddamn place in the world. The only things to do are drink, play cards, and play golf. And I didn't like to do any of them. Really, I don't know why I'm telling you all this."

"Let's go back. I'll be glad to listen."

She took her bow down. "I'm really good at this. Really. I really am."

He nodded politely. She reminded him of a woman he had trained. That woman had left her husband and three children in Philadelphia to come to Israel to be a fighter. She was willing, and learned quickly. But she had been enraged when they sent her to guard a school near the Lebanese border. She felt it was too much like being a housewife in Philadelphia. She wanted to be a general.

"Look!" said Betty Miller. "Did you see that?"

Glassman looked, but saw nothing.

"Wait here," she said. "Just for a minute. You don't know how to walk quiet in the woods. I'm going to bring it back and *then* we'll see what Bob has to say."

He hesitated. She stooped over, stringing an arrow to her bow, and moved into the bushes. He took a step forward, to follow her, and stubbed his toe on something. He looked down.

It was half covered with leaves, but he saw at once what it

was. Still holding the firewood, he moved the leaves aside with his foot. It was his Uzi.

He looked in the direction the woman had gone. He could see nothing, hear nothing. He squatted by the Uzi, wanting to pick it up, but to prevent himself, he held the more tightly to the sticks he had gathered.

These creatures had an ethic, he realized. The old woman was right when she said they would attack only with the weapons that . . . the humans . . . chose. Or were given.

They wanted him to pick it up. They had put it here for him. And when he did, someone would come out of the bushes with another Uzi. He was not afraid of that. It would be an even fight; if anything he would have the advantage, for surely they had no Uzis wherever these beings came from. He laughed at the memory of a young soldier proclaiming, in an excess of zeal, that the Uzi was a weapon sent from God.

It was not *that* good.

They might still hunt and kill him, it was true. He shook his head. He had only a vague memory of being attacked on the mountain, but he had resolved not to be taken by surprise again.

Yet there was another possibility. He had someone else to consider. He remembered what had happened to the woman from Philadelphia. PLO terrorists attacked the school—no doubt when she was thinking of what she would do when she was a general—and killed her, and seven children.

Betty Miller had confided in him, saw him as a friend. If she were in danger, must he not help her?

That was the argument he had been confronted with by his friends in Israel, after he had made his decision to fight no more. Pacifism was impossible when you were surrounded by enemies, his friends had said; you are taking advantage of those who have the courage to fight to defend you, said others who did not know him as well.

His ears burned with the memory of their accusations. It was not that he was lacking in courage. He dropped the sticks on the ground and advanced through the woods in the direction the woman had gone. But he left the Uzi behind.

Halvorssen saw the wreckage of the Millers' raft, still caught in the back flow of the falls, before he saw the figures on the beach. They began shouting and waving. He steered toward them.

Mkomo saw his intention and rushed back to the rowing platform. "Leave them!" he shouted. "Their troubles are not ours. Everyone must take his own risks."

Bjorn hesitated, then looked at his daughter. She had half climbed to the top of the flotation tanks. Bjorn took another look at the beach and saw that her boyfriend lay there, motionless.

"If we stop, the creatures will be on us. It's a trap!" insisted Mkomo.

Bjorn knew that he was right, but he also knew that if he turned to go on, his daughter was capable of diving into the stream to swim ashore. He looked for Bibi, before remembering that she was no longer there to restrain Kirsten. It was not so easy for him. He turned the boat, ignoring Mkomo's enraged shouts, and before long they had joined the others on the beach.

With their dry supplies, they made a meal. The boy rose from his deep sleep and looked around as if he could not tell where he was. When he saw Kirsten, it was as if he had regained something. She held him close.

Miller and Kosho explained what had happened, saying that Glassman and Betty Miller had gone into the woods to gather firewood, but had not returned. Halvorssen glanced once at Bob Miller, then looked away.

But Miller had read his accusation: How could you have allowed your wife to go into the woods?

"She wanted to," Bob Miller said, pulling at Halvorssen's arm, wanting to make him understand. "You don't know."

Halvorssen knocked Miller's hand away, immediately wishing he had not. "Don't I know? Until yesterday, I too had a wife."

Miller reacted by putting his head in his hands. Bjorn saw that he was crying, and left him alone.

They divided the remaining food among the group. There was little enough, but Kosho assured them that the old woman had said they would come to another lodge before long. Mkomo was anxious. "She did not guarantee you that we would get there alive," he said.

Halvorssen nodded. "We can fit you into our raft," he offered. "The river seems to have lost its ferocity." Mkomo spit into the fire.

"There is room," Halvorssen said firmly to him.

"I can't go," said Bob Miller. "I've got to find Betty."

The others exchanged glances. Janet Gore finally spoke. "Realistically, Mr. Miller, there would seem to be little chance. They would have returned by now if they were . . . safe.''

''You have no weapon,'' Kosho pointed out. ''And your son needs a father.''

Miller shook his head. ''Billy's old enough to take care of himself. A man's got to watch out for his wife. I can't just leave her here, even if . . .'' His voice lowered to a whisper. ''At least the others got a decent burial. I'm not gonna spend the rest of my life thinkin' that I just *left* her out here.''

The others silently agreed. Bjorn stood up and went to the raft. He brought back his .470 hunting rifle. ''This may help,'' he said, giving it to Bob Miller.

''Yeah,'' said Miller, patting the stock. He looked at Halvorssen. ''You understand.''

The Dane nodded.

Chapter Twenty

The Scientist twittered with delight. "You brought me a specimen! Is it . . . ?" he peered at the form that the Commander held across his shoulders. "Really?" the Scientist said. "Really alive?"

The Commander indicated that it was, setting the body of the creature down. The Scientist's fingers examined its garment fasteners. "A real Class B specimen."

"You are not to harm it," the Commander cautioned.

The Scientist hesitated. "I cannot be sure how it will react to the tests I need to administer."

"Then you will not administer them."

"But you gave me your word. That was the only reason why I came along. To find out . . . what the Discovery means. If you had not kept their existence as a Class B race a secret, the Guardians would have wiped out the entire species anyway. What does a single specimen matter?"

"This one means nothing. But one of them, the son of this creature, may have already made the Discovery."

"That cannot be possible."

"I have seen him using what appear to be Discovery powers."

"How could he have learned? Who could have taught him?"

They looked at the unconscious form of Betty Miller.

"In the usual way, our way, the parents prepare the children," mused the Scientist. "But if this creature could do that, you would not have been able to capture her."

"As far as we know," said the Commander, "they have no

Initiation Ceremony. Could the boy have learned about that from his contact with the Mate?"

The Scientist dismissed this idea with a gesture. "The Initiation Ceremony is a sham. It means nothing."

The Commander was shocked, deeply offended at this insult. He regarded the Ceremony as the central ritual in the custom of the People. "It is not a sham," he said. "It is the formal bestowal of Discovery."

"Ceremony. Ritual," the Scientist said contemptuously. "Only a way of formalizing what occurs naturally, and through practice. Many races, more primitive than ours, have similar coming-of-age rituals."

"But they do not have the Discovery."

"Quite true. The reason why has to do with their development, obviously. But we have never been allowed to study that, not even among our own kind. We have our own superstitions; we need to think that we are uniquely ennobled, to justify destroying all other races who might make the Discovery. We cannot admit the contradiction—cannot reconcile our belief that only the People can make the Discovery with our obvious need to prevent others from making it also."

The Commander turned away. "I understand now why the Guardians stopped you from continuing your work. Your attitude is an insult to the heritage of the People."

"Anything that adds to our knowledge of ourselves can only enrich our heritage."

"There may be some things better left unknown."

"Spoken like a Guardian. You know, if you hadn't done such an outrageous thing as to lead this illegal expedition, you might well have been chosen as a Guardian someday. You were considered to be among the very best of the Hunt Commanders."

"Until my earlier visit to this planet."

"So you returned, to salvage your honor."

"Not so much that, as to find a real challenge."

"Of course. Like our friend the Aging Master. He *is* one of the Guardians, you know. And what may surprise you, he agrees with me."

The Commander gestured for silence. "He could not." He stood up, indicating that he wished not to continue the discussion. "You will not harm her. I need her alive. It is the only way to capture her son."

"If he really has made the Discovery, it is not possible that both of you could survive an encounter. One of you must destroy the other."

"Not if he surrenders."

"Why should he surrender?" said the Scientist, but the Commander had already turned his back.

The Commander was removing the garments of the creature. "To save his mother," he said softly.

Bob Miller felt at home in the woods. From his boyhood, he had hunted all sorts of creatures—deer, wild boar, even grizzly—in the forests of the South and West. He moved quietly, stopping to listen to the sounds around him. It was too quiet. To his practiced ear, it seemed as if nothing lived in this territory. No birds in the trees, no insects, no small game. Yet there had been a deer.

His eye caught a movement ahead. He froze. Slowly, as if it were a branch moving in the wind, he lifted his rifle into firing position, his eyes straining to see the source of the movement, waiting for it to move again. He saw it, and only the thought that it might be Betty kept him from firing.

It was not the black color of these creatures' clothing. It was the green color of the flotation jackets that they all had worn. He stepped forward. "Betty!" he called.

"Who is it?"

Miller's heart sank as he heard Glassman's voice. "Over here," Miller called. At least, if one of them were still alive . . .

Glassman told him what had happened. Miller cursed him. "How could you let her go on alone?"

"She insisted. I thought she was going after the deer. I went after her when she didn't come back. Over there . . . I found her bow."

"Her bow? Oh, God."

"No, listen. It's very strange. There was no sound. I would have heard her at least . . . cry out, if . . ."

"Yeah. Maybe. Show me."

They went toward the spot where Glassman had been standing.

"There's nothing but the bow," said Glassman. "No blood."

"They must have taken her."

"I can't understand that. Last night, when they killed Ian Gore, they left his body. They could easily have removed it, if that was what they wanted."

"We don't know what they want." Bob Miller was trying to

avoid thinking of the stuffed grizzly that his father had kept in his den. The memory brought his gorge up, and he turned away from Glassman.

Suddenly Glassman pulled his arm. "Look," he whispered.

It stood there, thirty yards away. It was carrying some clothes. Betty's clothes. Miller swiftly raise his rifle, but the other shot first, firing, it seemed, from reflex alone. It seemed accidental that the slug reached its target.

The force knocked Bob Miller to the ground, and he gritted his teeth with the pain, trying to reach for his fallen rifle. As he attempted to pick it up, he saw that the shot that had only numbed his arm had destroyed the rifle, splintering the stock and tearing it away from the barrel. He waited, expecting the next shot to be deadly.

Glassman surprised him. He stepped in front of Bob Miller and charged at the creature. The sudden attack made it draw back a step. Bob Miller watched, wondering why a coward who wouldn't carry a gun would want to commit suicide in so spectacular a fashion.

The Commander timed the approach of the other creature, and at the last moment brought his gun around, smashing Glassman on the side of the head. The rabbi crashed to the ground.

Bob Miller ignored the pain in his right hand. For some reason, the alien was not going to risk shooting him from that range. It walked closer and held up his hand. He looked around. Bob Miller's jaw dropped as he saw Granny emerge from the bushes.

"Mr. Miller, the Commander means you no harm. He wishes to compliment you on your skill."

Miller was angry. "I wish to God my skill had been enough to blow his brains out."

"Yes, but the Commander is one of the best of the Hunters. It is not surprising that his skill is superior to yours."

"Well, what's he going to do? Why don't he kill me?"

"He wants me to tell you that your wife is safe, alive, and in good hands."

"Oh, my God. What are they going to do with her?"

"Calm yourself. The Commander would like to make you a . . . deal, I think you would say."

"A deal? Lord, I might as well be back in Dallas. This is the kind of deal I'd like to make. Hold a gun to a man's head, and then say you're willin' to bargain. But what in Christ's name could he *want*?"

"Actually, all he wants is your son."

The trap seemed perfect, and the Natural Hunter was right where he wanted to be. He had stationed himself on a dry rock in the middle of the river, armed with a spear. The Aging Master and the Gray Female were in the woods, one on either side. When the creatures in the raft saw him, they would turn. Which way they turned would be a matter of chance. But it would give him the target that he wanted. He wanted the black beast who had twice humiliated him. He chose the spear specifically for that reason. The Aging Master and the Gray Female had access to all the other weapons the things carried, except the spear. That animal was his alone.

The people in the Halvorssens' boat were exhausted. Bjorn's arms felt heavy, and even his eyes ached with the constant strain of keeping a firm course on the river. Even so, this journey must soon come to an end. The sun was low in the sky, and the old nana had said there would be a lodge at the end of the day's travel. The creatures apparently would not attack—they must be occupied with Glassman and Bob and Betty Miller. Bjorn felt an unwelcome sense of responsibility; the boy would now be his to look after, for his daughter, he could see, was enamored of him.

Then, as they rounded the bend, Bjorn saw the black creature on the rock in the middle of the river. He called out, but Mkomo, who had seen him too, had already rushed to the front of the craft.

Mkomo saw the spear the other held. He smiled, knowing this would be a contest. They would judge the limits of their range; whoever could throw the farthest with accuracy would be the winner. Mkomo admired this idea of a contest, the more so because he had never met a being who could throw a spear as far as he.

"Papa!" cried Kirsten from her place in the bottom of the boat, where she tended the still sleeping boy. "Turn the boat."

Bjorn looked uneasily to either side. Nothing appeared in the woods, but quite obviously the creature would not have exposed himself that openly in front of them without some kind of support. Bjorn regretted giving his rifle to Bob Miller. He could have easily brought down the creature.

That was what they were *meant* to think, Halvorssen realized. They expected him to turn the boat toward the shore. Therefore, he would keep to the center of the stream. He would have to rely on Mkomo's skill.

Janet Gore moved up behind Mkomo, drawing her .45 automatic. "I want him," she said. "It might be the one that killed Ian."

Mkomo brushed her back, wishing she wouldn't interfere with his concentration. "Your weapon has no range," he said. "The spear he holds will be in my heart before you can bring it down."

"You first, then," she said, "but when you miss."

"I shall not miss," he snarled. "Stay back!"

The boat moved forward, Bjorn steering it into the swiftest part of the current. He wanted it over with quickly, and whatever the outcome, he wanted to get past this place before any of the other aliens could make their appearance.

Mkomo measured the distance in his mind, then calculated the place on the river from which he could hurl his spear without fail. Surprisingly, he saw the creature's arm tense before the raft reached that part of the stream.

It loosed its spear. With a cry, Mkomo just had time to duck. The distance was too far; though the throw was accurate, he had the half second longer to react. He looked behind him as he heard the others cry out. The spear had gone through Janet Gore's chest, and she staggered backwards, still trying to raise her automatic.

Mkomo could not think of her; he turned back, saw that the place in the water he had marked was upon them. He smiled as he saw the creature unarmed. He threw, feeling the good snap in the upper muscle of his arm that meant the throw was perfect.

At the last second, just as Mkomo threw, the Natural Hunter took the only course open to him. He leaped with the full extension of his long, thin legs. The sight made the humans gasp. Mkomo's spear sailed harmlessly past its target, but even he felt a twinge of awe as the Natural Hunter's body sailed out over the water. He landed close to the opposite bank and immediately sank beneath the surface.

"Is it swimming toward us, beloved?" called Bjorn to his daughter.

"I can't see." She leaned over the side of the boat, searching the surface of the stream for air bubbles. "Oh, Papa," she called. "Get us past quickly." He needed no urging.

At the same time, shots rang out from the woods, and Mkomo turned to see another of the aliens run to the edge of the bank with a rifle. He grabbed for one of their own rifles in the bottom of the boat, but it was too late: they were out of range.

Their joy at reaching the lodge at last was tempered by the necessity of burying Janet Gore.

"It was not my fault," said Mkomo as they lowered her body into the ground. No one answered him. He seemed to be speaking to Janet Gore.

When they had covered her, Mkomo spoke more words. They were in his own tongue, which none of them understood.

When he finished, he looked around at them. "She would understand the words," he said. "She was of Biandra. I said the words one says for a warrior."

Kosho helped Kirsten to wake Billy, and they half carried him to the lodge. Kirsten was not bothered by the minor wound she had suffered in her underwater flight, but Charles, whose shoulder was still bandaged, lagged behind. Kosho dropped back to speak to him.

"Your father does not seem to be quite the man I remembered."

"When you took those photographs? They were really bad. You know, I saw them in a magazine in Switzerland. I never knew things were that bad in Biandra. The other kids . . . You know, that school had all kinds of crooks' sons in it. We used to laugh about it. Their fathers were dictators, organized-crime leaders, billionaires who made their money in all kinds of dirty ways, but they gave me the hardest time of all, because of your pictures.

"But you're right," Charles continued, nodding. "I think he's changed. He's scared. I understood what he said back there at the grave. He wasn't just saying words for a warrior. He was calling on her spirit for help. I think missing the dude that was on the rock got to him."

"A man who lives by power must live to see it ebb," said Kosho.

The lodge was warm, comfortably appointed as the other refuges had been, and held a groaning table of food. They attacked it with the hunger two days on the river had given them.

Warmth and food seemed to revive Billy to full consciousness.

Kirsten told him what had happened to his parents. He took in the story silently. "If only I hadn't been so tired," he said sadly.

"There was nothing you could have done," said Kirsten. "You did everything you could. If something happened to them, as it did to my mother, you must not blame yourself."

He gnawed on a piece of chicken. "No," he said suddenly. "They're not dead." He turned to Kosho. "I'm getting better at it. I can feel them out there. Mom's terribly afraid. I can't quite read her. I can't get to where she is. But I know she's alive. And Dad's safe. He's very near."

Kosho and Kirsten exchanged glances. "Maybe you'd better not tire yourself, Billy," suggested Kirsten.

"No," he said, shaking his head stubbornly. "Dad's coming. He's all right. He'll be here in a few minutes. He's got something he wants to ask me."

Chapter Twenty-One

Betty Miller was terrified. When she wakened, she found herself lying on her back on a cool, soft, mossy surface. She had been stripped naked, and one of the things was watching her. She was not bound, but as she moved to cover herself, she felt the creature stop her. It did not move; it only looked at her, but she felt it freeze some part of her brain, paralyzing her. It touched her again, far more intimately than if it had been touching her body. It controlled her, and she felt it soothe her, calm her in some way as easily as she might stroke a cat.

In spite of herself, she responded to the mind touch, and her fear gradually dwindled. She remained slightly uneasy, as if knowing that there were thoughts too terrible to think just beyond the reach of her mind. But she settled back, secure in the feeling that nothing could *really* hurt her.

She started again when the others returned, but the one who controlled her made her see that they meant her no harm. As they came to look at her, she felt that this might not be true. Their features were strange to her, but she found that there were certain differences by which she could tell them apart. The one who seemed most like her—was it a female?—had the same black sight-slit where eyes ought to be as the rest, but behind it she sensed a malevolence, an abiding hatred. Her controller had to work extra hard, she felt—was it a he?—to quell her awareness of that feeling.

They began to talk among themselves. She could hear only a series of meaningless squeaks, but noticed that they had many movements by which they conveyed meaning. She realized that if she exerted herself, she could reach back to the mind of the one who controlled her and understand them.

It shook her terribly to realize, for a second, what it was they were talking about. Her controller felt her awareness then, and reached farther (*Oh, damn him*, she thought) to make her go to sleep. But just in the moment when she felt herself losing consciousness she reminded herself with amazement: they were talking about Billy.

Billy and Kosho stood outside the lodge. Glassman and Billy's father had not shown up yet, and Kosho—despite his faith in Billy's ability—knew that even the wisest of men could be led astray by hope. If Billy were wrong, Kosho wanted to be there to soften the blow that the realization of the loss of his parents would be.

"What you said to me earlier," said Billy. "I've been thinking about it."

"What was that?"

"You know, about all this being an illusion of some sort. But look up. Could the stars be an illusion too?"

"It is possible. It would not be necessary, however, since we are obviously still on earth."

"Why obviously?" asked Billy. Kosho admired the question.

"All of us were brought here by a conventional transport. Jet planes are not capable of leaving the earth's atmosphere."

Billy considered this. "Could you tell where we were, on earth, by looking at the stars?"

Kosho looked upward, surprised at the simplicity of the idea. He blinked, trying to find his bearings. He stared upward for a long time. "I think . . . no, it is true. The constellations are unfamiliar to me. Either they too are an illusion or . . . wait! There is one other possibility. Let us ask the others."

Inside, they explained Billy's idea. "I do not recognize the conformation of the stars," said Kosho. "But it occurred to me that they may be the constellations of the Southern Hemisphere, which are different from those seen in Japan, Europe, North America." He looked at Mkomo. "Could you confirm my theory?"

"You presume I have a knowledge of the stars," said Mkomo. "We Biandrans are not a seafaring people."

"But you were supposed to be able to walk from one end of

your country to another without a guide. Was that a legend you created?"

"Not at all. It is quite true. You are perceptive. The people thought that I was able to find my way among them by magical means. It is clever of you to realize that I used the stars as a guide. My father taught me."

"Then perhaps you can guide us now."

Mkomo shrugged, and led the way outside. He stood for a while to accustom his eyes to the darkness of the sky. When he finally began to scan the constellations overhead, they saw his obvious surprise.

"Do you recognize them?" Kosho asked.

Mkomo waved his hand, turned himself in a circle to orient himself. "At first, I thought . . . but look." He pointed. "You see the group of four stars there, two of them very bright, the other two not so bright? They seem to form a cross."

"Yes." The formation was easy to pick out.

"That is what navigators call the Southern Cross. And there near it, a group of three, known as the Australian Triangle. Using those, I can pick out the others. But they are not where they should be."

"What do you mean?" said Billy.

Mkomo shrugged. "Their position indicates that we are thousands of miles south of my own Biandra. But if that were so, we would be in the regions of intense cold. We would be near Antarctica."

"That's right," said Billy. "I knew it."

Mkomo glanced at him. "Except, little boy, we are obviously *not* in a region of great cold. Even the snow-covered mountains of yesterday were a balmy Mediterranean resort compared to the cold that exists in Antarctica. And we stand here now, lightly covered. We would be frozen statues if we were that near Antarctica."

"But what other explanation is there?" asked Kosho.

"That the stars are not to be trusted," said Mkomo. "Just a moment ago, I thought you were a clever man."

"But that is impossible," said Kosho.

"With Western technology, nothing is impossible. Did you not think it strange that a mighty mountain region lay next to a wilderness river? How far have we traveled in three days? Certainly not a hundred kilometers. Such terrain as we have gone through has no natural counterpart."

"Yes, but . . . the stars cannot lie."

"We were willing to believe that the Americans had created this strange amusement park here, simply for pleasure. Now we are told that it is in fact the creation of creatures from another planet. Perhaps they are more powerful than the Americans, more clever than you Japanese. Then they could seem to make the stars move, if they wished."

" 'Seem to make,' " said Billy. "You see, Kosho? He believes it's an illusion too."

"Not so fast," said Mkomo. "What are you calling an illusion?"

"All this," said Billy, excitedly, sweeping his arms to take in the landscape. "Kosho thinks it's imaginary. And this afternoon, when I was asleep, I dreamed just . . . just what you said. That we were really in a place that seemed very cold, where the wind always blew, and everything was frozen."

Mkomo and Kosho exchanged glances. Mkomo laughed, and twirled his finger in a circle next to his ear. He looked at Billy. "You're telling me that all this"—he stamped his foot on the ground—"is not real?"

"I know it sounds strange."

"I prefer to believe that the stars lie," said Mkomo. "If what you say is true, then there is no hope for us. These creatures could make the rocks change to fire, the ground on which we stand turn into a raging sea. Is that not so?"

Billy admitted that this was true.

"Then why do they not do it, even to save themselves? You killed one, true or not? You took credit for it."

"Yes, but . . ." Billy paused. He could not expect Mkomo to believe what had really happened. He was not sure if he wanted him to believe. Or know.

"Why didn't the creature turn you into a toad? Why didn't the one I speared turn *me* into a toad? Instead, they ran from me."

"The old granny said that there were rules to the Hunt which they would obey," offered Kosho.

"Hah. Let me tell you, when your life is in danger, really in danger—you understand?—so that either you or another must die, there are no rules that you would not cheerfully break."

Their conversation was interrupted by a shout. They turned to see two figures emerging from the woods along the bank of the river.

"Dad!" Billy called out. "I knew you'd come!" He ran

toward the two figures, and Kosho nodded as he saw it was indeed Bob Miller and Glassman. *So he knew*, Kosho thought. *He was right.*

Billy reached them, embracing his father. "You're all right, Dad."

"Billy . . . your mother . . . I couldn't . . ."

"Don't worry, Dad, she's alive. I know it. I really do."

Bob Miller nodded. His son's sudden affection would make it difficult to tell him. But there was no reason to tell him. No one but the old woman knew what he was supposed to do to get his wife back. Miller had wanted to tell Glassman, just sort of to ask what he should do. But there was no point in that. Glassman might have told Billy, might have tried to stop what was going to happen. What he had to do.

Glassman still didn't understand why they weren't dead. Bob Miller's explanation that the old grandmother had come to save them didn't make any sense.

Glassman sat with Kosho in front of the dwindling fire now, retelling the story of what he had seen. The others had all gone to bed. The old woman had reappeared, telling them that their journey tomorrow should begin as early as possible, to avoid the heat. What heat? They were comfortable in front of the fire. Kosho had told him of the theory that the entire environment was imaginary, but Glassman was as skeptical as Mkomo.

Kosho considered the tale Glassman had told. "The boy believes his mother is alive."

Glassman nodded. "I found no evidence that she was harmed."

Musing, Kosho took another sip of his cup of warm sake. "We have seen them—the alien hunters—and they are eager to kill. Yet they did not kill you or Bob Miller. And they may not have killed Betty Miller."

"They wouldn't kill anyone not carrying a weapon."

Kosho shook his head. "Both the Millers were carrying weapons. My friend, I believe you are a skeptical man."

"That is true," said Glassman with a turning of his lips.

"I cannot expect you to believe me when I say that I believe the boy has some kind of powers that you or I can only guess at. Powers that may rival those of these alien creatures."

"*Mishegoss*."

"I do not know the meaning. Excuse me."

"It means I find that hard to believe. Look at him."

"In my culture, we do not always judge ability by the appearance of the one who holds it."

"You correct me justly. Even so, I have not seen the miracles you describe."

"I ask only one thing," said Kosho. "I wish you will help me to follow the boy and his father tomorrow."

"I might as well be with you as with the others," said Glassman.

Bob Miller could not sleep. It was not the pain in his bandaged hand. He was facing something his life had totally unprepared him for. The phrase for it was not in his vocabulary. It was a moral choice.

His wife or his son.

There was the possibility he might lose both. What if Betty were not even alive? The creature had shown him only her clothes—they were hers, all right—but that didn't mean she was alive. Nor did it mean they would give her back, even if he did turn Billy over to them.

Why in hell did they want Billy in the first place? They had plenty of firepower to just *kill* him, if that was what they wanted. But according to the old woman, the creatures seemed to feel that Billy was something special.

How could they think that? Bob Miller had been worrying about his son for years. Always in some corner, reading, or watching television. Never interested in getting some air or going out to the club or even finding some friends of his own. He never seemed to be doing *any*thing.

Bob Miller got angry again just thinking about it. His friends at the club had kids they could talk about. They were on the football team, or were about to get into a decent college, or were making money or winning prizes. Even the ones whose kids got into trouble had something to talk about. But Billy wasn't interested in anything. Bob didn't even think the kid smoked dope.

For someone who read so many damn books, you would think he'd at least make decent grades. But he barely scraped by. They had thought that sending him to Culver would do something for him—make a man out of him, anyway. But they sent him back, with a letter saying that he was "unsuitable." That was the word for him, all right.

There was a knock on the door. "Who is it?" Bob Miller

called out, looking for the new Purdy that the old lady had given him as a replacement for the one he'd lost.

"It's only me," said Billy.

Bob Miller turned on the light next to his bed. "Come on in," he said.

There he was, gangly and awkward, half tripping over his own feet. Miller felt a twinge of shame that he had produced such a son.

"I could feel you worrying about me, Dad," he said.

"Worrying? What do you mean?"

"Dad, I don't know how to explain it to you. I can read minds, that's all." At his father's look of fright, he added quickly. "I wasn't reading yours, though, Dad. I don't like to do it. It was just . . . I knew you were thinking about me. I thought you wanted to ask me something."

Bob Miller cringed and wanted to move away as his son crossed the room toward him. "Keep away," he said, raising his hand.

Billy looked at him in surprise. "Dad, I won't . . . Dad, you can't be afraid of me?"

"No, 'course not. I just . . . why would I be afraid?"

"I don't know," said Billy miserably. "It just seemed that way. Dad, I've just got to *talk* to somebody. I don't know what to do!"

"Damn it, what can we do? We're trapped, that's all. Maybe we can fight our way out of it somehow. Only thing we *can* do."

"Dad, you can't fight them. Something Mkomo said earlier set me to thinking."

"That black bastard's full of lies. Don't listen to him. Or the Jap either. He's filling your head with funny thoughts."

"No, Dad. It's me that's having the funny thoughts. Dad, all this around us is really . . . kind of make-believe. It's not real. But I can see through it."

"Billy, listen, son, it's all been too much for you."

"It is too much for me, but I'm not crazy, Dad, really. I've got . . . Something has *happened* to me. You know when I jumped in the water and swam ashore this morning? Dad, you know I couldn't do something like that."

"Well, a man sometimes responds to pressure, to danger. I knew a man who was chased by a bear once . . ."

"I know, but Dad, please listen. I changed into a fish."

Bob Miller stared. "Oh, my God, Billy."

He hung his head. "I know what it sounds like, Dad, but . . . aw, Dad, I'm just really sorry I can't make you understand. But, Dad, really this is true: I'm the only one who *can* really fight them. And I wanted to tell you—I'm going to go and help Mom."

"Wha-at?"

"I don't know if I can really do anything, but I'm the only one who can."

"No, no. Now listen, boy. Your dad knows best. I looked all over them woods for your mom. She isn't there."

"I know it, Dad. They're keeping her someplace. She's afraid."

"No. Billy, she'll be all right. She's not in danger."

Billy looked at him. "Dad," he said quietly. "How do you know that?"

"Why, *you* told me. And that Granny. She said so too."

"She did? When was that?"

Miller's eyes shifted away from his son's.

"Oh, this afternoon. Late. Out there. That's why I decided to come in."

"But, Dad, you acted like you don't trust her."

"No, but she brought . . . some of your mother's clothes. That tailored hunting jacket that she bought at Nieman's. She's just resting, or something. They're going to let her go."

"I don't understand that."

"Well, there's a whole *lot* here we don't none of us understand. But don't go off thinkin' you can do something by yourself. Stay with me, and if she don't show up, we'll try something. Trust your dad. Just get some rest tonight, Billy boy."

Billy hesitated. "Did she really say that?"

"Sure. Let's give it a chance. It makes more sense than running out there in the dark where them things are waitin' for you."

"I don't know . . ."

"Billy. Do as your dad says. He knows best."

"I wish I could make you understand."

"We'll think about it tomorrow."

Glumly, Billy agreed. After he had gone, Bob Miller lay awake for a long time. When he finally slept, he left the light on.

Chapter Twenty-Two

The sight that greeted Mkomo in the morning made him recall the conversation of the night before with Billy and Kosho. "So they are, perhaps, right," he muttered. Outside, the river seemed to have dried up. It ran now in a narrow trickle. The forest that had sheltered the lodge had utterly disappeared. Now, the terrain was only a vast desert—barren, dry, and hot. There was no longer a fire in the fireplace; heavy air conditioners made the temperature inside the lodge comfortable. But the sun was rising, and Mkomo knew what the old woman had meant when she warned them to get an early start. He went to waken Charles.

Kosho was awakened by the sun filtering through the window. He accepted their new environment with equanimity, and went downstairs to hear Mkomo urging his son to eat lightly, but to consume as much liquid as he could.

Gradually, the others made their appearance. The last was a bleary-eyed Bob Miller. He glanced at his son, who was in conversation with Kosho. "We're travelin' together, Billy," he said loudly.

Granny made her appearance. Mkomo rose from his place. "We know all your secrets," he announced confidently.

"Really?" she said. "It's enough to make an old woman blush."

Mkomo rushed to put his hands on her shoulders. "You will answer our questions, and you cannot escape so easily." Suddenly he was grasping at empty air. Granny was standing near the door. "It is not good for you to touch me," she said. "It might be dangerous . . . for you. And of course I will answer your questions."

"We know that the desert is imaginary," said Mkomo.

"Oh, I assure you it will seem quite real," she replied. "You will find it hot, and dry. And each moment you waste time it will grow hotter."

"Suppose we decide to wait here?" said Glassman.

"The air conditioners will not function," said Granny. "And there will be no more food or drink after you have been supplied with enough for the journey. The only way you can eat again is to cross the desert."

"How far?" asked Bjorn Halvorssen.

"Not far," she said. "Thirty miles, or forty-eight kilometers."

"I cannot walk that far in such heat," said Halvorssen. "Nor can my daughter. We are not used to desert conditions."

"It will be difficult, but not impossible," said Granny.

"Wait a minute," said Charles. "You showed us where to find snowmobiles before. You said we can have the equipment we want. What about something . . ."

"Dune buggies," said Kirsten, clapping her hands. "I have always wanted to travel in a dune buggy, the way everyone does in California."

Mkomo beamed. "Our children are worthy of their parents." He looked inquisitively at Bjorn Halvorssen, then at Kirsten. "You are not, by chance, related to the royal family of Denmark?"

"I'm afraid not," said Bjorn, not liking the way he looked at Kirsten.

"Only a thought," assured Mkomo. "But yes," he said, turning back to Granny. "We must have these . . . motorized conveyances."

"I don't think you're entering into the spirit of the Hunt," said Granny crossly. "It will take me some time to assemble them."

Billy sensed she was about to leave, and waved at her. "Granny," he said. "I want to talk with you."

"I am sorry, Billy," she said. "The Hunters feel you are . . . progressing enough on your own. I am forbidden to answer any more of your questions."

"I want one thing understood," said the Commander. "No one is to interfere with the boy or his father. I have arranged a meeting with them."

"I have no quarrel with that," said the Natural Hunter. "My quarry is the black one, the great one with his primitive weapons."

A retort crossed the Gray Female's mind, but she suppressed it. Instead, she leveled her gaze at the Commander. "From what you have told us, I presume you are afraid that this young one is capable of making the Discovery at any time. If he does, I assume that all the Old Rules are inoperative. I will not stand armed only with this thing," she said, waving the crude projectile thrower she had chosen for today's Hunting.

The Aging Master indicated his desire to speak. "The Commander has conveyed to me his confidence that he can subdue the young one. He has *not* actually made the Discovery. That should be apparent to all."

"Because we have his mother as a hostage," said the Gray Female. "And he has not come here."

"Is it your intention to bring him here?" asked the Scientist eagerly.

The Commander regarded him coldly. "If that is possible," he said. "But you must stay here to see that his mother does not send out signals to tell him where she is. It is possible that the potential for evolving to the Discovery came from her."

"I have her under complete control," said the Scientist.

"But you must keep her safe," said the Commander. "I gave my word on that."

"You gave your word? To an animal?" The Gray Female gaped, expressing her astonishment. "I thought you held your honor highly."

The Commander indicated his offense at her words. "Highly enough to fight in the spirit of the Old Rules. I fight these creatures on their terms. And they, too, have a code of honor."

The Gray Female glanced at the Aging Master to see his reaction to this improper assertion. He sat impassively, indicating neither approval nor disapproval.

"What about the one who carries no weapon?" she said. "Is that a mark of their honor?"

"The creature acted in a brave manner yesterday," said the Commander. "Though without a weapon, it attacked me. I had no desire to kill it, for I wished to establish trust between the boy's father and me. Eventually, however, one of us may wish to engage it without a weapon. Or we may wish to let it go."

"Let it go?" said the Natural Hunter. "I did not risk *my*

honor, and considerable expense, to look and then let go. I came to Hunt."

"Then let us Hunt," said the Aging Master. The discussion was over.

"One thing more," said Mkomo warily to Granny. "There is sufficient gasoline in these vehicles to take us across the desert?"

"Oh, yes," she said. "More than sufficient. You realize, of course, that since you chose to utilize this method of transportation, the Hunters may choose it as well."

"I have more experience with driving than they have," replied Mkomo. "I love to drive."

"That will be your advantage," said Granny.

There were four of the dune buggies. Mkomo and Charles were in one; Kirsten and her father in another; Glassman and Kosho in the third; finally, Billy and his father.

Mkomo took the lead, speeding off over the sand, seeking to test the limits of his vehicle by urging it up the nearest high dune. They heard his triumphant lion's-cry resound across the desert as his dune buggy topped the crest, all four wheels off the ground. With their oversized tires, low-slung construction, and roll bars, the dune buggies gave their occupants a feeling of invulnerability.

Mkomo was soon far out in front. Bjorn Halvorssen drove more cautiously, feeling the responsibility of having his daughter beside him, although she urged him to go faster. Her voice reminded him of Bibi urging him to accept the opportunity to go on this adventure.

Glassman was driving the third vehicle. The motor was high-pitched and noisy, but he was able to make himself heard to Kosho. "The Beast of Biandra doesn't realize how dangerous it is to drive through the sand this way."

"It does not seem dangerous," replied Kosho.

"This toy is not like a half-track. But even an army vehicle can turn over if you approach the dunes in the wrong way. Still, we could move faster than this if you weren't so concerned with letting the boy and his father stay up with us."

"There is a need," said Kosho. "Of that I am convinced."

Bob Miller wished the others would pull farther away from him. The old woman said they would come in sight of what would look like a ghost town. He was supposed to turn in there. He didn't know exactly how they were going to arrange this. He looked over at his son. Billy looked like he was perfectly okay. His eyes were staring ahead. "You feeling all right, Billy?" he asked.

"It's going to change soon," said Billy.

His father pressed on the accelerator. *The hell of it was, he sounded so sure of himself.*

Not long afterward, Glassman nudged Kosho. "They're going to make it harder than Mkomo thinks," he said. He pointed to a dark spot in the sky ahead that seemed to grow rapidly in size. "Mkomo's going to run right into it."

"What is it?" said Kosho.

"Sandstorm."

The Scientist walked over to observe the specimen visually. She felt fear at his approach. He sent out impulses that would calm her, but studied the source of her fear. He was surprised to see that the root of it was sexual. She felt vulnerable at being stripped of her garments, as if that alone might signal her willingness to a sexual approach, even though he himself must surely not resemble a male specimen of her species with mating intention.

That was a clue to their evolutionary success. He could see it in her body. The primary sex organs were interior, as in the females of most successful species, so her body could embrace and nurture the young for a period of time to allow uninterrupted, fully protected development. Yet this creature had secondary sex organs that were unusually protuberant, obviously with the intention of attracting a mate. And even the site of the primary organs was clearly marked by a patch of vestigial hair, pointing like an arrow. No wonder she felt that he would be urged into mating by the sight of her.

He soothed her brain. The Commander had forbidden him from experimenting. But the Commander was a superstitious fool, still believing that the Initiation Ceremony was the source of the Discovery power. Didn't he realize that just by controlling this specimen with the force of his mental energy he was experimenting on her?

This species was so unusually prolific, in comparison to his own, that they must have an inordinate amount of sexual energy. That fit in with the Scientist's opinion that the source of the Discovery was the urge to reproduce. In his own species, that urge was almost entirely channeled into a desire to kill. For the society, that had been good. They had not overpopulated their planet, as so many otherwise successful species had done. But somehow the unfulfilled sexual urge had enabled them to make the Discovery. He wished that he himself had been able to overcome his disgust for the physical necessities of mating. He had never had that experience. But this creature had. Perhaps, through her, he would be able to reenact those feelings that she had felt at the time of mating. He spread himself throughout her brain until he controlled her utterly.

Now he felt her fear, understood it. It was strange to him, and yet familiar. She too felt the disgust and shame he had felt when contemplating mating. He was surprised to realize that her feelings were so similar. Yet she had gone through it, for some reason that was utterly foreign to him. He let himself enter into the memory of it. *Bob likes it,* she thought. That no doubt referred to her mate. But who would experience something so revolting because another being wished it?

He had to start at a more primary level. He forced his way back to memories that had long been buried. He revivified the dormant cells, found himself in the memories of infancy. A helpless creature. Held close. Warmth, nourishment. He sucked at her mother's breast with her, understood the meaning of those secondary organs.

Another figure appeared in her memory. A great, heavy figure, rough. There was a smell associated with it. It was important, that smell, and the roughness of the hands. It separated the creature's feelings for all who came after into two categories.

Male, and female. The Scientist was intrigued. There was a greater feeling of separation between the sexes in this species than in the members of his own race. There was an emotional content to the sensation of separation. It had a great deal to do with the creature's willingness to undergo the mating process.

This separation was puzzling. It was almost as if the species were two separate, but mutually necessary, races.

The Scientist probed further. Throughout the youth of this creature its experiences reinforced the consciousness of that sexual separation. The countless ways in which it was emphasized were a fascinating mosaic, to one who saw the pattern. They lived together in small family groups, but there was always that separation, and as the mating awakening approached it grew more and more pronounced.

In her mind, he reached the time of mating readiness. He felt the creature's awareness of her own development, felt the unease, the embarrassment—all quite similar to feelings his own People felt. Yet there was a countervailing, in fact contradictory, feeling that made the experience of the growth of the body especially confusing. The Scientist felt it, and was totally in sympathy for her impressions of shame—for the contradictory feeling was an unwilling attraction for the opposite sex.

This was significant. Despite his revulsion, the Scientist made himself probe onward. In his own experience, the growth of the body had produced quite a different feeling. As he grew closer to the time when his sexual maturity was celebrated in the Initiation Ceremony, he had developed an aversion for the opposite sex. The reaction was normal in his species. The ones who fought most successfully against it succeeded in mating, and thus preserved the race. But normally, those who mated lost the urge to become . . . Hunters.

He withdrew, keeping only a soothing grip on her brain, for he realized that her feelings were becoming too intense for him to comfortably experience. He had reawakened years-old memories in her that he could not fully quell. She was at this moment yearning for a sexual contact.

The Scientist rested. He was determined to find out the components of that sexual yearning. He sensed that beyond it lay the Discovery-awakening. There was a path that these beings had chosen not to take. One that the young one, the offspring of this particular specimen, was now taking.

Why?

"Dad," said Billy. "There's going to be a sandstorm. We'd better look for cover."

At the same time, as Mkomo glimpsed the onrushing dark cloud, he saw racing along its edge toward him two other dune buggies. Confident that his speed had put him well in front of Miller, Halvorssen, and the rest, he realized that these other vehicles must contain the Hunters.

He swerved to his left, hoping to put the main body of the sandstorm between him and the pursuing ones. Even so, he knew that soon he must seek cover of some kind. The open vehicle would offer no protection against the blowing sand, and if caught without shelter he and his son might well be buried alive.

At the top of a dune he caught sight of something other than the endless sand. He could hardly believe his eyes, and thought at once of Billy Miller's warning that all this was a mere illusion. He was wary of a trap set to catch him and his son. Yet there was no other recourse. He swung the vehicle in the direction of what he had seen, and at the top of the next dune, with the sky growing darker every minute, he saw it spread out in the valley below.

If not an illusion, it was certainly a phantasm. What was the name for such a place? A deserted village, yet one that resembled those found in the Americans' western movies. A ghost town.

Chapter Twenty-Three

The Commander had ordered Granny to prepare this place as a refuge where he could meet Billy and Bob Miller. He was annoyed to see Mkomo and his son approach, and moved into one of the buildings where he would be out of sight. He had no desire to tangle with these two others at this moment. They were unimportant; sooner or later the Natural Hunter would overtake them and bag his Kill. The Commander hoped no harm would come to them here, however, for he wished to encourage the relationship of trust he had established with the father of the Discovery-bound youth.

Mkomo and Charles abandoned their vehicle and rushed for one of the buildings. The door was weak with dry rot, and gave inward at a touch. The interior of the building was dark; what little light there was came through windows coated with what appeared to be years of steadily accumulated grime and dust. "Be careful," cautioned Mkomo.

"There can't be anyone here, Pop," said Charles. "Did you spot them? They were way off, chasing us on their own buggies."

"I saw them. With luck, they will be diverted by one of the other groups. In any case, they could not find us here once the storm hits."

His words were cut short by the sound of another dune buggy motor, approaching from the same direction they had come. "You have that popgun loaded?" asked Mkomo.

"Sure," said Charles, confidently patting the holster where he had slung his Colt Peacemaker. "I'm itching to get another shot at them."

"You will remain absolutely quiet," said Mkomo, in a voice that achieved its desired effect. Mkomo peeped through a crack in the door. "It is only the Americans," he said.

Charles stepped forward, but Mkomo shoved him back. "Aw, Pop, there's safety in numbers," he said.

"That shows how little you learned in Switzerland. A man travels fastest when he travels alone." He looked at Charles. "Remember that I slow my progress for you only because you are my son. And besides, there is something strange about that boy. He knows too much. The Japanese believes he has special powers. Who knows? At any rate, it can only be to our advantage to let him encounter the Hunters while we watch."

Charles knew better than to argue with his father, but he didn't like the idea. The old man was getting slow. Kosho saw that, and so did everyone who saw him miss with his spear throw yesterday. If the American dude had special powers, then it would be better to stay with him. You had a better chance of getting out alive.

As Mkomo watched, the American father looked around at the buildings. He seemed to be expecting something.

"Dad, we'd better take cover," said Billy.

"Yeah, sure, it's just that I thought . . ."

"Dad, you're looking for something. Did you see someone else come in here? It wasn't Kirsten. She and her father found a rock formation to shelter them. They're all right."

Bob Miller cringed. He wished Billy would stop all that craziness. Maybe he would be all right in the hands of these things. Maybe they only wanted to get a close look at him. Maybe they could cure him.

"Dad! There's Granny!"

The old woman appeared at the other end of the dusty street. She was gesturing toward them.

"Stay here," said Bob Miller. "I'll see what she wants."

Billy did as he was told, but he followed his father mentally. He wished he had the courage to read his mind. His father was acting strangely. He was nervous, unsure of himself. It made Billy feel upset to see his father like this. He was usually so much . . . in command. Losing Mom had been a strain on him.

At a certain point, Billy felt a barrier. It was strange to him. He had experienced no limit like this to his power. He could feel much farther away, to Kirsten and her father. But there was something . . . a ring of power that was stronger than his, that kept him from following his father, even though he could still see him. He gasped as he saw one of the aliens emerge from a building. He started to shout to warn his father, but checked himself. The alien was unarmed, and his father clearly saw it. He even moved a few steps closer.

"Where is she?" asked Bob Miller.

"She is perfectly safe," said Granny. "She will be returned to you after the Commander has taken the boy."

Bob Miller shook his head. "I want her now. Here."

"That is not possible," said Granny.

The Commander decided to risk moving the ring of his power farther up the street. If he could catch the boy unawares, there would be no need to argue with this creature about details.

They're talking, thought Billy. *Granny is telling Dad what the other one wants. What? What could he want?* Then he noticed that the limits of the power he felt were gradually extending up the street on either side. Toward him. He sensed he was being encircled by it.

The answer flashed through his brain. *Me. It's me they want, because they're afraid. They know I've found out . . . what's really going on. And Dad.* He choked back a despairing cry. *He's going to give me to them.*

The Scientist tested the nervous system of the creature. He made her stand, walk, expel bodily wastes. She had a taboo against that, but he calmed her easily. She was as easy to control as the simplest lure. He made her lie down.

As he examined her sexual function, he found that there were, as in many advanced species, regularly spaced time periods in which a female was fertile. But amazingly, she responded to sexual stimulation even in times when she was not fertile. In fact, she could be encouraged to sexual activity at any time.

It was a staggering waste of energy. He explored her memories, and found that she was not unique in that aspect—it was normal. What a waste! All this pointless sexual coupling, yet they still had an advanced civilization, and one of them had even progressed to the verge of the Discovery.

He searched through her memory patterns, trying to find a reason for this incessant sexual responsiveness. He saw that it reached its height at a certain period not long after the sexual awakening. Yet, remarkably, they actually had a taboo against sexual contact just at that time. It seemed to be a taboo enforced by the elders largely as a means of prolonging their dominance over the family group. Many young people violated the taboo, as she had, but they did it in secret, and in most it brought feelings of guilt, further retarding their emotional and intellectual development. It was a strange system, seemingly designed to delay an individual's full acceptance into adult society for as long as possible.

The Scientist could see that although the female specimen had herself violated the taboo, and had knowledge of many others who had done likewise, she believed that her son strictly observed it. Her memory even showed the fear that he might not be developing his sexual powers normally.

Suppose, the Scientist thought, that the enormous sexual energy that flowed through him really had been thwarted. If true, then that would account for the excess of energy that had led him to attain the Discovery.

A hypothesis suddenly became clear to the Scientist. If they merely placed the boy into the proper situation, provided a willing partner . . . then his energy might harmlessly dissipate. He could, if the treatment were prolonged, even lose all memory of those powers he had already exhibited. It was marvelously simple. The Commander would be very glad to hear of this.

The flush of success emboldened the Scientist. He had, he believed, succeeded in finding a solution to their present dilemma, proving the value of his work to the expedition. When the Guardians heard of his achievement, they might well allow him to experiment further.

Or perhaps not. Superstitious fools like the Commander, they might throw a cloak over the entire matter. Ultimately, they were afraid of finding the true, natural source of the Discovery. Obviously, the case of this boy was unique to his species, so far as they knew. The explanation he had found explained only *why* he had made the Discovery. The physiological source of it—in this boy, and in the People—was still to be determined.

He must use this chance to find it in the only specimen he had to work with. Betty Miller lay exhausted, soiled, and drained. He had released his hold on her briefly in the elation of finding the solution. As he turned his thoughts to her once again, she tried to draw away from him. She was powerless, and felt his being violate hers once again, felt his touch on the synapses of her brain, the nerves of her body, her organs. . . . She fought unsuccessfully to keep him away, then searched within herself for a place where she could remain herself.

He felt that fright, experienced her flight, and decided to allow her the freedom to explore her own potential for power. An incredible thought occurred to him. Was it possible that she could be brought to the Discovery while he was within her?

He followed her, pursuing her to the core of her being, that part of her that she considered self. He was not surprised when the chase led him downward to the sex organs. But Betty's spirit did not reach them; it veered away.

At the very lowest tip of the creature's spine, there was a focus of energy that seemed to have no physical function. She retreated there, and he probed, pried at the hiding place. Suddenly he was aware of a change—from that intense point of energy, the female turned like a cornered animal to face him. He felt the immense force of the entire race located there. *Life force! The source of Discovery!*

The spreading ring had not yet closed around Billy. In his mind, he extended himself backwards, finding the opening. He could still escape. Not by running, nor with the dune buggy. He could feel the strength and speed with which the ring was closing. He had to change. He had to remember what he had done before.

He thought of Kirsten, saw her huddling in the shelter she had found with her father. He looked up. The dust cloud had darkened the sky and was nearly upon the little town. Billions of particles of dry desert matter. He struggled to reach up there, felt himself flowing into the cloud of particles. Then he was among them, hidden, dissolved in the storm, only one particle among many. He was the storm, of it, within it, among it. A moment before it was mindless, a great force of power moving randomly. Now he was its mind. And he turned and blew away.

The Commander closed the ring, but then realized that it was empty; the boy had already fled. He shot out probes, searched for him . . . in vain. He was gone. The Commander felt the emptiness of failure and the subtle vibration of fear.

Bob Miller turned as the sky suddenly lightened. He saw the empty dune buggy. "What the hell did you do with him?" he shouted directly at the Commander, ignoring Granny, who put a hand up to stop him. Miller sidestepped her and leveled his shotgun at the Commander. His finger had just begun to pull back the trigger when a blast from another Purdy shotgun disintegrated his upper torso, spreading what was left of his body along the empty, dusty street.

The Aging Master stepped from the shadows of the building nearest them. He felt no particular satisfaction; the Kill held no honor, coming as it did from ambush. All he had really done was to embarrass the Commander; it occurred to the Aging Master that the Commander was extremely careless to have successfully led so many Hunts.

The Commander made a gesture of utmost humiliation.

"You have lost your prey," said the Aging Master sternly.

Mkomo had witnessed the disappearance of Billy Miller and the death of his father with the terror of a man who believed that at its most elemental level, the world really is irrational, controlled by magical forces that only the strongest could control. He was stunned by the realization that the boy was, in fact, possessed of powers that were greater than he thought possible. He turned toward his son.

And found that he had gone.

Charles had decided that the time had come to strike out on his own. When he saw Billy disappear, he realized that his father was no longer the strongest, the all-mighty, the all-powerful. There was someone else who was far better equipped to save him.

But as he emerged from the back door of the ramshackle building, he had been surprised by the appearance of the Gray Female. He did not know it was her, saw only that one of the alien creatures was dismounting from its dune buggy. It was less than thirty yards away. Charles drew his Colt and fired at it while its back was turned.

He heard the whine of the bullet ricocheting off the metal frame of the dune buggy. The creature turned. It was wearing a holster and gunbelt, with a weapon like his. It drew the gun now, but did not fire. He fired again. No effect. The creature began walking toward him.

Mkomo, hearing the shots, rushed to a window that overlooked the scene. He nodded. *At last you have gotten yourself into real trouble,* he thought. *Because you deserted the protection of your father*. Mkomo's hand tightened on his spear. He could rush outside and defend his son, but the beast had a pistol.

And the noise might draw the attention of the others on the opposite side of the building.

Mkomo shrugged. What would happen would have happened sooner or later anyway. Charles would never be strong enough to have ruled an empire, no matter how much education he was given. And what he had told the boy earlier was true: Mkomo would himself have a greater chance of escaping without the worry of providing for Charles's safety. If he did get out of this situation, there would be more women in Paris, in Africa. But there could be other sons only if he himself escaped to sire them. Mkomo thought of the clean hotels and lively women he had enjoyed so much. As for Charles . . . Mkomo knew when to cut his losses.

The Gray Female had tested the ridiculous weapon earlier. Such practice was advisable when opposing species who had chosen unfamiliar weapons. She knew that the projectile thrower was not accurate at this distance. He might, by sheer chance, hit her, but in the meantime he was expending ammunition. There was the smell of fear about him. She knew at what point she would reach the usable range of the weapon.

Charles fired two more times, seeing the bullets kick up dust in the street beyond his target. It seemed terribly unfair to him that it wasn't working out the way it did in the western movies. His father had been right: the Americans always lied.

Still, the creature approaching him had not fired. Perhaps, Charles thought, he could turn and run. Pop was inside somewhere. He'd think of something. As he moved toward the building, however, the Gray Female fired and brought him down.

The shot was not a good one; it had hit Charles in the upper thigh of his left leg. He could not believe the pain, and wiggled about in the dust, trying to make it to the door. "Pop," he called. The Gray Female drew closer, watchful. Yet no others appeared in response to the creature's cries. Her second shot, at point-blank range, went between the eyes.

Mkomo retreated from the window, silently crossing the room, alert for the sounds of an enemy. He peeped out the front door. The other aliens and Granny were nowhere in sight. He ran outside, started his dune buggy, and fled back into the desert.

Kosho and Glassman were struggling to right their dune buggy. When the storm approached, they had been unable to find shelter. Overturning their vehicle and crawling underneath it had been their only recourse. But though the storm had rushed directly toward them, it veered away at the last minute.

Kosho had had the distinct impression that he heard Billy's voice as the storm passed by: *Kosho, I'm all right. Get away from here. Don't go into the town.*

Now, as Mkomo approached at breakneck speed, they waved, calling for him to stop. The Emperor grimly ignored them, charging by without a glance in their direction.

After a few minutes work, they set the vehicle on its wheels again. "What now?" asked Glassman. "Do you want to continue to follow the boy and his father?"

Kosho told Glassman what he had heard. Glassman really did smile now, a broad grin that had no mirth in it. "You have faith in him," he said.

"This is so," said Kosho.

"You are a man of many achievements. You have a learned, subtle mind. You have experienced danger yourself many times."

Kosho bowed his head in acknowledgment of the praise.

"So why have you now placed your faith in a callow, helpless youth who has never achieved anything or showed any promise of becoming anything?"

"Promise," said Kosho, "may appear in strange ways. I have seen people devoted to many causes that seemed strange or unworthy to me. Even Mkomo had followers who believed in him, believed that his leadership was good." He sighed. "In this boy, I see . . . forgive me . . . a potential for command of the forces of nature. He has the ability to perceive beneath the surface of things."

"To be in command of the forces of nature? He is not even in command of himself."

"He seems to be working on that. As his command of himself grows, so may his command of other forces. The two do not necessarily go together."

Glassman made a gesture of contempt. "You sound like a convert to a new religion."

"I hope it is not as limited as a religion."

"There we agree. The last thing the world needs is another religion."

They climbed into the dune buggy. The rabbi's foot struck a metal object that had slipped from underneath the seat as they righted the vehicle.

"Don't you believe any longer in your own religion?" asked Kosho.

Glassman reached down and picked up the Uzi. His eyes glowed with anger that the old woman had placed it there. He waved the weapon in the air. "Here is what all religions become in the end. All the noble words and ideals expressed so piously. Why is it that they find their fullest expression in this?"

Kosho felt an empathy for the rabbi's anguish. "It may be that ideals need defending."

"This is not a defense, this is an aggression," replied the rabbi. "It is a failure, an admission that ideals are not enough." He seemed about to throw the weapon into the sand. Kosho gently placed his hand on Glassman's shoulder.

"What of life? Is that worth defending?" said Kosho.

Glassman glowered at him. Slowly he lowered the weapon and returned it to its place under the seat. He said nothing.

Chapter Twenty-Four

The Scientist realized with a thrill that he had unleashed the source of this race's primal power. Such an achievement had never been accomplished before, with any of the numberless races that the People had encountered. It would lead directly to the source of life itself, all power.

It resembled a serpent as it uncoiled and lashed angrily at his alien force that was invading the body of its host. The Scientist pressed back, confident that his superior power could control it.

And indeed it moved away from him, receding in a manner almost seductive, as if it wished him to follow. He felt its singular quality as the embodiment of a female life force, female to his own People as well as to this race of the blue-green planet. It was the female innate, and as it receded he felt himself yield to the desire to follow.

It broke through some barrier within her body and reached a passageway that led upward along the spinal column of the creature. He moved after it, feeling a strong desire—which he identified abstractedly as being sexual, though he had always been averse to sexual feelings—that made him wish not to let it escape.

In the path of the ascending force there appeared a center of power that his physiological examination had not previously revealed. The serpent entered it, gained force from it, and passed beyond it with its power and seductive allure intensified. The Scientist was increasingly held by its appeal.

There were more of these power centers at regular intervals

along the passage. The serpent gained power at each, requiring the Scientist to exert more and more of his own power to follow and control it. His own body now lay abandoned next to hers, resting on the cushion of damp, decaying swamp vegetation that the Hunters had created in imitation of their own world. So much of his own force was expended in keeping pace with the growing power of the serpent that he had only enough left to keep his body's own life system going at a low level.

As they passed through the fifth of these power centers, he realized that to follow he would temporarily have to abandon his own body altogether, leaving it for the moment lifeless and defenseless. That would require his using the Discovery. But the journey must surely be nearly at an end, and he could risk those few moments of utter concentration that it would take to follow it to the end of its journey. Besides, the sexual allure was almost irresistible for one who had never felt this kind of attraction in such intensity.

As they passed into the skull and into the sixth power center, he had a moment of fear. It was his last chance to pull back. He felt the power of it energizing his own life force to a peak that he had never before experienced. This must surely be the source of the Discovery, and his soul, which was ultimately that of a Hunter, impelled him to leap into the unknown power that lay ahead.

The final center lay at the top of the head, and he realized that it contained the twin, yet opposite, of the serpent that had lain dormant at the base of the spine. It was the male principle, and he understood in the final moment of rational thought left to him that it was this underlying tension between the two halves of the self, straining to unite but never able to, that was the ultimate source of the power behind the Discovery. More than that, it was . . . but the coils of the serpent unwound with a swiftness that terrified, its mouth opening. The Scientist strained to pull back, but it was too late.

The minds of the two alien creatures, man and woman, violently fused, shattering the Scientist's being into an infinity of fragments swept by the movement of the engulfing serpent, a movement that had no limit, ending, or beginning. No senses, body, mind. All there was, is, ever had been . . . bliss, ecstasy.

Light! An ocean of infinite, conscious, timeless light flashed across all space in a single harmonic pulse. Had there ever been anything stranger than the unexpected union of the earth woman with the creature who had traveled untold light-years to achieve a destiny greater than any he had dreamt of?

In his storm form, Billy sensed the flashing, and that it was the soul of his mother. He sent himself out to the limits of the power at his command, but even if he died, he could not follow her. Her soul touched him, lovingly, but she was unaware. His mother was gone forever, and he was left alone to honor her memory, and to wonder.

The storm spent its force. Billy resumed his ordinary form not far from the place where Kirsten and her father had taken cover. They saw him coming, apparently from the midst of the storm, and called to him. He reached out with his mind and felt the warmth and love they offered him. Gratefully, he leaned on the emotional support they offered, and at last collapsed into the arms of the one he loved.

"Kirsten," he gasped, "Mom and Dad are dead."

She held him tightly, the only response she could make, and he lapsed into unconsciousness.

"He is making a habit of falling asleep when he meets you," her father said with gentle humor. "Why is that, I wonder?" Kirsten waved her father away.

Bjorn thought sadly of Bibi. *She should have been here. But that is our nature. Too short a life. Regeneration, begetting, implies death. When the two of us lay together and conceived our Kirsten in joy we prepared the way for our own deaths. What makes us continue? That love that they feel for each other now*. He would not disturb them by telling them that they were beginning the path to their own deaths. *We only realize that when it is too late*.

Mkomo drove wildly, roaring across the flat spaces, up and down the dunes in his path, his buggy leaping from the top of each mound of sand, higher and higher. He was fleeing spirits. In this land where miracles seemed commonplace, his thoughts carried him back to the village of his childhood, where the magical powers of the shamans were taken for granted.

He had always feared the vengeance of the dead, but in his mastery of the shaman's art he felt he could protect himself against those he had slain. Now he felt himself powerless and alone. He thought of Janet Gore, who had died because he had missed his spear throw; of Charles, his ill-begotten son who had died as he watched, died calling out to him. He fled them, feeling that their spirits pursued.

In defiance, the only recourse that had never failed him, he drew his spear and called out his lion-roar. Nowhere had he encountered a creature who could stand against him, he reminded himself. He was the Emperor of a great nation.

Ascending the side of the highest dune he had yet encountered, he was startled by the appearance of another vehicle that cleared the lip of the dune from the opposite direction.

He saw at a glance that the buggy contained one of *them*—the black-clad Hunters. It was bound on a collision course for Mkomo's own vehicle, apparently propelled by the creature's belief that mutual destruction was the only way of taking him.

The thing in the driver's seat was in clear sight, and amazingly close. Mkomo's arm rippled with the instinctive effort of throwing the spear. As he grunted with the force of the throw, he knew that his aim was true.

But he watched in dismay as the creature duplicated—mimicked—Mkomo's earlier action on the snowy mountainside. It flung itself over the side, and let the spear harmlessly bury itself in the driver's seat of the vehicle.

Mkomo now realized the creature's true intention, and swerved to avoid the collision. His action was too late, and the two dune buggies smashed together and rolled down the slope of massed sand, reaching the bottom in a fiery heap.

The Natural Hunter had thrown himself clear. He watched the fused, burning wreckage with a twinge of regret that his plan had worked so well. He had thought not to kill the creature with a machine, but to force him to dismount. Carrying the spear that he had intended for the creature's heart, he stepped cautiously down the hill of sand.

The flames and smoke rose rapidly, obscuring his vision, but his Hunter's awareness alerted him to the sight of something moving in the midst of it. Or was it beyond it?

"Look!" said Kosho. He and Glassman were still better than a quarter of a mile away, but they could see the column of smoke that rose from the wreckage of the two vehicles. Kosho turned their buggy in that direction, and Glassman's hands tightened on the Uzi.

* * *

Mkomo carefully kept the burning wreckage between himself and the creature. Several of his ribs were broken, and he had struck his head on the side of the vehicle when it overturned. He could feel blood coursing down his temple. But the realization of the danger had brought a swift return of his reflexes.

It would be a matter of timing; each of them held only one spear. He who chose to throw first must find his target or be left naked.

He darted to one side, momentarily exposing himself to the enemy, hoping to draw his spear. Too quick—there was no throw, but now the creature circled around to that side. Mkomo matched his steps, keeping the wreckage between himself and the other. But as the creature circled, it gradually advanced, narrowing the circle in which Mkomo could move.

Mkomo had played a game like this when he was a child, learning to separate an antelope from the herd, working to turn it by allowing it to scent him, and then moving the quarry closer to where the elders waited to kill it. If the game were done alone, it was necessary to force the animal to turn against an obstacle—a stream or a wall of rock, where it would have to turn and be killed.

He was the prey now, as well as the hunter. There were no obstacles in the desert, and no fear in the adversary he faced that would cause it to turn and run blindly. Onward it moved, slowly but inexorably cutting off Mkomo's field of maneuver. Soon it would be close enough so that one of them would have to risk a throw through the fire itself.

They heard the roar of the approaching vehicle, and the same thought occurred to both Mkomo and the Natural Hunter: Was it friend or enemy? Whichever, the time for decisive action was now near for one of them. Neither, however, could afford to wait to find out which one.

The Natural Hunter ran with his spear drawn back as if to throw. He feinted toward his left, and Mkomo turned to the right. The Natural Hunter anticipated this move, and lunged in the other direction to counteract it. He did not have a clear shot, but enough of Mkomo was visible to make a hit possible. The Natural Hunter's spear covered the distance between them in less than a second. He allowed himself a moment of satisfaction as he saw it strike the thickest part of the creature, where its heart lay.

The force of the blow spun Mkomo half around and carried him downward into the sand. He was alert enough to land on his right side to keep the shaft of the spear in his chest from striking the ground. The blade had missed his heart, but if he had landed on that side, the force of his fall would have enlarged the wound.

Mkomo rose to his knees, holding his spear at the ready position, in time to halt the creature rushing toward him. He grinned in satisfaction as he saw the creature dart from side to side in an attempt to throw off his aim. Slowly, conserving his energy, keeping his eyes on his adversary, Mkomo struggled to his feet.

He took a step forward, testing his ability and strength while attempting to force the creature into outright flight. The alien stood fast, seeming to realize that if it turned to run, it would be making itself a blind target.

Mkomo felt his strength ebbing with the blood that pumped out of the wound. The step had jarred the spear that rested in his body, its point protruding from his back and its shaft sticking out in front like a grotesquely long organ. He remembered a woman in Paris who would have been excited at the sight of it.

The creature tensed for Mkomo's throw, ready to leap once more at the sight of his muscles tightening. Mkomo remembered that earlier leap, on the river, when the creature had avoided his throw. He forced himself to take another painful step forward.

The sound of the dune buggy roared clear now as it crested the last dune between it and the battle. It would be in sight, if either of them looked to the side, but Mkomo's eyes held the Natural Hunter's sight-slits in a firm grip. The one who looked, each knew, would be the one who lost.

Kosho motioned toward the Uzi, but the rabbi saw that the angle was bad; Mkomo and the creature were too close to each other, and he might hit both of them if he fired. *Why not?* Glassman asked himself, and raised the weapon.

Though Mkomo did not raise his eyes to the approaching dune buggy, the Natural Hunter took advantage of the moment when Mkomo was distracted by the sound. He leaped forward, crossing the distance between them in less time than the blinking of an eye. Mkomo instinctively turned to protect the arm that held the spear. As he did so, the protruding shaft of the weapon in his chest struck the Natural Hunter.

Mkomo was far heavier than the alien, and the weight of his

body behind the shaft made it a weapon that knocked the alien to the side. Mkomo's right arm whipped downward, propelling his own spear into the body of the alien, just below the neck.

Kosho heard above the roar of the motor the high-pitched squeal that was the anguished last cry of the Natural Hunter. Then he heard Mkomo's triumphant lion-cry, resounding over the desert and then dying to nothingness as Mkomo's body fell on top of that of the alien. Glassman lowered his Uzi.

By the time they reached the wreckage it was all over. The blow that felled the alien had turned the spear in Mkomo's body, and his blood now mingled in the sand with the green slimy fluid, like algae-infested swamp water, that ran from the body of the Natural Hunter. Their duel was finished. Neither had found the other as weak as his usual prey.

The Japanese and the Israeli stood looking down at the bodies. "Shall we bury him?" Kosho said at last.

Glassman looked around at the silent desert, realizing that it was not empty. Yet he remembered that Mkomo had uttered words over the grave of Janet Gore. He looked at Kosho. In both of their traditions was a reverence for the dead. Glassman nodded his head toward the wreckage of the vehicles, which was still flickering with flames. "A funeral pyre," he said.

"For both?" asked Kosho.

Glassman shrugged.

As they were struggling with the bodies, there came the sound of another vehicle. Glassman ran back to get the Uzi. As it came into sight, however, they saw the dune buggy that contained Bjorn Halvorssen and his daughter. Wedged in between them was Billy, unconscious.

Kosho rushed forward as they slowed to a stop. "Is he wounded?" he asked anxiously.

"He does not appear so," said Bjorn.

"His father?"

"He told us his parents are dead," said Kirsten.

Kosho grunted, and bowed his head. Behind him, the fire was greedily consuming the new material it had been offered.

They traveled together, following the path of the sun, which was the only landmark they had. At last Glassman spotted the refuge, incongruously modern, like a motel in the midst of what seemed like a trackless desert.

"Do we go on through the desert in the morning?" asked Glassman.

"In the morning," said Kosho, "there will be something else here."

"What, I wonder?"

"Granny will tell us."

Glassman shook his head. "*Meshugge*," he said. Madness.

Chapter Twenty-Five

But Granny did not come when they called her. There was the usual table of food and drink, and the refuge was comfortably air-conditioned, but no one appeared to tell them what came next.

"Perhaps they've gone away," said Bjorn Halvorssen.

The three men mused on this. Kirsten was nibbling at a bit of salmon near the couch where Billy lay sleeping.

"If they have gone," said Kosho, "then this would not be here." He knocked on the heavy table, held aloft his cup of sake.

"It could have been prepared in advance," said Glassman.

Kosho spread his hands. "It is all being prepared now. It depends on their presence. I told you what Mkomo thought . . . that we are really somewhere near Antarctica."

"Then what are we supposed to do tomorrow?"

"I think," said Kosho, "they expect the boy to tell us."

The Commander had been enraged when he found the bodies of the boy's mother and the Scientist.

"Perhaps the one you say has made the Discovery found its way here," suggested the Gray Female.

"Then its mother would not be dead," pointed out the Commander.

"But if she were already dead when he arrived?"

"But how? How?" The Commander nearly overcame himself with fury. "I formally ordered him not to perform any experiments on her."

"There seems no mark on her body."

"That was not the kind of experiment he was interested in. We know all there is to know about this species' biology."

"Perhaps not all," suggested the Aging Master. "If they are capable of making the Discovery, our survey teams certainly never picked it up."

"They don't really know what to look for," said the Commander. He gestured toward the Scientist's body. "He thought *he* could find it."

"Perhaps he did," replied the Aging Master. "If so, he seems to have left no record of what he found. For us, the immediate problem is that we now have to think of another way of controlling the boy."

"He doesn't know that his mother is dead," said the Gray Female.

"He knows," said the Commander. "He sensed her life pattern last night. Now he will feel it gone."

"You do believe, then, that he has made the Discovery."

The Commander hesitated. "I believe he has certain aspects of it, like a bright child in our own society. But he has not gone through the Discovery ceremony."

"Then the three of us, using our full Discovery powers, could easily overcome him."

The Aging Master signaled his disapproval. "This is a Hunt conducted under the Old Rules."

The Gray Female turned to him, and visibly suppressed a rude retort. When she finally spoke, it was with respect. "Four of us have already died."

"That was why the Old Rules were suppressed. It is precisely that aspect of the Hunt that makes it forbidden. It is also that which makes it the only noble form of Hunting."

"The Rules were intended to allow the game an equal chance—not to put ourselves at a disadvantage."

"That is true. Perhaps not all of us fully appreciated what the implications were of allowing the game an equal chance." The Aging Master stressed the word "equal." He continued, "It did not mean the slaughter of particularly ferocious animals who might be exhibited to frighten children. It meant that there was as much a chance of their conquering us as there was of our subduing them. Of our four losses, only one was credited to the boy. And that Kill of his was made against the one of our party who chose to use the Discovery, as you seem to be recommending.''

''And we have taken seven of them, in fair combat,'' said the Commander. ''That proves our superiority.''

''Our superiority will only be proven when we have killed them all,'' said the Gray Female.

The Aging Master gave her a long look, and the Commander felt the sadness that was implied in it. ''Our superiority will be proved if we uphold our honor,'' the Aging Master said.

They weighed the implications of his words. ''I beg leave to be excused, if there is to be no more discussion of this,'' said the Gray Female. ''I wish to practice with the weapons I will be using tomorrow.''

The others nodded their assent. ''If you have no objection,'' said the Aging Master as she rose to leave, ''I would like to be allowed the privilege of confronting the one remaining creature who carries a sword.''

The Gray Female deferred to his request and departed.

The Aging Master turned to the Commander. ''You did use your Discovery power to restrain the boy this morning.''

Though the Aging Master's tone was respectful, the Commander felt his words an accusation.

''I only set limits to his power. I did not use it to harm him. I intended that he should come willingly.''

''What did you intend if he *did* come with you willingly?'' asked the Aging Master.

''I . . . the Scientist wished to study him. He thought he could determine the source of the Discovery.''

''I thought that a worthy purpose,'' acknowledged the Aging Master. ''Yet you see there the results of the Scientist's work. What if that had happened to the boy?''

''Perhaps that would have been best,'' said the Commander.

''Do you really believe that? You would not have experienced sadness?''

''I have killed many times.''

''And you never felt it . . . saddening?''

The Commander expressed surprise, but it was a formal expression. He kept his true feelings to himself.

''I read the reports of your Hunts, including the ones on which you led tourists. I am, as you have guessed, one of the Guardians.''

The Commander made the formal gesture of respect that was owed a Guardian, but the Aging Master waved it by. He spoke slowly: "A majority of the other Guardians will express their disapproval of my actions, should we return and the story of this Hunt become known. I will be required, in honor, to end my life voluntarily."

The Commander's expressed astonishment was real.

"And of course," the Aging Master continued, "they will take immediate steps to destroy this race. *That* will not sadden you?"

The Commander's answer was slow in coming. "It would seem . . . a waste."

The Aging Master nodded. "I sensed your feelings from the tone of your reports. That was why I desired to come on this Hunt, with you as Commander."

"Because you knew . . . they were about to make the Discovery?"

"No. I have seen many races about to make the Discovery. I was personally in charge of exterminating them."

The Commander's bewilderment showed. "Then how can you . . ."

The Aging Master nodded. "Why have I not made the required report to the other Guardians? That once again a race is endangering our unchallenged superiority?"

The Commander indicated assent, then inquisitiveness: "Because you too . . . felt sadness?"

"Not in the way you mean. Exterminating a race is a question merely of exerting the Discovery on a wide scale. I am capable of that. One never sees the game, its bravery or pain. No, the sadness I felt was for our own People. For what has become of them."

The Commander's lack of response was a clear indication that he did not understand.

"Look at what has become of them," the Aging Master continued. "You have led many young People on Hunts. Did you consider them worthy of the Hunting tradition of our race?"

The Commander could not assent, but said, "Yet there are some . . . the ones we brought . . ."

"Yes. I allowed the Golden Female to come. I encouraged the Natural Hunter. And the Gray Female . . . I owed her the chance. She and I were almost mates. But she chose another. He was killed on a Hunt on which I participated. One of the last of the Old Hunts. She thought that I could have saved her chosen.

That was true, but it was in a situation in which it would have been dishonorable to intervene."

"But the others are, were, worthy Hunters."

"They were utterly unprepared. Because they had never really faced game under equal conditions. I see now that the Hunting ability . . . must be developed. We are not innately superior."

"Except through the Discovery."

"And our use of that has made us corrupt. We cannot truly stand equally against these creatures, who know how to respond to challenge. Our young People have never faced challenge. Nothing can challenge us. Unless we allow it."

"But then . . . it *was* wise to ban Hunts conducted under the Old Rules."

"Wise . . . until we meet a race that has made the Discovery on its own."

"That cannot happen."

"It nearly happened *here*. You yourself reported that the scouts grossly underclassified the species. Even so, you withheld the knowledge of how far they had really progressed."

"I did not know."

"You knew enough to want to return. You knew that one of them had used a Discovery-powered weapon."

The Commander had no response.

The Aging Master reached out his hand and actually touched the Commander, who strove to maintain his dignity at this unexpected intimacy.

"If you had not met this race, you would someday have been one of the Guardians," said the Aging Master. "You might have led the effort to regenerate our race. You were worthy."

The Commander opened himself humbly to the Master's praise.

"Even now, though the Guardians will never accept you, you still might accomplish that purpose."

"How?" asked the Commander.

"By initiating the boy into full Discovery powers."

Billy awoke with his head in Kirsten's lap. His opening eyes met the delighted, concerned gaze in her own. He was in ecstasy and pain at the same time. The knowledge of the deaths of his parents was an empty ache in his mind, like a missing tooth that had been pulled. More, he felt the pain of awareness of everything living around him. It was like being in a room with many different stereos, all playing a different record.

It was almost too much for him. He felt himself sinking back again into unconsciousness to get away from the chaos that filled his mind. Then a thought, one random set of words, struck him, as he noticed it in Kirsten's mind: *Billy, we need you.*

He took that thought, concentrated on it, and gradually made it rise above the other thoughts till it drowned the rest out.

Billy, we need you. He relaxed, looked up at her, and she understood. Not really understood how he was doing it, or what her importance was in his ability to do it, but knew that he knew. They shared that knowledge. They smiled at each other.

"Are you hungry?" she asked. He was surprised. He hadn't yet been able to think of himself like that, as something separate from the others, with needs that were different, all his own. He would have to remember that, after all, he still had his body to take care of.

He nodded, and she moved gently away from him, propping his head on one of the pillows, and went off to get him food from the table.

He felt a little panic as she moved away from him, afraid that by breaking the physical touch she would move away from him inside as well. He sent out another kind of touch, and realized that he was seeing through her eyes.

More than that. She was selecting things from the table that she thought he would like to eat. Chicken, good; but she liked other things—fish, mainly—that he *didn't* like. Salted cod, anchovies, eel. He *hated* eel, gagged at the thought of it. Only, now, seeing the food through her eyes, he was feeling it, tasting it the way she thought it would taste. He liked it because she liked it.

She brought the plate back, smiling at him. He could see her smile through his own eyes, but at the same time he was still able to look out through *her* eyes, and he saw himself the way she saw him.

He was more astonished by that perception than by anything else that had happened to him. The way she saw him—it wasn't anything like he thought himself to be. It was still *him,* but he was tall, strong, fairly good-looking. He was brave, resourceful, intelligent, and sincere. Even beyond that (*How could this be?* he wondered), he was even somewhat sexy.

He ate, realizing how hungry he was, and tried to withdraw from her mind. He concentrated on the food, but found that without sharing her feelings for it, it was still mostly repulsive to him. Guiltily, he allowed himself to remain in her mind, to share her feelings about the food. But in doing so, he realized that she was looking at him. And he felt what she felt.

The others came over and sat silently nearby, waiting for him to finish. He kept their thoughts firmly away, not able yet to deal with all of them at once. But when he finished, he had to look up, acknowledge that they were there, wanting to ask him things. He waited for them to speak, knowing that it was easier to sort things out if their thoughts were spoken, one at a time.

"Billy," said Kosho, very gently. "You have achieved something. You are master of yourself."

"No. Not that," Billy replied. "But, you know . . . I can *do* things I never could before."

Kosho smiled.

Billy could see, without probing Kosho's mind, that he—like Kirsten—had an image of Billy that was different from Billy's own. Billy did not want to go into Kosho's mind to see what it was. It would be too confusing.

"The old nana won't come when we call her," Bjorn Halvorssen said. "Do you know why that is?"

Billy thought. "She can't . . . can't give us any more help. There's something wrong, but I can't quite understand what it is."

"Have the Hunters left?" said Glassman.

Billy looked at him, surprised. "Oh, no. They still . . . want us. More than ever."

"Especially you, I suppose."

Billy's face changed. His eyes filled with alarm. "No, that's not true. In fact, one of them . . ." He strained for a moment, and then found that he had lost contact. He sighed. They had sensed him, and erected a barrier.

He looked up at the faces around him. "There are three of them left. And they all have different feelings. It's very hard to separate them."

Glassman muttered something. Only Billy understood what he said. "It isn't *meshugge,*" Billy said earnestly to Glassman. "I know why you find it hard to believe. Sometimes I think I can't believe it, except that it's happening to me."

"It is not happening to us," said Glassman.

Billy nodded. "I know. You want me . . . to show you." He shook his head earnestly, meeting Glassman's eyes. "But if I did

. . . it doesn't really matter if you believe me or not. We'll still have to go out there tomorrow."

Glassman shot a look at Kosho. "No miracles?" Glassman said wryly.

"Not a religion," Kosho said.

"I have seen many religions, but never a miracle."

"You'd better watch out if you're making fun of Billy," interjected Kirsten.

"He was not making fun, beloved," said her father. Halvorssen turned to Billy. "We are depending on you to tell us what to expect tomorrow."

"Oh, that," said Billy. "It's not difficult, exactly. Not like . . . what we've already gone through. We could walk through without any trouble, except that they'll be out to kill us."

"What will it look like?" asked Halvorssen.

Billy shrugged. "It's supposed to look like a city."

Glassman laughed. "If I see a city out there tomorrow, then I *will* believe."

"It isn't important, Mr. Glassman," said Billy. "Really, it doesn't matter if you believe. But don't forget to take your Uzi."

"Spoken like an *alte bubba,*" said Glassman. "A true Granny, to you."

It was late, but the three men had still not gone to bed. At first, they had stayed together talking out of delicacy, for Kirsten and Billy had gone upstairs, and they obviously wished to be alone. Eventually, the drinks had made their conversation less a matter of duty. The three discovered that they genuinely liked each other, and they traded stories about their experiences. At times, the talk turned melancholy as they remembered those who had died, and faced the realization that they might themselves die tomorrow, but another round dispelled the thought and they considered that, after all, there might be a treasure, and they might share in it.

Someone's reference to a sexual exploit caused Glassman and Kosho to exchange glances. Bjorn saw what they were thinking of. He patted his knees and leaned toward them unsteadily "You need not worry about Kirsten. She knows about boys."

"But does he know about girls?" asked Glassman wryly.

"You are not . . . a father?" asked Bjorn.

"No," said Glassman, softly, remembering something.

Bjorn nodded. "We are very wise, we old ones, and we

sometimes make ourselves forget what it was like, back then. But if we are honest, we will let the young people have their way. If we try to hold them back, pretend that they do not have the same feelings we have, it is because we want them to remain as children. If we understand that they must grow up, then to ourselves we seem that much older. We have reached another stage in our lives, are that much closer to death. So we do not inquire into these things too closely."

The others nodded, and poured themselves another drink.

It had not been at all like Billy expected. Not that it wasn't good—it was just very different from what Brian McConnell had described. He wondered if Brian had really made it with Shelley Sue Dennison. Even so, it was a lot different between Billy and Kirsten.

There was the difference, of course, that he could see things as Kirsten saw them, and if he had wanted to . . . but he had shut off the sensations coming through her mind when he realized that she was excited by him. He couldn't have taken it. Even so, for a second he thought he was going to come as soon as she started taking off her clothes and he realized what was going to happen.

He had regained control; it had all worked out, and when it was finished, she whispered to him, "I love you," and he could feel that she had really thought he had done all right. He lay drowsing, listening to the sounds of her regular breathing, keeping himself just on the verge of consciousness because he wanted to let himself enjoy the memory of it for a while longer.

Then he realized that something had happened. Something *else*.

Because he couldn't hear the thoughts from downstairs anymore. He didn't have the realization that everything around them was only imaginary. He sat up. It was really dark inside the room; only a crack of light shone under the door. Before, even though it had been just as dark, he had sensed the objects in the room, knew what lay outside, and what was beyond *that*. Now, he couldn't see anything.

He had lost it. All his thoughts were back inside him. He knew, without attempting it, that he couldn't change now, couldn't move except with his body, in the usual ways.

He turned on the light. Kirsten stirred and rolled over under the sheet, away from the bedside lamp. He sat next to her, remaining tensely silent until her breathing resumed its regular pattern.

There was a movement in the corner of his eye. Granny was here.

"Billy," she said crossly. "I've been calling you."

She didn't know, he realized suddenly. He suppressed the thought instantly, leaving behind only a tingling awareness that he mustn't let her know.

He pulled the sheet up over himself shyly. "Granny, you're not supposed to be here."

She waved her hand impatiently. "Why are you doing that now?"

He frowned. "I thought you knew everything. You're not supposed to be here. Go away."

"Billy, I have something very important to tell you."

"I know all about it. Go away. I don't want to listen."

"The Commander wants you to come with me. Right now. He wants to tell you something."

"Tell him that didn't work. He tried to catch me earlier, when he killed my father."

"That wasn't the Commander who killed your father. He's very sorry about that."

"Tell him we'll meet tomorrow. And that I'm going to kill him."

"Billy, he only wants to give you an equal chance."

"He wants to take my powers away from me, so he can kill the others. He's not going to. I know all about the Discovery."

"Billy, this is all bluff. You don't know. But the Commander will tell you about it."

He took in a deep breath, wondering how long he could keep this up. He spoke as sternly as he could, trying to sound like his father: "Granny, I command you to go away. Now."

She looked at him strangely, and he worried that she had guessed. But she disappeared.

He turned off the light. He was no longer sleepy. He began to try to remember what it was he had done first, how he had discovered how to do it. But the thought kept creeping into his mind: *What am I going to do tomorrow?*

Chapter Twenty-Six

The sun rose. The three Hunters walked through the city that had been created, searching for a place to confront the game.

The Aging Master was bemused by the structures that towered overhead. He had not thought of a race capable of making the Discovery as living in dwellings like this. They reminded him of dwellings erected by certain peculiar species, sharing a common low-level telepathic awareness so closely that they might be said to have only one mind among them. Yet the species that was dominant on this blue-green planet was said to be fiercely individualistic, and had clearly demonstrated their innate aggressiveness. *Such an active race,* he thought, *living in such proximity, must have difficulty in maintaining the system of social etiquette.*

The strangeness of his surroundings made him yearn for his own comfortable dwelling, with its garden of plants and plant-animals brought from other worlds. It was a small dwelling, designed for the simple life of a Person living alone. Smaller than the dwellings of those People who chose mates and raised young. Yet it was comfortable, and it afforded the distance from others necessary for peaceful contemplation. He would never see it again, he knew. Whatever his success today, he would not choose to return to a public disgrace. The thought filled him with a desire to meet the prey. It had been a long time since he had felt that.

The Gray Female separated herself from the other two and went to the section of the city that the game would enter. She did not want the other two to hinder her, with their talk of Old Rules and honor. She would not use the Discovery, unless it were necessary. But if the adept boy attacked her, she would retaliate with all the force at her command.

The Aging Master—or so he was known now; she had known him when he had another name, and even before that, when both of them had children's names—spoke of honor. What did honor mean? She knew that he had killed untold numbers of defenseless creatures with his exercise of the Discovery. Yet he had withheld that power when it was needed—needed to save her chosen mate—and called *that* honor. It was jealousy; it was his revenge. And because of his sense of honor, she had been required to live alone, and had never borne a young one. The only pleasure left to her was killing, and she would assert that right. When she had killed the one with the sword, there had been an easing of her rage. Satisfaction. And again when she killed the stupid one with the projectile thrower. She had allowed herself the sensation of pleasure by probing his mind at the last moments, sharing his surprise at death.

Now there were five more. Five more chances to feel that same pleasure.

The Commander wandered through the streets, alone now. The Aging Master had found a spot that suited him. The Commander knew that he himself must find a place to make his stand, but his Hunting instincts were strangely dull. He could not reach the mind of the boy, and it disturbed him.

Why had the boy not come when he called? He did not trust the Commander, of course. But the Commander had sent the guide, which had been created as a symbol of trustworthiness, and it had not been able to bring the boy either.

Perhaps it was because the boy's senses were keen enough to make him realize that the Commander was not, after all, entirely sure of what he was doing. The Aging Master's argument had been troubling, although powerful. Their People needed an adversary, needed the experience of real danger, to regenerate themselves. To become again a worthy race.

To initiate the boy into full Discovery powers would be to create an enemy. Even though the boy would not be strong enough, by himself, to utterly destroy the People.

Or would he? The Commander was troubled by the thought of initiating an alien creature into the uttermost secrets of the

People. It was like the stories that every species had . . . of mating with other species. To create monsters of myth.

There was no doubt that the boy had qualities that would have made him respected as a Person. He was brave, intelligent, resourceful . . . yet so were many beasts that the Commander had encountered.

That did not make them People.

The Commander thought about another aspect of the Aging Master's revelations. The Aging Master had desired, at one time, to mate with the Gray Female. He had wanted a child, had wanted to regenerate himself.

That had not come to pass. If it had, the Aging Master would not have developed his skills to the point where he was acknowledged the supreme Hunter. He would not have been one of the Guardians, none of whom bore or begot progeny.

Yet he had confessed to the Commander that in his old age he would willingly have given up those achievements if he could exchange them for offspring worthy of the name of Hunter.

Rationally the Commander understood the Aging Master's emotions. The Commander had seen that family bonding was strong among many species, even his own. He had observed parents of other species sacrifice themselves for the sake of the safety of their offspring. That was an instinct necessary to the survival of species.

Yet in his own people the mating instinct was weak; they had to overcome their own feelings to experience it. Those who successfully mated were thought to have reduced themselves to a lower social scale. Even the pleasure of having offspring was not enough to induce many of them to mate.

The Commander unwillingly faced his own emotions: he admitted that he himself would have liked to have a child. What the Aging Master urged him to do was to do just that, without the necessity of submitting to mating: to administer the Discovery Initiation to this boy, he would have to assume the role of the father. For only parents could guide their progeny through the Initiation Ceremony.

The Commander felt himself gravely troubled at the thought. He was glad the boy had refused. It would be unnatural.

Billy awoke with a terrible headache. Kirsten rubbed his back and his temples to take away the pain. But the feeling of her thighs astride him made him yearn for her again. When he rolled over, she giggled and scampered out of the bed. "Not now," she whispered. "The others will be up soon."

One of them was already awake. Glassman saw from his window a sight that threatened to overturn his conception of what was reality. They were, in truth, on the edge of a great city. It has come to pass, he thought.

It was a strange, fairy-tale city. He could pick out the towers of New York, but there were other buildings that he did not recognize, and small cottages that seemed to belong to villages. He realized that it was an amalgam of the cities of earth.

Truly a fairy tale. And the boy had said it would be here. What did that make him?

The rabbi opened to the Psalms of David and began to read. It did not give him the peace he craved. His eyes strayed to the Uzi, lying next to his bed. He bowed his head.

They gathered downstairs. A breakfast was awaiting. All of them had by now seen the city, and each was silently contemplating the meaning of it.

Granny did not come, and the others looked to Billy. He smiled shyly at them, glad that his headache was gone. Yet when he tried to see what they expected of him, when he probed their thoughts just a little, the pain in his head returned. He would have to do it on his own.

"We won't need anything except the weapons," he said. He held Kirsten's hand, then reached out for Kosho. The Japanese waited for what Billy would say. "We have to try," was all Billy could think of. He opened the door and led them outside.

The thing they noticed first was the utter silence. The canyons of the city towered over them, making them uneasy. Any of the windows of the countless buildings could hold a hidden Hunter in wait.

Only a light wind, carrying with it the scent of the sea, gave a sense of movement. There were no sheets of newspaper blowing in the wind, no dust. No piles of trash in front of the buildings. No smells of food, nor stains on the sidewalks. It was exactly as if it had been built just for them.

They were an odd-looking group. Billy went first, his hands thrust in the pockets of his jeans like any teenager in any number of cities. His girl came sprightly along next to him. The slight bulge in the back pocket of her own jeans, and a jewel-encrusted handle half exposed, showed that she still carried her weapon.

Bjorn Halvorssen, tall and alert, held his huge double-barreled hunting rifle at the ready as he scanned the empty windows.

Kosho's eyes flickered to the dark shadows of alleyways and entrances; he had tied a red braid around his waist to hold the ancient samurai sword; he walked with his hand on the sharkskin grip. Around his head was a white kerchief; on the front he had drawn a Japanese character in what appeared to be red ink. It was, in fact, written with his own blood.

Last came Glassman, the point man, eyes dull as he pondered the strange circumstances that had brought him here. He carried across his arms the ugly, deadly Uzi.

They found a car parked at a curb on one of the empty streets, as if its owner had just left it. Glassman tried the door and found it unlocked. A glance inside showed him that the keys were in the ignition.

"Let's go," he called to the others. They looked at Billy, who shrugged. They piled into the car. Glassman drove, with Halvorssen on the passenger side, the nose of his rifle sticking out the window.

In the back, Billy sat between Kirsten and Kosho. Billy and Kirsten held hands and seemed to have eyes only for each other. Glassman observed them through the driver's mirror, and thought with amazement how unconcerned they seemed to be—with everything except each other.

The rabbi was not unacquainted with love. He had seen it in the kibbutzes, in the towns under attack, even in the conquered Arab territories. He had noticed the same phenomenon—the utter isolation from the events around them—in lovers everywhere. They might participate in those events, might fight bravely, work hard, suffer, triumph . . . but there were always these moments of isolation in which the world was locked out.

He himself had never experienced that feeling. He had been friends with women, slept with some of them, but none of them had ever had the single-minded attraction for him that he was compelled to acknowledge as love.

There had been a young woman in New York. They had shared intellectual interests, enjoyed going to lectures, concerts, and museums together. They had enjoyed bed together as well. But when he announced his decision to go to Israel, expecting that she would accompany him, she refused. Looking back on the affair later, he realized that what it had been was a mutual need for companionship. Only that. Shared interests were not love. He had seen that later.

Now, glancing at the two in the back seat of the car . . . he envied them. Perhaps that was the path not taken, the one that is always wondered about. If he had stayed in New York, continued his studies at Columbia, perhaps the companionship could have blossomed into love. Love did not always strike at first glance, the way it seemed to with these two; it could develop over time.

But he had not stayed. He chose the other path. He pursued an ideal.

His eyes flickered back to the road, then back to the lovers, who had not changed their position. He had not found an ideal; what he had found was a cause, and he had fought for it, sacrificed his life—years of his life—to it.

It had not brought him the satisfaction that these two felt.

"Fog," said Halvorssen.

Glassman snapped his eyes ahead, and he saw the street ahead dissolve into the gray bank of mist. He slowed the car, and as it entered the fog they found themselves blinded, unable to see more than a few feet away.

At the next intersection, Glassman turned to the left to see if they could move around the fog.

"Do they want us to move in this direction?" Kosho asked Billy.

Billy reluctantly broke eye contact with Kirsten, still clutching her hand. He had been trying to rediscover his awareness, but found that he could not even enter Kirsten's mind. He could not tell the others of the loss of his powers; they would only be frightened.

But now, as he mulled over Kosho's question, he realized that he had a very dim awareness of what the others in the car were thinking—not detailed and precise, the way it had been, and maybe no more than an intuition. But he felt their fear, and it seemed to carry over into his mind.

The fear brought him the awareness of the three Hunters. One of them was near. "It's a trap," he said. "They want to turn us away from the fog. Go back the other way."

Before the rabbi could decide whether to believe him or not, the windshield shattered. Glassman swung the wheel instinctively, and the car bumped over a curb and struck the side of a wall.

Bullets struck the side of the car where Halvorssen was sitting.

Glassman heard the Dane's hunting rifle fire, and tried to reverse direction. The crash had immobilized the front wheels; the car wouldn't move.

Glassman seized his Uzi and rolled out of the driver's seat onto the pavement. Using the car as a shield, he stuck his head up, trying to see where the shots were coming from. He could see only fog. He fired a burst from the Uzi, hoping to draw return fire.

There was silence. Glassman looked inside the car. None of them seemed to be hurt. Halvorssen was stretched out full-length on the front seat, but aside from a few minor cuts from the glass, he was uninjured.

Glassman jerked open the back door. "Out, out," he called, relieved to see that none of them was wounded. They tumbled onto the sidewalk beside him. Halvorssen wiggled across the front seat and joined them. The five crouched behind the car.

Glassman looked at Billy. He saw someone frightened and confused. Glassman gritted his teeth and asked, "How many are they?"

Billy shot out a probe, feeling the weakness of it. He encountered nothing, but remembered the sensation he had had just before the crash. "Only one, I think."

Glassman nodded, and looked around for another place of refuge. He pointed. Not twenty feet away was an alley intersecting two buildings. He looked at Billy. "There," he said. "Go."

Kosho put his hand on Glassman's arm. "They might hit him."

Glassman jerked his arm away. "Someone has to risk it. If they fire, I will be able to see where they are firing *from*. If he has the power you say . . ."

Before anyone could stop him, Billy had jumped forward and ran crouching toward the alley. Glassman turned just in time to see flashes of gunfire in the fog. He leveled his Uzi and laid down a devastating pattern of fire in that direction. "Go, go," he screamed to the others.

They ran. In the alley they found Billy, unhurt.

"Keep moving," said Halvorssen. "Get to the other end. He'll follow us."

But Glassman, seeing the others reach temporary safety, had made his decision. The boy, whatever else, was courageous. Perhaps . . .

Glassman shrugged. They were in love. If they were lucky, they could avoid the Hunters. Chances were that they would die. If they did not, perhaps they could come out to someplace where they could enjoy their love.

He had had his chance at that, a long time before. If he escaped from this trap . . . there were waiting for him only the choices of killing or not killing. Neither had brought him satisfaction.

Better to stay here, and if killing was what he must choose, then best to try killing something that desired to kill him. If he must face death, then best to face it for two who were young and who loved.

Once he had made the decision, he knew it was right. He felt the doubts and rationalizations drop away. He was in his element. He knew what to do. Knowing that, again, was all the peace he could hope for. He knew what he was.

Chapter Twenty-Seven

They reached the other end of the alley and came out on a broad square. Halvorssen waved them back.

"They may be waiting there," he whispered. "I will go first. If you hear nothing, follow me." He looked at his daughter. Her eyes were filled with tears. He put his hand on her shoulder. "None of that, beloved," he said. "Your mother and I . . ." his voice broke, and he turned his eyes away. "We always raised you to be brave. To take risks."

"Papa . . ." She looked at him, blinked back her tears, and nodded.

Halvorssen looked at Billy. "Take care of her," he said.

Then he was gone, his tall form disappearing quickly into the fog as he ran. They heard his footsteps for several seconds after they could no longer see him.

Then, nothing.

Kosho looked at Billy. "What is out there?" he asked.

"Kosho . . . I don't know. I can't sense them."

Kosho seemed to understand. He nodded slightly. "You will concentrate," he said. "It will return. You are capable of it." Then he too ran out of the alleyway and disappeared into the fog.

Billy looked behind them. "Glassman. He hasn't followed us."

Kirsten only looked at him, trusting. He felt the burden of making the decision on his own. He took her hand, and realized that she would go where he would. But he also felt her expectation that they would go. They squeezed each other's hand, hard, and ran.

* * *

Halvorssen ran swiftly, holding his rifle at the ready, but to his relief found no enemy in wait. He reached the other side of the square and looked back. He could see nothing through the fog. He crouched silently and listened. "Kirsten," he called. "Over here. It's safe."

The Commander heard him, although he did not understand the words. The Commander was looking for Billy. He knew the creatures would travel in a group—that was characteristic of them, although the lure of a treasure hunt had been designed to split them into competing parties. Somehow, whenever they felt in danger, this species would instinctively coalesce into a pack. That alone should have marked them as primitive, and must have been one reason why none of the scouts thought them capable of the Discovery.

The Commander could turn it to his use now. This creature was obviously separated from the others. If its cries were to bring the others to it, then the Commander would have the boy within his grasp.

Kosho stopped in the center of what seemed to be a limitless square. It was clear that there were no opponents here, although he had not overtaken Bjorn Halvorssen. He was not so much concerned about that as he was about losing sight of Billy.

Kosho peered back through the fog, listening for the sounds of Billy and Kirsten approaching. There was only silence. He began to retrace his steps, thinking that they might still be in the alleyway.

Instead of the alley, he found himself passing into a broad walkway lined with the fog-shrouded shapes of trees. He shook his head, irritated that he had lost his way, but then the soothing sense of a familiar spot came to him.

There had been elements of the city that reminded him of New York. He had seen other streets that reminded him of Paris, especially the broad boulevard on which they had traveled earlier. One could not be sure, and in fact, if the city were only imaginary, it might be part of any city. Or parts of many.

This particular pathway reminded him unaccountably of the outer garden of the Meiji Shrine in Tokyo. Of course, it was not. But the sight brought back those same feelings he had felt when he walked through those gardens. They had been built to celebrate the resumption of the imperial line, but at the same time

Japan was meeting the West. Old and new somehow entwined here. Kosho touched his sword, thinking of the elements of ancient and modern cultures that he himself embodied.

He stopped. Up ahead, beneath the trees, a dark form slowly emerged from the fog. It was one of them. There was no place to hide, and Kosho stood stock-still, hoping not to be noticed. The creature came nearer, walking slowly as if it were taking a peaceful walk by itself.

Then Kosho noticed the sword hanging from the other's belt. It was the twin of his own sword. And Kosho saw the purpose of all this—knew that the illusion that lay over everything had lifted. He had been drawn to this spot for one purpose.

The alien creature stopped and looked at Kosho. Its intention was clear. Kosho bowed, and accepted the challenge.

The sound of his sword sliding from its scabbard was like the drawing of a great curtain. The past was present. All that he had read about and imitated was now real. The answering sound of the other sword being drawn completed the change.

Kosho had read hundreds of times *The Book of Five Rings*, the lifework of Shinmen Musashi No Kami Fujiwara No Genshin—the great swordsman known as Musashi. It was a work designed to be studied and absorbed over the course of a lifetime. It had prepared him for this moment. Before long, he would discover whether his preparation had been adequate. He advanced on the opponent, adopting Musashi's stance: head erect, the line of the neck straight, vigor throughout his body, strength in his legs. The combat stance that one must practice in everyday life. He remembered the comforting words that Musashi had written more than three hundred years before: "The way of the warrior is resolute acceptance of death."

Glassman waited silently. The creature out there would have seen the others run into the alleyway. There was a chance it would be fooled into thinking all of them had escaped, or that the one they left behind was dead. If so, it might show itself.

There were a few bursts of gunfire. The rabbi recognized the sound of the weapon. He was facing another Uzi. Its owner concentrated on firing into the car—a waste of ammunition, calculated Glassman. There was a short pause, and then the firing began again. Glassman knew that his only recourse was to remain hidden and hope that a chance round did not ricochet off the car or the wall behind him and whirl crazily into his body.

A longer silence followed. Glassman lay completely flat on the pavement, risking the loss of full mobility to get a look at the area beyond the wrecked automobile. The fog still restricted visibility, but it was less dense near the ground.

He spied a shadowy movement just beyond the limits of his clear vision. Then it receded, disappeared for a second, then appeared again, a few feet to the left of where he had first seen it.

Something was moving out there in the fog, and evidently it was seeking to circle his position. He had to move, but to leave the shelter the car afforded would make him an easy target. He rolled underneath the automobile, bringing the Uzi up beside him. He cringed as it struck against the pavement, making a metallic scrape that seemed magnified by the cramped space he was in.

Even so, the additional few feet he drew closer to the enemy gave him a better sight. He could see the legs of the black form now, standing like thin pillars. It had frozen at the sound, and gave Glassman a shot. He held the Uzi on its side, trying to bring its barrel parallel to the ground, and pulled the trigger.

Billy and Kirsten, their hands clasped tightly together, ran toward the spot where they had seen her father disappear. She was, he could feel, stronger than he, and he need not fear that she would tire. He had the sense now of imminent danger . . . of Hunters all around them in the fog.

They stumbled over the curb on the opposite side of the square. In trying to keep from falling, they lost their grip on each other. They turned instinctively, breathing hard from the exertion of the run.

"I don't see Papa," Kirsten said anxiously.

Billy tried to sense where he was, but his weakness and the disorienting sensation of the fog kept him from pinpointing Bjorn's location.

"He's near," Billy said. "Listen."

They heard the sound of Bjorn's voice, softly calling, but it seemed to come from all around them. Kirsten pulled at Billy's hand. "He's over here," she said.

He shook his head, but followed her.

The deafening sound of the .470 hunting rifle filled their ears. It echoed off the buildings, invisible in the fog, and the echoes sounded over and over again down the canyons of the city.

* * *

When Bjorn had seen the approaching creature, he had fired without thinking, making his aim poor. He had only alerted his enemy, who dashed off to the side into the safety the fog offered.

He hesitated, feeling defenseless. The creature had held no weapon that he could see, but that did not make him feel any safer. He thought of Bibi, lying peacefully under the sandbank, and of the words the rabbi had said over her. A phrase repeated itself in his mind: "Though a multitude of my enemies set upon me from all sides, I am not afraid."

Bjorn knew that his duty now was not to save himself, but to save Kirsten. The boy had said there were three of these creatures. If Bjorn could kill only one, even at the cost of his own life, there would be two. One of them was back there with Glassman. If only the boy had sense enough to flee with Kirsten, then they might have a chance. But they might come toward the sound of the shot. He had to act quickly.

He ran up the steps in the direction the creature had taken.

Glassman fired burst after burst, raking the Uzi back and forth to cover any lateral movement the creature might make. At last he stopped. He had no refills for his clip, but there was half a clip left, he judged.

Fear rose up in him as the fire returned. He could no longer see the legs of the creature, and the bullets were ricocheting off the pavement in front of him, sending sparks of light up into the fog, making it difficult to tell where they were coming from. The creature was firing from a slightly higher vantage point, so that his position under the car sheltered him from a direct shot, but the sparks from the ricochets drew nearer, walking across the pavement toward the car, as the line of fire was adjusted.

He rolled quickly back to the other side of the car again. He had two choices: he could make a dash for the alleyway or he could emerge to face the enemy, hoping to sight its position before it could react.

Glassman was not trained to retreat. Israel's position as an isolated entity surrounded by foes who wanted its total destruction had made retreat the same as defeat. Habit made his decision for him.

He stood up quickly by the trunk of the car, the lower half of his body still shielded. Incredibly, he saw the thin form of the enemy in profile, the barrel of its Uzi raised. He could not miss despite the fog. He fired, emptying his weapon at the creature, then stopped in bewilderment as the racket of the Uzi echoed around him. The other did not fall or even react. Glassman's blood turned cold. He heard a sound to his right and looked.

The bullets ripped through his chest, slamming him backward until the wall of the building stopped his lifeless form. Still holding the Uzi, he slipped to the pavement.

Warily the Gray Female approached, alert for a feigned death. There were creatures capable of that, she knew. She had seen an animal on another planet with a compartmentalized body that was capable of suffering the complete loss of one part of its body and maintaining life in the others.

This race was not like that, she reminded herself. Or it was not supposed to be. There were already too many surprises on this Hunt.

As she advanced, however, she sensed it. It was not through her Discovery powers, which she had used to create a mirage of herself to draw the animal's fire. It was a sensation that she had felt too seldom, could never get enough of. It brought her a feeling of fulfillment, as if the void in her life had for a second not been there. It was the sensation of death—that she had once more taken the life of another creature. Possessed it.

She touched the body of the creature with her foot. It still held tightly to its weapon, she noticed, and she thought that, whatever else was or was not true about them, they were born naturally to kill. Perhaps the Scientist had been right—that they were capable of making the Discovery and becoming true Hunters. All the more reason why all of them must be destroyed. She felt not the slightest shame for violating the Old Rules to destroy this one.

She looked around. Its action had allowed the others to escape, for now. Perhaps that was their weakness. For true Hunters did not Hunt in packs of animals that acted as a unit. She would not give up her life for another. In that, she thought, was the strength of the true Hunter.

The Commander had reclaimed his weapon. He had hoped by showing himself defenseless that the creature would hold his fire. But the animals were too aggressive. And they were frightened. It would kill him on sight, and he heard it now, stepping closer through the fog. Stalking him.

The realization sent a feeling of cold fury through the Commander. He had not come here to be stalked by an animal. He had come to prove his prowess as a Hunter, not to show his ability to draw a half-grown beast into a trap in order to bestow on him the greatest attribute of the most powerful form of life in the galaxy.

The Commander raised his weapon, which matched that of the creature that dared to stalk him. That advantage—that the creature was experienced in its use, and he was not—was enough for a Hunter to offer.

The Aging Master thought the same thing as he beheld his opponent. He was delighted as he saw that he had made the correct choice of weapons. The first time he had held it in his hands at the Hunting Council he had admired its beautiful craftsmanship. The crudity of a cutting weapon was more than overshadowed by the aesthetic pleasure of the immaculately finished blade, its silver sheen tinged by a hint of blue that indicated its strength, its ability to cut through other metals without shattering or nicking. The groove along its side was obviously intended to allow the life blood of an opponent to escape easily, so that the deepest possible cut could be made. Even its curve, subtle and perfect, showed the Aging Master how it was to be handled.

He looked at the creature who held a similar weapon. This was the opponent he had crossed the galaxy to test his skills against for one last time. The creature, still some distance away, made a bow, obviously the form of a ceremony. The Aging Master imitated it, then followed the other's lead in holding the weapon above his head with both hands.

In that position they advanced on each other, each conscious of the subtle choice implicit in each step, the positioning of the foot changing the angle of the body in relation to the other, one move countering the other as each fought to attain an advantageous position from which to strike.

The Aging Master let the other take the lead, but he learned more of the tactics with each step. In one step, the creature moved almost imperceptibly to one side. The Aging Master corrected the angle with his own next movement, keeping his body fully facing the other.

Gradually, they began to circle each other, each step committing the other to another step around the circle to maintain the balance of position. The Aging Master sensed the dulling effect of this movement on the senses, so that eventually when he would make the anticipated next step the other would seek to reverse the movement and strike.

Quickly as the thought came, the Aging Master struck first, bringing the sword down with all his strength. He was surprised by the instant change in the other's stance, from offense to defense, as he blocked the swift movement of the Aging Master's sword with his own blade and then moved immediately to the offensive again as he slid his own blade down that of the Aging Master's.

The Aging Master felt the strong blow of the opponent's blade drive downward to his hand guard, nearly driving his sword from his grasp—as it was obviously intended to. He withdrew quickly, flexing the fingers of his hands to revivify the sensation in them, and found himself forced to retreat farther, step by step, as the other followed up his advantage with a series of slashes.

The Aging Master fended off the ferocious attack with a series of defensive maneuvers, blocking the opponent's sword with his own and continually moving backward. Fortunately, they were in a large open space, and he could not be pressed against an obstacle.

Even as his mind concentrated on parrying the lightning-swift blows, the Aging Master felt a deep satisfaction. At last he had found an opponent who could push him to the limit. Even as he feared for the loss of his own life, he marveled at the sensation. This was truly a race that could, if allowed to develop, be equal to his own—to provide the challenge that he believed the People needed. He hoped that somewhere the Commander was encountering the one among them who could make the Discovery.

Chapter Twenty-Eight

Billy struggled to catch up with Kirsten, who kept vanishing up ahead in the fog. He could feel the panic in her mind, even now that they were separated physically, and he knew that his powers were slowly returning. What was it Kosho had said to him? "You are capable of it."

That was true. He had done it, and so he must be able to do it again. But his power was strongest when there was great danger. Though they were frightened now, there did not seem to be immediate danger. At least, not to him or to Kirsten.

He hurried after her, reaching out for her shoulder, clasping it and turning her around to face him. "Kirsten, you mustn't get away from me. Slow down."

She clung to him, and as he felt the warm contours of her body, he experienced in a surge the renewed ability to know what she was thinking. It was all jumbled together—her sexual attachment to him, the anxiety she felt for her father, and the belief that he, Billy, could somehow keep them safe.

The confidence she felt in him transferred itself to his own mind. He felt what she felt, and his own doubts dropped away. He began to reach out again, searching with his mind through the fog. Suddenly he came alert as he saw, as clearly as if they had been actors on a stage, the Commander and Kirsten's father stalking each other.

She felt his alertness and alarm. "Billy, tell me . . . what is it?"

"I have to . . ." he groped for the words to explain it to her, distracted by the attempt to translate for her the images that his mind was immersed in. "I have to help him."

She held to him with a strength that had fear behind it. "Don't leave me here," she pleaded.

He struggled for control of himself. He could move now, if he concentrated really hard, conquer the air again, make himself into something that was nearly beyond the limits of his understanding . . . but he was tied to her, his body held fast, and if he disappeared from her grasp he knew the shock would be too much for her.

He probed farther, trying to enter the Commander's mind with his own, felt his attempt noticed and then slapped back viciously. *Keep away,* came the thought, but not in words, just a sensation of outraged anger. *Never touch the mind of a Hunter,* came the thought.

The first shot—he heard it with his mind, saw the flash, but realized that Kirsten heard it as well—was not far from them. It came from Bjorn's rifle. There was the sensation of pain radiating outward from the Commander's mind, and then more shots.

He felt as if he stood in the crossfire between them, and he struggled to hold the shots back as he had the arrows aimed at his mother. But his power failed him. He had not yet developed it to the point where he could handle and control so many sensations at once.

He caught only the thought of Bjorn Halvorssen, a weak thought mingled with pain—it was of him and Kirsten, Bjorn's image of the two of them and his deep hope and approval. Then the source of the thought faded gradually like a dimming, flickering electrical surge. It went out.

Billy groped, looking for other thoughts. He found the mind of the Commander again. It was weakened, mixed with pain and the effort to regain control. The mind behind it slapped at Billy's mind again, but he pressed through the barrier. What he found there, only on the surface of the mind—for it was a mind that worked differently from his, had too many memories that were utterly beyond any point of reference for him—was something that astonished him.

A mind that, in a different way from Kirsten's or her father's, had a respect for him. *You are growing stronger,* came the approving thought. It approved!

Tell me, Billy said, daring to try to send his own thoughts into the complexity of that brain. *Tell me how I can do this. Tell me what I am.*

Come to me, came the reply, and Billy shrank before it. There were too many other thoughts, conflicting ones, behind that, and for a second he saw himself as the Commander saw him. He shrank away, broke contact completely, and fled.

"Run," he whispered to Kirsten. She obeyed, wanting, he knew, to ask him about the shots, fearing to know what had happened. He would tell her—he cringed at the thought, but he would *have* to tell her—but only when they were safe.

As they ran, though, he felt the futility of it. When he broke through the Commander's barriers and touched his mind, he realized that he had established a link between them that could not be broken. He would have to learn how to set up his own defenses, for now the Commander could find him wherever he went.

Kosho remembered word for word the advice given in *The Book of Five Rings:* stick to the enemy like lacquer to a vessel. . . . Cut, seek always to cut.

There were words of caution, and words of relentless attack. The swordsman who knows the Way completely will know when to use one, then the other.

Kosho felt that it was the time for attack. He forced his opponent back, step by step, slashing, seeking for the weak spot in the defense.

As his thrusts rained down, however, he realized that the enemy was parrying each of them successfully. Though on the defensive, its reflexes were quick, as quick as Kosho's.

Kosho realized that at some point one of them would make an error, the tiniest error that would enable one of them to break the cycle of endless cut, thrust, and parry. When the moment came, he must be ready to switch his own method, to press his own advantage or to counter quickly the advantage inadvertently given to the other.

Already the other had learned how to parry his blows to prevent him from sliding his sword down the blade of the other to get nearer to the body.

What was unknown as yet was the matter of fatigue. Kosho knew that at a certain point in time his own reflexes must relax for a second—less than that—in the way that an overexerted muscle must momentarily relax. He did not know, yet, the limits of fatigue in the creature. He must have some limit—Kosho would not allow himself the weakening fear of suspecting that there might be no limit. It was alive, as he was, and therefore must at some time weaken, rest.

He thought he felt a weakening in the other, and the sensation gave him the strength to intensify his attack. With each renewed thrust, he felt the sword of the other lower, inch by inch.

He struck! Cut, pressing as deeply as he could, then withdrew quickly for the next blow, the one that would finish the other.

In the excitement of the moment, the first time he had ever felt a real sword cut into flesh, he allowed himself the luxury of elation.

It was his mistake. Without warning, the other struck back, causing Kosho to reflexively lift his blade in defense.

And now the tide of the battle instantly changed. It was the enemy who forced him back, cutting with strength that seemed unabated by the wound it had received. Kosho moved to the side, seeking to circle to take away the strength of the attack. Remembering to keep his feet moving as if they were steps taken in tranquillity, without crossing his legs or feeling the need for haste; he moved and felt the other move instinctively with him, keeping fully faced toward Kosho, keeping up its attack.

The sound of the blades was like eagles screaming. Again they had set up a rhythm between them. Cut . . . parry . . . cut . . . parry. Kosho realized that when that rhythm had established its own inevitability, then one of them must seek to break it by changing tactics. It was a risk, but the greater risk was that the other would strike first.

Almost at the moment of his thinking it, he realized that the other had changed the angle of his thrust by the merest fraction. Kosho's realization saved him from the sudden lowering of the enemy's sword to a side position, and enabled him to jump back in time to avoid being decapitated.

Even so, he had changed the angle of his arm to bring his own sword down to parrying position, and the side blow caught him on the elbow.

Cut, he realized. He himself was cut, and the second realization came to him: it was as the masters had written. It did not hurt. The razor-sharp edge of the blade entered his flesh and withdrew without the sensation of pain. It was only the brief moment in which he felt pressure against his elbow that let him know that he had been cut at all.

The danger was that the lack of feeling in the cut would deceive him into thinking he could make the same movements as before, with equal strength. The cut had not severed a muscle, but it had opened blood vessels that gave strength to the muscles in that arm. Eventually, perhaps without his realizing it, the arm would weaken. If then he struck with the full force of his other arm, expecting the injured arm to exert its full power, the path of the sword would alter. It would miss its target, or give his enemy room to maneuver.

He knew this, and would adjust. It was possible that the enemy would not realize the effects of his own cut.

The Commander searched with his mind for Billy. The pain from the wound the creature had inflicted on him at the end, exposing its own position and giving the Commander just enough time in which to fire and kill it, was distracting him. It was not a serious wound, but the projectile had been large, ripping through the flesh of his leg, immobilizing him.

He could, he knew, use the Discovery to change his body and take another form. Even that would have a defect that would reflect the diminishment of his own person, but he would be more mobile.

To use the Discovery, he realized, would at this point be ignoble. He had gone beyond the commands of the Guardians, true; but it was for a purpose, the attempt to test himself on equal terms with a creature who had not made the Discovery.

The boy had spoiled that. Yet the Aging Master was right: the existence of the boy had presented them with an opportunity not only for themselves but for the People that might never come again. He *had* to reach him, and to do so he had to somehow win his trust. He had felt the boy withdraw in fear. That was understandable. What must have it been like for the first of his own People who had made the Discovery? And that Discovery was made in solitude, without the immediate threat of a Hunting party that had shown its ability to kill others of its kind. The boy had had no parents who could carefully inculcate him into the mysteries of Discovery power. Only the Commander could do that now.

The Commander's probing mind found that of the Gray Female. She was exultant, and did not bother to conceal her feelings. She had, the Commander saw, no fear of the boy. She felt the same toward him as she did toward the others—to her, they were merely animals whose slaughter would gratify her. She had killed again, he saw, and the kill only intensified her blood thirst for other kills.

He had to keep her away from the boy. Where was he?

Billy and Kirsten lay gasping under some trees in a park. They had run as far as they were able. Wet from the fog, they lay grasping each other in an embrace of desperation. He drew strength from her, fighting against fear, sending his mind out wildly in all directions.

He realized he had to control himself. He slowed his thoughts, let himself feel the limits of his body, the points at which it touched her . . . drew mentally away so that he would not be distracted by her feelings of need.

Their position became clear. He could now sense the others, as if pieces on a city-large chessboard. He saw the Commander, but drew away from him before he could sense Billy's mind. Then he saw the Gray Female, still armed with the Uzi. He touched her mind briefly enough to see the dead body of Glassman, and he felt her elation. It revolted him.

Where was Kosho? Then he saw. Physically, he was not far away, but he had been difficult to locate because his mind was absorbed in one purpose. Billy watched the battle between him and the Aging Master, touched the mind of the third alien, and came away with even more confused impressions than when he had entered the mind of the Commander.

He had received the impression of great age and wisdom, yet a vitality and vigor that were nearly overwhelming. Billy realized he had drawn strength from the contact, and that the other had not seemed to notice. Compelled by curiosity, he returned to that mind.

The Aging Master's keen awareness had observed the touch of Billy's mind on its first contact. He had not permitted it to distract him—*could* not, in the heat of battle. But a cautionary thought formed within the complexities of his mind. It was the boy; neither of the other People would risk touching his mind, for whatever reason, while he was in the midst of combat—or indeed, at any other time.

When the second touch of the boy's mind came, the Aging Master allowed himself to devote a portion of his consciousness to it. He felt the boy's curiosity, his puzzlement at the experience of being within a mind so foreign to him.

The Aging Master knew that he could, if he wished, suddenly turn the full force of his powers on the newly-awakening mind that had committed the ultimate insult of probing into his thoughts.

The Master's mind, which had destroyed worlds, could snuff out the boy's consciousness and make him as if he had never existed. He could do this in so short a time that it would not even disturb his concentration on the battle he was desperately engaged in.

As a Guardian, he was obliged to do that.

Instead, he held back, fascinated by the spectacle of a mind making the Discovery—a race making the Discovery for the first time. The Aging Master felt an emotion he had not thought himself capable of: he felt benevolence. It was like the sensation those who had borne children spoke of—the sensation when they conferred upon their young the power of the Discovery by letting them probe their parents' minds. He had not thought anything could still make him happy.

Kosho noticed that the reflexes of the other showed signs of becoming automatic, as if the other were tiring mentally. Kosho knew that he himself was tiring, but tried not to let the realization daunt his effort. He had to exert himself to the utmost, mentally denying fatigue as long as possible.

He remembered Musashi's advice for a maneuver to use when tiredness seems inevitable: strike at the heart. He timed the rhythm of their continuing exchange of blows and parries, and at the second when he exerted himself to parry the strong downward thrust of the other's sword, continued the motion with an anguish of effort and turned the blade from a square-on position, showing the point of his blade for the first time. He thrust it deep within the chest of the other, withdrawing instantly.

The other drew back, and Kosho raised his sword quickly for the finishing blow. His sword wavered in the air, faltering. The other raised its own sword one last time, but Kosho could see that the blow must be feeble.

His hesitation cost him. Instead, the downward blow was immensely strong, stronger than Kosho could have believed possible, and Kosho was not in a defensive position. He parried the blow weakly, knowing that he had let his guard down too soon. He felt the Aging Master press the crossed blades down, forcing them toward Kosho's face.

The Aging Master felt the pain in his heart and knew that he was dying. He made the last noble effort—to kill that which had killed him—but used a precious part of his wavering power to grasp at the mind that was within him.

Billy felt himself enclosed by a gigantic hand. He was utterly unable to resist it, and he felt the message it wanted to give him: *You are to Hunt. That is your purpose and meaning. Seek yourself a name, the name of a Hunter.*

Then it thrust him from its brain, leaving him dazed. He was back in his own body, lying next to Kirsten. He could not hear the message of the Aging Master that was meant only for the Commander.

The Commander heard, alert and waiting as the signal of death came from the Aging Master. He knew that he was to be entrusted with a Death Wish:

Our race must renew itself by challenge or die. To deny that need is to succumb to decadence. You must give it to them. Give them the challenge.

One other heard the message—the Gray Female, who recognized it as a Death Wish. Momentarily, she was stunned at the realization. She denied it.

She hated him, it was true, but she held tightly locked within herself the memory of a time when she had felt otherwise. If he had not been the one to allow her chosen mate to die, they might even have renewed their courtship. That was not unseemly. But instead she had nurtured her anguish, the resentment she felt toward him, and they had fallen into the familiarity of old friends who have an unspoken grudge between them. They knew each other better than they wanted to.

Now, to have it happen again . . . from beasts of this class . . . She gave a low cry to erase the knowledge of what had taken place. But the memory remained.

Her hatred rose to the surface. There was only one among them who could have had the power to surprise the Aging Master and kill him. She rushed toward the spot from which his Death Wish had come, gathering the full force of her anger and continuing the journey with the power of the Discovery.

Billy felt her coming and shivered. He raised himself and looked again at the figures in the garden. Kosho stood there, cut and bleeding, looking down at the Aging Master.

* * *

Kosho had received a wound on his forehead, which bled into his eyes. He blinked it away. The other had slumped to his knees, and remained there, head bowed.

To Kosho, the enemy's position suggested that he must perform the final act of honor. He raised his sword and brought it down swiftly, decapitating the foe and assuring that he would suffer no longer.

Suddenly there came a sound like the rising of a great wind through the trees, and Kosho turned to face the source. His eyes widened.

Billy touched Kirsten's shoulder. She turned to look at him. "Don't watch," he said. "I'll come back."

But she did watch, and saw him slowly dissolve into a form that had only vaguely the outlines of a human. He was a gray mist, very much like the fog itself, and it began to rise.

She heard—no, felt—his touch inside her brain, the soothing message *I'll come back,* and despite her terror, she felt calm. The mist rose, brushing against her lips like a kiss, and she felt a pressure close her eyes gently.

She wanted to scream, but she remembered the comfort he had given her, and tried very hard not to. He wanted her to wait. She didn't understand what he was doing, but she knew, somehow, that it would be all right.

He rose into the sky and faced what Kosho had seen.

Kosho had been a boy living on the outskirts of the city of Nagasaki when the fireball rose over the city. His parents had been farther towards the center; no trace of them was ever found. When the air-raid sirens went off, he ran from the field where he was working toward the shelter of a farmhouse cellar. The initial shock wave had knocked him flat, and that probably saved him. He had been burned slightly on his back, but he had not been able to look toward the source of the wind. His eyes were saved. Others later described to him what they had seen: those whose eyes were now empty sockets.

He looked toward the end of the garden and saw what could only be that same awesome terror. But it moved much more slowly, as if he were seeing it run through a projector in slow motion. He tensed for the blast, and then overhead he saw the immense gray cloud that rushed toward the fireball. It bore no resemblance to Billy by now, but he heard Billy's voice from the midst of it. *Get down,* it said.

Kosho saw the meeting of the cloud and the fireball; the force of the collision reverberated throughout the garden, ripping up the trees and tearing flagstones from the ground. Kosho fell, realized that his wounds had robbed him of all strength, and despite his wish to watch, fell into unconsciousness.

The Gray Female had been taken by surprise, the Commander realized. She had put up no defenses at all, and somehow the boy had seen through to the essence of the illusion. He had chosen just the right counter-form to drain her of power, and by the time she realized her mistake, he had her mind enclosed in his.

Even so, she should have had the agility to escape. But as the Commander observed the struggle between the two minds, he recognized certain motions that only the Aging Master had been able to perform. They were not elegantly done, with the strength and finesse they would have displayed if the Master had completed them himself, but they bore his stamp.

Just before the Aging Master had signaled his Death Wish, the Commander had sensed that he had expelled another from his mind. It was almost unthinkable to contemplate: he had allowed the boy entrance to his own thoughts. And the boy had learned.

Even in the midst of the struggle, the Commander could have intervened, could have swayed the contest in favor of the Gray Female. But that was not the way of Hunters. She had chosen to use her Discovery powers; it was she who had established the rules of this contest.

And she was not equal to it. The gray cloud grew larger and larger, taking within itself the fireball that had rushed through the skies. Slowly, inexorably, the fireball ceased to burn, until only a flickering tongue of fire struggled within the heart of the cloud. As the cloud snuffed it out, the Commander heard the dying cry of the Gray Female. She left no Death Wish—only a lingering feeling of hatred and threats. Then, emptiness.

It began to rain, in torrents that washed the garden stones clean of the blood of alien and human. The Commander felt the water rolling down his body and looked upward to experience its cleanliness. Soon, he knew, the boy would exhaust himself. He did not realize that he was young, and had even now much to learn.

Chapter Twenty-Nine

The rain revived Kosho. He tested himself, and realized he must get to some place of shelter to bind his wounds. He staggered to his feet with the same iron discipline of spirit that had enabled him to kill the Aging Master. He looked down at the corpse at his feet. *I never knew his name,* he thought. He slid his sword into the scabbard at his belt and began to walk painfully through the garden.

Not far away, he found Kirsten under a tree. She told him what had happened, what she thought she saw.

Kosho nodded and looked upward at the clouds, which were beginning to clear.

"Can he . . . come back?" Kirsten asked.

Kosho thought. "He has discovered the secret of *utsuroi,*" he said.

"What is that?"

Kosho smiled slightly. "It is difficult to understand or explain this concept. In Japan, we admire the beauty of nature. But it is not merely for its beauty. We look at the cherry blossoms, which bloom only for a short time and then fade. If one returns for the cherries, it is possible to understand that the blossoms have become the cherries. And in winter, the blossoms, the cherries, the leaves have gone. There is only the tree. And yet there is still the promise of the blossoms that will come again. If one is able to return, one can see them again. But the following year the blossoms are not the same—nor am I the same. I may return to the same spot, but I am older and the blossoms all look the same, but they are different."

"You're right," she said, shy but smiling. "I don't understand."

He patted her hand. "It takes many years of visiting the cherry blossoms in spring before one understands. And then, even then, one sees only that things may change and yet remain the same."

"Are you talking about Billy? Are you saying that he is the same?"

Kosho glanced upwards. "To our eyes he is not the same. Yet to himself, he has merely learned how to assume another form. He is the same, to himself. He has only advanced farther in knowledge. He has learned to command the ability to change. As you grew from a child to a beautiful young girl, and will someday be an old woman. Did you not remain yourself?"

"Yes, but . . . this is different."

"Only beyond our comprehension. It is the same, to him."

"But I want *him*! I want him back the way I know him."

Kosho smiled "Then I think he will return. But you must understand that"—he shrugged—"he will never again be like us."

"But will I be able to see him . . . *you* know."

"The way that is most familiar to you."

"I guess that's what I mean."

"Perhaps." He pointed to the clouds overhead. They were drifting toward the sea. The wind had changed. "We must follow him. I do not know what we will find, but we can only follow."

They walked through the empty streets of the city together. He felt weakened by his wounds, and was grateful for her assisting arm. She was strong, this girl. Kosho wondered about last night, wondered if they had made love together and if there would be a child of their union. These were questions it would be impossible to ask, but in time they would be answered.

The clouds gradually faded from view. They came to the edge of the city, where cold and lifeless waves lapped against a wall. Shelter was there. They recognized it, for it was the only structure that was lighted, looked as if it might be a place of life.

They saw Billy lying there on the pavement.

Kirsten ran to him with a cry, and Kosho plodded after her, thinking, *He has tired himself. He should not have changed back. He returned for her*. He nodded. *That is the part of him that has not changed.*

Kirsten carried Billy inside by herself. As before, the refuge was comfortably furnished, with a table of hot food and many kinds of drink. There were also bandages and medicine. Kosho began to clean his wounds, watching Kirsten trying to revive Billy.

She looked over at him. "What can we do?"

"He is not injured," said Kosho. "He is only tired, as before. He has not learned to gauge his limits. That is because he is young, impulsive, wants to do everything within his power. However powerful he has become, he has still the weaknesses of youth."

"We have to help him."

"He will be helped if he senses you are here, concerned about him, and healthy. Eat something. You remember last night? He awoke when you were eating. He took something that you brought for him. He enjoyed it."

She looked at him doubtfully. "Is that all I can do?"

He paused. "Perhaps you can look and see if I have covered the cut on my head with this bandage."

She came and fussed over him. She took the entire bandage off and replaced it. Doing, she felt useful. It gave her contentment.

"Kosho," she said.

"Yes?"

"Do you think . . . Papa . . . and the other one . . . are dead?"

He bowed his head. It was better to tell her the truth. "They must be."

"Billy . . . couldn't save them?"

He sighed, and shook his head. "I do not know what he is able to do."

They ate, with an eye on Billy, and found that the food slowly revived their spirits. When Billy finally stirred, Kirsten was there with a plate of food. He smiled weakly at her and took some of it. She was eager with questions, but a look from Kosho stopped her. It was better to wait until Billy felt like talking.

He finished his plate of food. "I'm thirsty," he said. "Is there any lemonade?"

They poured it for him, and he drank glass after glass of it. Kosho marveled at his capacity, and then remembered the rain.

Billy looked at them sheepishly. "I'm sure *thirsty*," he said. They nodded.

He hung his head, and they could see he had something he wanted to say. With an effort, he met Kirsten's look.

"I'm sorry," he said, "that you saw me."

She was puzzled. "I don't understand."

"I mean . . . you saw me change. You know."

She shook her head. "But that doesn't matter." She moved closer to him.

"It doesn't?" he said, staring back at her. "I mean, I thought you'd be frightened. You *were* frightened."

"Yes. I was." Her blue eyes were full of happiness, and very close to his. "And then you touched me. No one else ever touched me like that. Inside."

He blushed. "Yeah, but . . . that's just like . . . a trick. I made you be calm. But you were afraid of me."

"I know," she said. "But I'm not now. I never will be, because I know you would never hurt me. Because I love you, and you . . ." She waited.

He stammered, but he got it out. "I do. I love you too."

Kosho discreetly rose and moved away. They were kissing.

Perhaps he should not be doing that, Kosho thought, remembering Billy's apparent loss of power that morning, and guessing the reason for it. *But that is not for me to say,* he realized.

Billy did realize it, as he felt himself become excited. He wanted her very badly, knew that she would go upstairs with him and they could be as happy together as they had been last night. But he had to make sure that they could get away together, so that there could be other nights. Gently, he pushed her back. They looked at each other, their breath coming in gasps.

"You don't . . . want to?" she asked, her hurt apparent in her soft voice.

"I do, I do, but listen. There is still . . . one of them out there. And there's tomorrow."

"Oh, no," she moaned, holding him close. "We won't. Please. We'll get away. Where's the old nana? Just tell her . . . or *you* can do it. Take him, too," she said, nodding toward Kosho. "You can do it."

"I can't yet," he said. "I'm not strong enough. I don't know how. And when . . . last night . . ." The words stuck in his throat, for they were painful to say.

"Didn't you enjoy it?" she asked.

"Oh my God. That's not it. I . . . Kirsten . . . I love you, but I just can't right now."

She leaned close. "Let's try. I'll help," she whispered.

"No, really . . . I've got to stay . . . I can't do that, with you . . . and keep my power for the other."

She frowned. "Now I understand," she said, and he was surprised at the change in her voice. "Samson and Delilah," she said, becoming angry at the thought of it. She pulled away from him, folded her arms. She stuck her lip out in a pout. The sight of her lip made him want to reach close and touch it, but as he tried to do so, she angrily pushed him off.

"Don't touch me, then," she said. Looking at him, she added, "And don't touch me with your *mind,* either."

"No, Kirsten, you've got to listen," he said. "That . . . other one . . . out there . . . he's coming after me. He wants me to go with him."

She flashed her eyes at him. "And you'd go with him rather than with me?"

"That's stupid," he said, realizing that he had put it badly.

"So now I'm too stupid to understand these things. They're boy things, I guess. You're going to try to tell me that with boys it's different. I've heard that before. Though not," she added, "as an excuse for keeping *away.*"

He hesitated, tried to think of something to say that wouldn't make it worse. He looked at her. She was angry. He knew he could make her happy with a touch of his mind. But she was right. That wouldn't work. It would only seem to work. Then there would be no Kirsten for him to love. There would only be himself making love to himself. He might as well be using Brian McConnell's books.

"I love you," he said quietly. "I want you, I do. But tonight I've got to protect you."

She shrugged, but seemed to relax her hostility a little. "Let's fight them together. Let me help."

"He's too powerful. I can't . . . *we* can't. I have to let him come. If I have to, I'll give myself up for you. I'll make him let you go."

"No," she said. She stood up and ran across the room to Kosho. "He wants to leave us again," she cried. "Tell him he can't. We'll protect him. We've got to help."

Billy sighed. He went to her and took her in his arms. "You can wait then. But it won't do any good."

Hours went by. They waited, the three of them, together. Billy and Kirsten on the couch, Kosho with his sword at the ready near the table. Kosho had begun to try a little of the sake. It seemed to ease the pain, and yet he was able to keep his head clear. From time to time Kirsten would pour Billy a glass of lemonade.

With Billy's arm around her, Kirsten at last fell asleep. Kosho rested his head on his arms, but his senses were alert, watching the door. Billy was tired too, wanted to sleep, but knew that he must stay awake.

At last Kosho's head began to droop, then snap back as he caught himself. Billy spoke softly to him, "Kosho, there really isn't anything you can do."

"My sword served me this afternoon. You saw what it can do."

Billy let himself reach out to the older man. He touched his brain, trying not to let him know what he was doing. He felt guilty at feeling the things he found there. Kosho was far better at just about everything than Billy could ever imagine being. And yet, because of this, which seemed like nothing Billy had ever *earned* with the discipline and diligence that Kosho had . . . Kosho admired him. Billy moved within the brain of the samurai, and let him sleep.

As Kosho slept, Billy carefully disengaged his own mind, and waited. He did not wait long before the voice sounded clearly in his own mind. *Come,* it said.

Where? he thought back.

You will come, the voice said. *In your own body. You will find the way.*

Give me your word you won't harm them. That they can go.

They will not be harmed. Whether or not they can go depends on the outcome of what will take place between us.

You want me to fight you?

Come.

Billy opened the door of the refuge and stepped out into the darkness. As he had sensed, the city had disappeared. It had never really been there. The ocean was there, he could tell by the sound. Waves lapped against the beach in unceasing rhythm. He went down there, nearly to the water, and walked along the sandy beach. His shoes hampered his movement, and he took them off, along with his socks. He felt the grains of wet sand well up between his toes.

The night was warm but dark. There was no sight of the moon or the stars. Overhead was a vast shroud of dark clouds, not even perceivable as clouds. He could not see, with his eyes, but he knew where he was going. He felt the power strengthen in him, felt himself coming nearer to the one who called. Who waited. He began to strain against the bound of his body, wanting to reach him, but controlled himself, forced himself to walk. It was his planet, and the contact with it gave him the advantage.

He arrived. There was an unspoken meeting of their minds.

What do you want? Billy asked.

The other let himself appear to Billy, let his body appear. It was not dressed in the black outer garment.

Underneath, it was gray and glossy like steel, and iridescent in places, with what looked like scales. The Commander stepped closer to him, and Billy saw that he moved with pain. He saw the wound in the Commander's leg. *It will heal by tomorrow,* came the other's thought. *You must remove your own garments now.*

Billy obeyed, not thinking to question, feeling the unexpected air against his skin. It was a new experience, one that made him feel closer to the sand and water that lapped upon it. Why hadn't he realized before that the clothes only separated him from . . . the rest of the world?

We wear these garments, as you do, to bind our identity, came the Commander's answer. *Here, we must put them aside.*

Why?

Because you are to be told the final secret. Who you are, what you are. That you are part of everything, as it is part of you. Yet you have a separate existence. Feeling the greater existence, you will realize your ability to control it. You will realize the power of your self.

Why are you showing me this?

Because you are . . . worthy of being a Hunter.

Why?

That, no one can tell you. It is what you are.

Not yet. I can't do everything you can yet.

I know.

You could still kill me.

Perhaps.

Why don't you?

Because . . . I have another duty. I may yet kill you. You must be careful of asking too many questions. There was one of us—he died with your mother—who was like that. It is better to accept things as they are.

I can't help it.

Because you are not yet a Hunter. You must learn. Now . . . come close. Let me touch you.

I don't want to.

The voice in Billy's mind grew stronger. *It is because you are repelled at my shape. I am also repelled at your shape. You are not the son I would have chosen.*

I am not your son.

Whose son, then, are you?

Billy tried to remember, tried to speak his father's name, but the creature had taken it from his mind. He looked at the repulsive figure and stepped forward.

The Commander felt the repugnance at touching another, but even more so that he must touch . . . this one. Even now, though he was obeying the Aging Master's Death Wish, he was not sure if he were not committing some grotesque violation of the most sacred moment of the People. He forced his hands outward and touched the boy on his shoulders.

They both shuddered at the contact, feeling the alienness of each other course through their bodies. Billy nearly lost control of himself when he experienced the memories of the Commander, laid fully before him. Then the words came, bringing his consciousness fully alert, awesomely experiencing the mystery of their meaning:

I give you command of air, water, earth, and fire.

Command of space and time.

Command of self.

Power that is without limit.

Yet the greater power is of the self, the essence of the universe that makes order out of chaos, energy from matter, and matter from energy.

The self. The universe.

Always to rule.

Billy staggered, his legs weak as the power of the Discovery surged into him. He wanted to explode outward, soar beyond the planet, experience everything that he sensed lay beyond. The universe.

The Commander's fingers pressed deeply into his shoulders.

You must keep your body.

I don't need it.

You may leave it, or change it, or do with it whatever you will. But you must keep it as the repository of self. Without it you would expand forever into the infinite space of the universe.

I could do that.

And cease to exist as self. There are some who have done it, and their names are forgotten.

My name. The one . . . the old one who died. He told me I must seek a name. You must give it to me.

If you are worthy, I will give it to you.

How can I become worthy?

Tomorrow, you will leave the others and go into the sea.

It is not a sea.

It is what we think it to be. We agree that it is a sea. The contest is equal, for the water is my environment, and yet the sea is of your planet.

And then?

I will test you.

We will fight.

We will test each other. And if you are stronger, you will have your name.

And if I fail?

Then you will not have a name, and your planet will not have a name, and the People will come to destroy all life upon it.

Chapter Thirty

The Commander rested on the floor of the ocean, preparing himself for the contest. In the Initiation Ritual of the People, the contest was only symbolic. The parent would test the child, but in the end would allow the child to win, to emerge victorious and gain the last step that would earn it a name. Neither would die.

In this contest, one of them would die. He would give the boy a name only on the point of death.

For if the Commander won, his only chance of returning home with honor—or safety—was to extinguish the threat to the People. And if he lost, it would mean that the boy truly was able to challenge the People's supremacy. It would mean that the Commander had allowed the unthinkable to happen: another race would have made the Discovery. Better then to die here than to return home for the punishment of the Guardians, which would include death, but not a noble death.

Kirsten and Kosho found Billy sitting on the beach, looking at the water.

"We were so afraid," said Kirsten. "We thought you'd been . . ."

He smiled at her, a tender, tolerant smile as if she were speaking of something very childish. She was surprised. Before, he had never seemed older then her; the look he gave her now was like the looks her father and mother had sometimes shown her. She touched his shoulder. "Are you . . . all right?"

"I've changed now, Kirsten," he said. "I'm sorry."

"There's nothing to be *sorry* about," she replied. "All that matters is that you're safe. Did you . . . kill the other thing?"

He shook his head. "No. He . . . gave me the power to kill him."

"And you didn't?"

He smiled at her again, only now it was a bit infuriating. He looked at Kosho. "Do you understand?" Billy said.

Kosho looked toward the sea. "That is the final step in the Hunt," he said. "The treasure is there, after all."

Billy nodded.

"Who cares about the treasure?" Kirsten said. "Look at what it's cost us already. Our parents . . . the others."

"It brought you to me," said Billy.

"You never talked like that before," she said suspiciously.

"I told you I loved you," he said with honest puzzlement.

"But you never said the things boys say when they think they can talk a girl into bed."

"But . . . we already . . ."

"Maybe you fooled me then."

"Kirsten," Billy said, taking hold of her hands, "you don't really believe that."

"Well . . . maybe not. But if you really meant the things you said, you won't go after that stupid gold. You'll . . ." She trailed off, uncertain.

Kosho spoke earnestly. "Gold is not the treasure that he must go after."

She nodded, tears coming to her eyes, disconcerting both Billy and Kosho. "Now," she said through sobs, "he just wants to kill."

"I don't *want* to, Kirsten," Billy said. "But I can't help what's happened to me."

"What is it, then?" she pleaded. "What has happened to you?"

"I don't really know," he said. "I know that I can enter your mind, or Kosho's mind, or *anybody's*, I guess. And I can change shapes. And last night . . . he told me that I could do a lot more."

"Well, then, why don't you just take us all away? Why do you have to go back?"

"Because he'll follow us, even if I could take you away with me. And . . . because I have to have my name."

"Your name? You have a name."

He shook his head. "Among"—he nodded toward the waves—"*his* people, there are children's names. That is what I have. It's a child's name."

"It's good enough."

"No."

"How stupid," she said, breaking fully into tears now. Angry at herself, and at him, she got up, walked down the strand, and stood with her back turned.

Billy looked helplessly at Kosho. Kosho regarded him steadily.

"The name is only . . . a ritual," said Kosho. "It means nothing. You are you. Take what name you will."

Billy held out his hand, and Kosho took it. Kosho was surprised to feel his hand clasping that of a warrior, strong and confident. It was so very different from the way Billy looked. But then, Kosho reflected, he had seen him do very unusual things. *One cannot judge by the way he looks,* he remembered himself saying to Glassman. That was still true.

"I will do what I have to do," said Billy. "Will you wish me well?"

Kosho bowed his head. "I wish you strength and peace."

"Thank you," Billy said. He stood up and walked over to Kirsten.

"Will you wish me well?" he asked her.

She turned to look at him, and threw her arms around his neck. "You're so foolish," she said. "I love you. Please come back. Promise me."

He smiled in the same way he had before. "If I come back," he said, "will you still love me?"

"Idiot," she said, and kissed him.

After a time, he separated himself gently from her. There were tears in both their eyes. He turned and walked into the surf.

Kosho walked over next to her, and Billy slowly sank beneath the waves. "He cannot hold his breath for long under water," she said. "I can hold my breath longer than *he* can."

Kosho clasped her hand. "He is different now."

Inch by inch, he disappeared beneath the surface. Kosho sensed that if they could see underneath the water, they would find him changing form into something that would undeniably be no longer human. What he would become . . . perhaps it was better that neither he nor Kirsten could see.

* * *

Billy felt the Commander's presence below as soon as his feet touched the water. It wasn't as difficult as he had feared—not like the other times. He had no doubts at all about putting his head under water. There was no difficulty about breathing. He could adapt to the new environment without really thinking about it. He remembered that his own people had come originally from the sea, and the memory of that carried with it the knowledge of the sea as home.

He found his own thoughts falling away as he dropped slowly through the water. He was part of a gigantic chain of being, and the lives of all those individual beings who had gone before ended with him. He might be the last link, or only the middle, for he felt his potential to carry on his new strength. But there was something he must do first, for himself and all the others before and after.

The water was only a place in which to live. And the touch of the water all around him, inside of him, reverberated with the knowledge that something else—something foreign—was within the water too. He gathered the knowledge of the water within himself, changed it, and expelled it in a rush, energized with the thought that the Other must be destroyed.

The Commander received the challenge and disposed of it quickly, turning the angry water back into the environment that was like his own. There was no need to move. The boy would come. The boy was already here. The Commander charged the water with energy that would attack the boy's brain waves.

The attack momentarily stunned Billy, but he analyzed the source of his confusion and grounded it with the enormous source of water that he commanded. He spread his power as far as he was able, aware now that they were fighting for command of territory. He must not confine himself to the limits of his own self, limited to his own senses, heightened though they were.

His thoughts swarmed outward until they met the Commander's. At the point of contact, the water boiled and hissed, creating unstable molecules that formed and reformed themselves in a chain reaction that created more and more energy out of the conflict of matter.

Both the combatants sent their forces toward the points of battle, pressing more and more strongly against the limits of the other. Caught up in the thought that this was the sole area in which the conflict would be decided, Billy poured himself into it nearly to the limit.

The Commander's sudden thrust caught him unawares. From underneath, from the bottom of the sea itself, the Commander created pockets of poisonous, painful gases that floated upwards toward Billy's body, attacking the source of his thought.

Billy felt the first painful destruction of his personal cells, and withdrew some of his resources to charge the gases with molecules that reduced their potency.

The Commander renewed his attack on the limits of Billy's space, threatening again to overwhelm him there.

Confused, unsure how much of his resources he should commit, Billy struck downwards to the bottom. It was earth, earth itself, the same as the land above him, and he felt that he still had full command of it. He dissolved it as deeply as he could.

The Commander's body, heretofore secure in its resting place, suddenly tumbled downward, upsetting his equilibrium and his concentration. It gave Billy time enough to organize his perceptions of the struggle.

Angry at having been attacked from a point he had left undefended, the Commander struck back in force.

Billy had not been expecting fire. Here, the blazing wall of exploding molecules attacked the water near to Billy, turning the oxygen and hydrogen into a roaring, consuming ball that threatened to extinguish his self in an overwhelming agony of heat.

He drew on the only source he could rely on to lower the temperature—once more, the seemingly endless supply of the ocean.

But as he did so, the Commander again pressed in with his own volumes of liquid against the limits of Billy's space. If the attack were left unchecked, Billy would find himself encircled. Yet he suddenly withdrew all his forces for a moment into his own body and dove with all the force he could muster.

Confused by the sudden collapse, the Commander pressed forward blindly, hoping to destroy Billy utterly with one intense effort. He groped within the maelstrom he had created, looking for the tiny, hidden self that would be his prey.

But Billy had escaped, leaving the ocean for the moment to his attacker. Changing form as quickly as he encountered the earth, he assumed the form of a great burrowing thing and drove ferociously to reach down, down, impossibly deep, searching for the inner core of the earth itself.

Where the fire burns eternally.

He struck it, became one with the molten matter at temperatures impossibly high, and then turned to allow its unleashed force the channel he had dug for it to escape.

The force of the pressure carried Billy's fire-form with it, and by the time it reached the ocean floor it was traveling at a speed that propelled it up through the depths to the surface.

Billy felt the Commander's body tumble helplessly against the onslaught and groped for him, trying desperately to find and touch him.

Kirsten and Kosho, alone on the shore, were tumbled off their feet by the immense earthquake that rocked the land. The forces Billy had unleashed caused a tidal wave that rolled northward, rippling and gaining strength toward the islands thousands of miles to the north. The inhabitants of the islands had a legend to account for such phenomena: "The gods of the sea are fighting," they told each other.

Billy's loved ones crawled away from the roiling sea, only to meet Granny once again. "Come with me," she said. "They're going to endanger you if you stay here."

"Granny," gasped Kirsten, "is he still alive?"

"Can't you see, child?" Granny said. "He's trying to become a Hunter."

"Oh, God," Kirsten said in despair. "What if he does?"

The Commander propelled his body upwards, trying to get away from the sudden source of power and heat. He absorbed and quenched the fire, changed, and then dove again. Below, he would find the boy, who had now proved himself the master of the four elements. There was no point in continuing to attack each other in this way, until the limits of the planet were drained.

They met, drawn to each other unerringly. Billy knew now as well as the Commander did how to recognize the thought that signaled the originator.

Their contact was marked by a repulsion like that both had experienced the night before when the Commander had touched the body of the boy. Only now, the force of the repulsion was enormously greater, now that they had worked up the intensity of hatred that lay between them. The urge to kill was less strong than the mental aversion they felt for each other. The mental force expelled both of them away from the contact.

Mine, was the thought Billy sent toward the Commander's being. *This world is mine. You do not belong here.*

I take what I please, came the Commander's reply. *I rule where I go. I am Hunter. I command.*

You do not command me. Give me my name. I have fought you, and you did not win.

We are not yet finished.

An enormous shape appeared in front of Billy. A great creature, larger than an ocean liner, it sprouted heads with rows of jagged teeth that slashed at the water, seeking Billy's form. It carried with it the light of a creature that existed forever in darkness beyond the reach of any sun—a glowing, iridescent brilliance that was intended to illuminate its prey.

Billy struggled to control his fear. He too changed shape, took the form of a shark as large as the other creature, and lashed into the heart of the glowing form, ripping and tearing the heads from the body of the creature.

Their contact with each other was more secure this time, and they held together in a grip that bonded their minds. The Commander's memories were Billy's, and Billy's thoughts were the Commander's.

Rapidly, they borrowed images from each other, changing forms as quickly as thought. The water became murky with the colors of their mutually shed blood. Each continued to flay flesh from the other with teeth, claws, horns, and appendages that had no name but whose purpose was to grasp, grind, sever, and crush.

Like sharks whose feeding frenzy at the smell of blood causes them to tear at each other until both are destroyed, the Commander and Billy fought almost without rational thought. The meeting of their minds, the exchange of thought, drove their mutual hatred to an ever higher pitch.

With his power tested to the utmost, Billy fought within himself for more resources. He searched his own mind and the Commander's for new means of fighting . . . of killing.

At last he came to the kernel of himself that was truly his—all that was left. As he prepared to throw that into the battle too, he realized that that was what the Commander wanted. For the other reserved that part of himself.

Why?

Billy probed as deeply as he could, till he found that part of the Commander that matched Billy's own essence. He would have called it soul, and he saw that there was a word for it in the Commander's own language. The Commander sensed Billy's touch, and threw up his defenses to prevent him from reaching there.

Why?

Billy felt the Commander's attack slacken as he devoted his energy to protecting the core of his being. Not merely protecting it—hiding it. There was something there that the Commander wished him not to know.

The physical struggle of their forms gradually reduced its ferocity. The Commander was trying to disengage himself, break the physical contact that had enabled Billy to probe so far. They reverted to their own forms, with Billy grasping the Commander like a lover, holding as desperately to him as life itself.

He thought of Kirsten, and the way he had held her in the moment of their lovemaking.

That was the difference.

The thought coursed through him like an electric shock, magnified by the realization that the Commander was trying to quell it.

He thought of Kirsten, used a precious amount of his remaining energy to reach out for her . . . found her. He touched quickly inside her brain, revealed himself to her. He could not take her against her will. *I need you,* he told her.

Kosho and the old granny were surprised when Kirsten suddenly appeared to lose consciousness. They tried to revive her collapsed body, with no success. *It must mean he has lost,* thought Kosho. *I will be next*. He drew his sword, intending to use it on himself. Granny saw his intention, and they struggled for the weapon.

Kirsten went where Billy took her, unable to comprehend the sensations that he was experiencing. She felt him drawing on her energy, not knowing where they were going, or why. She loved him.

There were two of them now, and Billy used the fresh reserves of energy to increase the strength of his grip on the Commander.

This is your weakness, Billy told the Commander. *You have no love. No one to help, or be helped by.*

Those who are chosen, who choose, replied the Commander,

must Hunt, not mate. It is not possible to do both. A Hunter must Hunt alone.

It is possible for me, said Billy. *I have done it.* With the new vigor that flowed through him, he spread through the Commander's body, possessing and controlling every atom of it, leaving free only the last volitional portion of the Commander's mind—his solitary soul. Billy felt it, that soul, like a hard husk that he could crush with the power still within him.

Name me, Billy called. The husk of the Commander's soul moved desperately within Billy's grasp, struggled to disperse itself, to destroy itself, but Billy held it together, willing the Commander's existence.

Name me, came Billy's command again. The Commander thought, with the little freedom Billy permitted him, of the Aging Master's last words, his Death Wish.

Only, thought the Commander, *he did not realize that these beings may be even more powerful than he thought. Or perhaps he did. Perhaps he believed that there was yet something for the People to learn. He spoke of challenge. It falls to me to give it to them. And perhaps destroy the People.*

If they can be destroyed, came his own rejoinder, *then they were not worthy, after all.*

Now he knew. And agreed. And responded.

You must kill me, he said to Billy. *You must promise. If name you, you must kill me.*

I will kill you.

You are the . . . Other Hunter.

Billy crushed the essence that was all that remained of the Commander. There was no cry, no Death Wish, for the Commander's wish had already been granted, and his atoms spread throughout the endless chain of atoms that are not self, but chaos. Inchoate, and thus unthinking and unaware.

Epilogue

Billy sent Kirsten's energy back to her body. She awoke in time to stop the struggle between Kosho and Granny.

"He won," she said simply.

"That . . . is not possible," said Granny.

"But it is so."

Granny seemed to fade before their eyes. She—and her clothing, shoes, glasses, hair, flesh—gradually lost color, and they could see through her as if she were a ghost. But just as they expected to see her disappear entirely, she seemed to catch herself.

"I am still here," she said, in a faint, old-woman's voice that they had to strain to hear.

Kosho realized the import of what she was saying. He looked around. They were on an empty beach, with sand dunes stretching inland as far as they could see. Nothing grew upon the sand, but the waves continued their unending roll against the shore, and the air was warm.

"The illusion," he muttered. "He can maintain it."

When Billy destroyed the Commander, he felt the memory of how the illusion was made. He felt the responsibility for it descend upon him, and thought at first that he would not be able to bear it. He was weakened after his long battle, the struggle to change shapes. Then he realized that it was not something he had to concentrate on constantly. He had only to will it. And Kirsten and Kosho were still up there, depending on him.

The sea seemed cool and restful. The silence was soothing, and he could, he knew, rest there indefinitely, building up his strength.

For what? To find the answer, he would have to return to those who loved him.

He remembered that there was something still here. He went deeper for it, and found it. The aliens had never thought it would be claimed, but they kept their word. It was not an illusion. It was real, something that they had brought with them.

He took it up to Kirsten. A lover's gift.

"It . . . doesn't look like I thought it would," said Kirsten.

Billy sighed. He thought she would be pleased.

"I'm . . . much happier to have *you*," she said, reading his disappointment. She kissed him, and that made everything much, much better. They went off together, leaving Kosho to contemplate the wonder of a thousand ounces of pure gold.

Granny nudged him. "Better wake up," she said. "You know what they're going to do?"

Kosho looked at her. "I have a good idea. It is not for me to interfere."

"If they do, he'll lose the power to maintain this illusion, and you'll be sitting out here on an ice field in temperatures too low to maintain life—*your* life, at any rate."

Kosho ran after them, stopping them before they entered the refuge. He was at first too embarrassed to explain what Granny had told him, but Billy understood.

He commanded Granny to come to them.

"I am a Hunter now," he said. "My name is the Other Hunter. I command you. It is by my power that you exist."

She nodded. "I have closely examined the rules that were the essential part of my understanding when I was created. You are quite correct, even though this eventuality was not foreseen."

"Tell me, then, how we can get away from here."

She shrugged. "By your power. But it is still my duty to advise you."

"Go ahead, then. Quickly."

"You can recreate the plane that brought you here. I would advise that, for although you are now accustomed to travel without conveyances, it is a long journey and would tire you. And it would disturb your friends, who are not Hunters. If you allow me the power, you will find I can accomplish the task and the journey without tiring you."

"Do that."

"There is something else."

"Come *on*, Granny. We don't want to stand around here all day."

"You were going to the refuge with the intention to mate with your friend," she said sternly.

"Oh, my God . . . you didn't have to *say* it. I don't want you to say things like that. Understand?"

"Very well. But if you are to maintain the powers of a Hunter, you cannot mate."

He stood there. Kirsten looked at him. "Is that true? Billy . . . that isn't true, is it?"

He met her glance sheepishly. "Well, sort of. But . . . they're all dead. We've got the gold. We'll wait until we get back, that's all."

"Where are we going?"

He thought. "Anywhere you want. Though I'd just as soon not go back to Dallas."

"And then?"

"Well, we'll find somebody to buy the gold. Kosho, you can help us, can't you? Part of the gold is really yours."

Kosho nodded. "I have no need of more money, even though I would like to keep the sword. But I will help you, yes. It will not be difficult. Things are easily arranged when one has much money."

"Well, *that's* all right then," Billy said. He smiled at Kirsten. "By the time we get to Denmark, I can learn how to speak Danish."

"If you use your powers."

"If you let me."

"But is what she says true? If we . . . I mean . . . then you won't have that kind of power?"

He frowned. "It happened before. But the power came back."

Granny stamped her foot. "Tell her the truth. If you continue to expend your energy in sexual contact, you can never again be a Hunter."

He scraped the sand with his toe, then made a little of it rise in the air like a miniature whirlwind. He looked shyly to see if the others noticed. "That was true of the Hunters. But I may not be like them. Anyway, there's no danger now."

"But there is," Granny said. "The other Hunters will come. You are a great danger to them."

Billy shook his head. "The Commander hid from the others the knowledge of where he was going. He thought that when I had the . . . Discovery . . . I would use it to attack them. That's what he would have done. But I don't need to. Nobody there knows about me. And you can't tell them, if I—"

"If you take away my existence. But before you do that, let me warn you that although they do not know of your Discovery, they know where your planet is. They came before. Soon, some of them will come again. The People keep all the species in the known universe under surveillance. They will find you. And you will need your power to oppose them."

Kosho raised an eyebrow. Kirsten looked worried. Billy noticed, and was irritated. "What good is having this power if I can't . . . have you, Kirsten?"

She smiled uncertainly. "But what if what she says is true?"

He took her in his arms. He felt the way she responded to touching him. "Maybe we shouldn't . . ." she murmured before he kissed her. But she didn't push him away.

"The plane," he said to Granny after a time. "And when we are safe, you will come back and bury the Commander's ship under the ice cap. And yourself with it. Then you can wait."

"You'll need me," she warned.

But he had resumed where he left off.

Kosho, at a discreet distance, was first to hear the airplane in the sky. He looked up and saw the approaching Boeing 727 with relief. He wrapped his hand around the hilt of his sword. The boy had been right about everything, so far. It was wise to trust him now. Perhaps he was also right to do what he was doing now.

But when Kosho had first heard the sound of the plane in the sky, he had been afraid for a second that it was something else.

Sometime, he thought. *But how soon?*